BLAH BLAH

GERRY CRYER

BROVARY
LIMITED

ACKNOWLEDGEMENTS

Maria Hampshire has again guided me patiently through all the trials and tribulations of editing and production. There have, of course, been many others who have helped me get this far, with encouragement, advice, reading and editing. Thank you to you all.

DEDICATION

This book is dedicated to all those people who, to themselves and the rest of the world, are honest and open. It is a difficult stance to take but if we respect honesty and tolerate differences then the world might be a much better place.

Alexandra, again you have been my inspiration and I owe you more than you can imagine.

Chapter I

Waking at five on a winter's morning for a drive to Faversham railway station isn't high on my list of the one hundred recommended things to do before I die; but I do it five days every week. There are days, albeit few, when at five a.m. England is wonderful and the chore is a delight. This was not one of those days; freezing cold, damp and still very dark. On the platform the station café is, as ever, shut. It's never open at times when I travel. Every day, as I pass by, I read the sign that says it opens at eight and closes again by five, and despite my expectations, each day my hopes are dashed. It opens at hours when there's little demand and is another example of British entrepreneurship at its best. This thought makes me smile and I remember the famous (or probably infamous) words of George Bush: 'The problem with the French is that they don't have a word for *entrepreneur*'.

What a prat. But at this early hour, even thinking about the many failings of George Bush doesn't bring lasting cheer.

Faversham railway station in East Kent is depressing at any time but at six thirty on a winter's morning it encapsulates many of my core images of hell and in that it's not far behind Munch's *Scream*, the paintings of Hieronymus Bosch, and some of the lyrics of Cat Stevens. Each day as this journey wears me further down, it seems to be more frequently that I think about Hell, and the pain of eternal damnation, and commuting at winter on British Rail seems an apt analogy.

Today, as I stride up worn and wet concrete steps I try

and lift my mood and I imagine my version of heaven and being attended by either a scantily dressed Kim Basinger or bikinied Gwyneth Paltrow and understand that in my enjoyment one man's Heaven must be some other woman's Hell. On the other hand maybe Gwyneth would find that more appealing than having to listen to Cold Play albums all day? Of course it could be that I'm already in Hell and this is my penance, and then only submission and supplication are my routes to salvation. A drip of cold water from a hole in the roof falls down my collar and stirs me from these thoughts and I'm back in the real world.

I look around. There are knots of other commuters waiting for the train to take them on their painfully boring, ninety-minute journey to work in London.

It was about three years ago when I joined the regular travellers in the underworld and first started making this journey. It took a few weeks to establish my regular waiting place on the platform. All my fellow travellers in Hades know where we like to stand but it took time to work through the options.

In my first weeks I travelled in the front carriages but there the train fills up too quickly and is overcrowded, so I can't stretch out. Worse still, on wet days there's always someone standing and dripping water from their coat on to me (and as I sleep these are the worst of all wet dreams), and even worse I may have to speak to Jonathan or John. Both always travel at the front of the train for the simple strategy to save a minute on arrival, to get to a job that they, like all the others, seem not to want to do. Jonathan is one of my best friends and I would be happy, even delighted, to chat at six in the evening – especially at a local pub. It was in the Red Lion, on a Thursday evening, when I tried to explain why I always just walked on by. He didn't really understand but promised to try to describe my motives to John the next day. First thing in the morning I don't talk to anyone and I don't want anyone to talk to me. Thinking about Jonathan describing my motives makes me feel like a criminal because each crime has a motive. Criminals are social outcasts and that is what I am as I nod my acknowledgements, head past them as they wait in their places on the platform, and move on to my place, knowing that they would be talking about the criminal, the early morning social outcast.

Today there are no interlopers (or as I call them, transients) standing on my space. That's good. I hate having to nudge them away with that this-is-my-place-and-you're-new-here-so-fuck-off look. Transients are the unfortunates who are making a one-off special visit to London and at this time in the morning it can only be for a job interview. Madame Tussauds is bad enough tourist fare in mid-afternoon and then only after a healthy lunch and the induced drowsiness of a few pints of English beer; but it holds no delight before the time when even pubs are not allowed to open. A transient may of course be returning to a home in London after an all-night tryst with a beautiful or even buxom Kentish maid, but the idea is of course totally ridiculous. East Kent is not famed for the beauty of its women and then even the simply fair are far less accommodating than their sisters in Essex. No. No one ever comes to East Kent for a tryst. As I look at any transient, I hope that this awful first experience is sufficiently horrible to deter them from ever taking any job that would demand this level of early-morning commitment. That's why I feel totally justified in being rude and even (if the moment demanded it) physically threatening. It's for their own good.

We are mainly men waiting, and there's only occasionally a woman, who invariably has that weary look of middle age wondering why she is commuting and not living on the Costa del Sol with fun, freedom and the frivolity of sun, sand and maybe even once again (in her slightly sad life) extraordinary sex, but I know that she is not thinking about sex, or even love. It's the wrong time of the day. It's early in the morning and already she has washed some dishes, filled and started a washing machine, made and eaten toast, showered and dressed and arrived just in time for the train. Time doesn't allow time for cleansers, makeup, lipstick, scanty panties or an uplifting bra. Not for her love and sex on the six thirty-three to Cannon Street.

The younger travellers, girls mainly, only start to commute nearer to London for the evening discos and parties and they never bother us in Faversham. I miss them on the platform as we need a new generation to come through. I wonder how we commuters all start middle aged. Have we all missed our teenage lives and just land here, grey and boring?

Now I'm in my rightful place and, as with Jonathan thirty paces earlier, I nod a good morning to those around me. Once I actually opened my mouth to say something but the interest to communicate had vanished before a vowel or consonant emerged. I probably looked as if I was doing no more than trying to catch a fly in my mouth but even that caused no consternation with my fellow travellers.

Once, feeling more reckless than normal as I remember, I thought I might try to travel in a carriage at the back end of the train but still I fretted through all the journey that a runaway train would ram us as we waited in a station, or in a whiplash accident we would be flung off the bridge over the Medway (or as I prefer to call it, the Styx, being the river that separates the world of the living from that of the dead). Even as we travelled I was sure that every noise was a sign of impending doom and I failed to relax properly. What should have been a chance to catch up on sleep became a nightmare. A nightmare that was all too much. So I stay at my place in the middle of the platform.

I once tried to explain this to Jenny, my wife, and I think she understood because she was nodding but then she seems to nod at just about everything I say, so I can't be altogether sure. In fact she nods so much that she looks like one of those little toy nodding-head dogs who sit in the back of cars. The head is nodding but their only concern is that the car is moving; they have no interest in the direction it's going. So it is with Jenny. She hears the words but nothing of the content and direction of the conversation. Jenny only nods. I was so worried that I wondered if I should take her to the doctor to be scanned, to make sure her head was still properly connected. I thought that maybe I should, but then I started to think about something else and the thought left me, as did the image of arriving home and her head dropping off as she nodded to my words. Once I was telling her about my morning platform-positional problem (as I've come to call it), and she nodded and I decided I wasn't really too upset whether she understood or not. When I tried to explain that the middle wasn't just the middle but there was a front-middle and a back-middle, I knew she wasn't interested. Why should she care? After all, while I was trudging through that misery every morning, she was still fast asleep in bed. Well, I assume she was. I know if it were me, I wouldn't wake up to say goodbye.

Anyway, my decision today is to stay in the middle of the platform, just under the station canopy. It's not raining now but on another day it might be and I don't like to get wet. I parked my car with the minimum out-in-the-open walk to stay dry. So why get wet on the platform? Raining or not, we're all creatures of habit and recently habit seems to be the norm for me. As I said, we all have our places on the platform; I'm roughly in the front of the middle of the platform and the train. We see the train come towards us and the door is right in front of me which, of course, is another reason why I'm standing exactly where I am.

Today I have my briefcase as well as an overnight bag, for tonight. Another business dinner and I can't get back to Faversham, so I'm planning to stay at the company flat. This means I have to place two cases in the rack above the seat and there are scowling looks from other passengers as I randomly move their cases and handbags to make room. Everybody and everything has its place and that includes the luggage racks. Next I fold and place my overcoat with my luggage and, finally, as I'm properly perched in my corner seat, I settle down in purgatory.

I like taxonomies, so I categorise my fellow passengers into four sorts: newspaper-readers, book-readers, chatters and sleepers. With the demise of the over-large broadsheet, watching newspapers being unfurled is not the fun it used to be. Waiting for the unexpected right hook or back-handed slap as pages are turned and folded is now a generally forlorn hope.

The book-readers divide their solace into action pulp fiction or romantic fiction: men read the former and women the latter. The occasional sight of a classic stirs me but I wonder who can read Dickens or Ovid at seven in the morning. Some time ago I concluded that it was just the cover that was the classic, and the pages were filled with pulp fiction or romantic fiction or, even more likely, just pictures. I did once think that I should ostentatiously read *Publius Ovidius Naso* in Latin so that I could turn to the carriage and quote '*Fac tibi consuescat: nil adsuetudine maius*' and ask if anyone agreed.

The chatters I hated even more. I know hate is a strong word but they really do annoy me to a point where I would happily stand up and hit them; but the British don't do that, so I sit there, my journey totally ruined. While they chatter I sit in silence with both my temper and blood pressure rising, composing wonderfully vitriolic, scornful speeches which are never delivered. Unless the content is last night's erotic dreams, which of course it never is, everything at that time of the morning must be trivia; but trivia they talk. The chatters are always women.

And finally there are the sleepers. Often they'll start out as a newspaper-reader or book-reader but soon their eyes close and their heads nod down to their chests and the snoring starts, and it's always loud. Very loud. You can hear a sleeper from twenty feet away, but it's much worse if the sleeper sits next to you. As they sleep and their head drops they slump. Slumping forward is fine and often slightly comical as we all wonder if they'll finally fall to the floor, but slumping has three dimensions and invariably the sleeper slumps to the side – and if I'm unfortunate enough to be sitting next to them, it's always in my direction. They may be clean and showered, plump and over-perfumed but at that moment they're like a tramp in the road, and must be avoided. The spirit of the Samaritan is missing at seven o'clock, so you don't want to touch them to put them back in an upright position. Even touching them seems like a major intrusion into their private space and sleeping body, in full public view. Clearly, as they have their nose in your crotch, they have none of the same inhibitions. But something has to be done, so with a gentle push and minimal bodily contact, you try and return them to a vertical position and (if you're totally honest with yourself) a slight lean away from you, just a little beyond the upright, so their next slump takes them into someone else's lap.

Of course I'm in a unique fifth category. I may look as though I'm a sleeper because my eyes are closed but really I'm a *thinker*. Sometimes, but rarely, the thought for the day comes to me in the car as I drive from Canterbury and across the motorway to Faversham. Normally, though, my inspiration comes to me immediately as I sit and close my eyes. I try not to solve all the world's big problems in a single week. I did try once but then my day at work was wasted because I had to spend it composing letters to *The Times* or *Guardian* or *Economist* magazine with my solutions to all kinds of problems. I never sent the letters as I assumed the establishment would find it all too radical. I wrote and sent a single letter to *Marie Claire* but I never checked to see if it was published.

Some days – usually the ones when Jenny hadn't been sexually forthcoming the previous night – I wonder how many of the women are wearing panties and if it's uncomfortable or cold sitting panty-less on the train. I mean do women sit on their skirts or do their skirts ride up so they sit on their panties? It's a question I have considered many times, of course, but if they don't wear any panties then they are sitting on a bare arse. If only those fetishists who like to smell women's panties knew what delights the commuter trains really offer! I also wonder if they carry a spare pair of panties in their handbags in case there's a medical emergency. Sadly these thoughts of mine are getting more common. I look at the newspaper-reader in front of me and check out the headline:

PRIME MINISTER'S BIG PROBLEM!

For a fleeting moment I wonder if it's a medical complaint or whether it's an exclusive interview with his wife. Boringly I assume it is a political piece. I'm not keen to find out more about its subject now, because the first thing I read at work is the news digest. What did Paul Simon say? *I get the news I need from the weather report.* With careful planning I can even manage to miss that on the radio. Actually the planning doesn't have to be too careful because at home, at five o'clock in the morning, I've never been able to switch on the radio for fear of waking Jenny. Who knows – if she was to wake up suddenly to news of storms in Forties, Cromarty and German Bight, her head might fall off. As I carry that horrendous thought of her head bouncing down the stairs and chasing me out to the car every day, I can't care about anything else and I don't even manage to switch on the radio while I drive. If I did, I would catch the first half hour of the farming news.

For one week I did manage to turn on the radio and I became addicted. I knew all about the issues facing modern kale farmers, and even all the pork prices. I became so interested that I researched (at work of course) everything I could about kale. There's a lot to know. Did you know that during the war the Dig for Victory campaign encouraged all us Brits to dig up our front lawns and local parks and plant kale – we were asked to replace our manicured striped lawns with military rows of leafy green veg? I didn't think you did, and nor did any of my work colleagues.

'But it's so easy to grow and fills in all those missing nutritional bits we need because of rationing,' I told them. Most had to remind me that we no longer have rationing, but I had a smart answer.

'You don't actually know what kale *is*?' I would answer in an accusatorial tone, normally while jabbing a finger to stress my point. I knew I was on the high ground, so as they shook their heads (I never feared that any of theirs would fall off and was happy to press my case) I would tell them all, as I had learnt the definition from *Wikipedia* by heart. 'Kale or borecole is a form of cabbage (*Brassica oleracea* of the Acephala group), green or purple, in which the central leaves don't form a head. It's considered to be closer to wild cabbage than most domesticated forms. The species *Brassica oleracea* contains a wide array of vegetables including broccoli, cauliflower, collard greens, and Brussels sprouts. The cultivar group Acephala also includes spring greens and collard greens, which are extremely similar genetically.'

I could see from their faces how impressed they were with my knowledge (or more accurately, I could see from their retreating backs how impressed they were).

If it wasn't kale, it was the idea of pig farming, in miniature, that held my thoughts. I could clear a space for a few pigs in the garden. I wouldn't have any of those Asian pot-bellied ones that became so popular a few years ago as household pets. When you're ill, allowing a faithful dog to curl up next to you in bed is an appealing prospect, but could a snorting pig ever give the same love? And why Vietnamese? What the Vietcong couldn't achieve maybe their pigs will? Maybe one day we'll hear that they've all joined forces against the imperialist oppressor and there will be an army of potential suicide pigs blowing up synagogues in an Arabic, al-Qaeda or Communist plot. I suppose we should be grateful that Jews and Muslims have such an abhorrence of pigs or we might have a whole new terrorist threat to manage. No, I would rear proper, English-type pigs that we could slaughter and eat. I started to salivate as I thought of a Sunday roast lunch of Charlie's leg, and if a friend should ask me why the pig was once called Charlie, I would suggest in a roundabout sort of way that it was homage to a drug-taking, hippy-loving, self-sustaining youth, in just the same way I named my set of labrador dogs, Buddy and Holly. My farming phase lasted no more than a week or so and I returned to the silent drive, much to the relief of my colleagues at work.

So what's new today? I thought as I sat in my seat on the train. So what? The Prime Minister has problems. Well he always will. That's the nature of the job. I scan the other newspaper-readers. Another headline:

QUEEN VISITS LEEDS

I bet she isn't on an early train out of King's Cross trying to decide where to sit and wondering if a previous passenger in a short skirt had been reading an erotic Mills & Boon while not wearing panties. Maybe she has a tough job, but there are some perks, like never having to do anything for herself. Tudor monarchs had serfs to clean their bottoms, wear their cold shirts to warm them up or, when they were young Princes, to take their beatings – whipping boys. Does our current monarch have such luxuries? That must be a real joy and I think I would trade all her problems for the pampering she enjoys. An irreverent thought forms, suddenly, of a time a couple of decades ago:

'Philip, I think it's time the country had an heir to the

> *throne.'*
>
> *'Quite so, Lizzie. When would be a good time?'*
>
> *'Her doctor says ten days from now.'*
>
> *And taking the toast already buttered and covered with a rough-cut orange marmalade all ladled and spread by his personal butler, Philip said, 'I'll send someone round to fuck her then,' as breakfast continued.*

Maybe I'd be a particular favourite of The Queen, chosen to make Diana pregnant and produce an heir to the throne because her husband failed so many times? I'd be a great choice. Not quite as old as Charles (but that might be an advantage), highly intelligent and pretty accomplished at rugby, with no deformities other than a weak knee (which was a sporting injury anyway) and I'm extraordinarily well endowed – but maybe that would be a disadvantage if I'm not supposed to wake Diana up during the act. Whatever, I'd be a prime candidate. I can imagine getting a phonecall from Philip and being summoned for three consecutive nights' work … And then, in the twenty-first century, the Queen would want to see me again, because her grandchildren are such a benefit to the 'family firm' and what with the arrival of Will and Kate's own progeny she wants to reward me. Of course, as Will's secret father, I can't join in with the celebrations, but I'm a very proud viewer of the TV coverage.

'That's my boy!' I mutter to a startled fellow passenger. The train pulls into a station and I half stir to let an overweight woman out and a gaggle of school kids in. Then suddenly the door opens again and the Queen climbs in.

'Sir Tommy,' she says (of course I can't tell anyone I've been knighted – it's just one of my little secrets) 'Your help has been invaluable. What would you like to do for your country? I'll tell that toad of a Prime Minister to make it happen.'

I think for a moment. Like praying, I know I shouldn't ask for anything for myself. That would be greedy. What should I ask? I think for a moment longer.

'Ma'am, I would like all of your subjects to be emaciated.' I think for another moment: was that the right word? 'I'm sorry, Ma'am. I meant I would like them all to be emancipated.'

I think again. Maybe I was right the first time. After all, we're always being told that we're all too fat and that we eat too much. Maybe it would be better if we were emaciated. Then we could charge people for rail tickets according to their weight. Children would still get cheaper tickets because they weigh less, and parents who let their children become obese would pay the penalty in extra fares. And if they couldn't afford the money? Well, so be it. The kids would have to walk and then, when they had burned off some calories, they could start to use the train again; a wondrous, virtuous circle. Just think of the opportunities. We could discriminate against refugees and dissidents trying to get into our country not by their colour or point of origin, but by their weight. I can imagine immigration officers at Gatwick or Heathrow.

'I'm sorry, sir, but you're not allowed into the UK because you're too fat.'

'But I have a doctor's certificate saying I've got big bones,' says the fat American.

'I'm sorry, sir. We no longer accept the "big bones" argument – only a body mass index certificate.'

There would be positive discrimination against fatties. Our supermarket trolleys would be automatically scanned for total calories. We could have ration books again, computerised of course, to limit the food we could eat and I would be on TV extolling to all the benefit of kale. Police would stop us on the street to measure our body mass index – not to check whether we're drunk. If people were thinner they wouldn't be able to drink so much anyway. Now that would be good, too, and with a fitter nation, if we could get the policies right, we might even win more medals at the Olympic Games and other important sporting events – although we would still be useless at the shot putt. Never mind. We could tease the Americans for being overweight.

And diplomatically we would be friends with all the countries in the developing world as we start to look more like them: gaunt, thin – and, yes, emaciated. Economically we would be like a new family of the thin and we would want to buy all the things they sell, like fresh fruit and healthy food. We would not be a G8 or G20 combined by economic output, but a grouping based on body sizes and diet. We would use less petrol in our cars carrying all those fewer kilos around the countryside. Girls and women would do wonders for the fashion industry, buying more clothes for their new slim-line bodies. Only the panty industry would suffer because they'd all be so much sexier and none of them would wear panties in the mornings to work. What a good idea. One of my better ones.

Ma'am, I was right the first time. I would like to see all your subjects emaciated.'

And just as I am about to be secretly ennobled, the train pulls in to Cannon Street abruptly and I wake from my half sleep. Now that would be good politics, I think as I take my two cases off the rack and the passengers disperse. By the time I step onto the platform it's nearly empty, as usual.

Everyone else has raced ahead, no doubt with Jonathan in the lead. Why are they all in such a hurry? Do they love their jobs and workmates that much?

I stroll casually to my office in Wollacott: the bank that calls itself The Bank of The City. Sometimes I think they should be explicit and say which city. They assume everyone knows it's the City of London, the financial centre of the world. But it could have been Fray Bentos, an obscure city in Uruguay, or maybe Tomsk or Omsk in Siberia. Who knows how people read this marketing bumf? I've been Director of Economic Research for nearly five years now and as usual Jane, my PA, is there to greet me with a double espresso in hand.

'Morning, Tommy. Good journey?' The same words of greeting every morning.

For a moment I think of telling her about my plans for the country. She would do fine in my new world – beautiful, slim and clever – but she wouldn't understand.

'Normal thanks, Jane,' is what I say, but I fail, as always, to add sarcastically that I love getting up at five thirty to drive through the ice and rain; it's heaven, and ninety minutes rattling about on a cold British Rail train just fills me with joy, but none so much as the joy of seeing you, Jane, and that espresso. Even if I had sufficient energy or interest to tell her this obvious truth, she would stop listening after a few words; she was long gone and already back to her desk.

Chapter II

Work is the usual mixture of mundane and boring and I wonder what would happen at Wollacott if I didn't exist. Would anything change much? I decide quite rapidly that hardly anything would be different. I know this should upset me because we all like to see purpose behind our effort, but my purpose, for many years now, has simply been to take the money and do as little as I possibly can of those tasks that I find uninteresting or mundane. Because so much of what we all do is exactly that – I do very little. The reality is that now I've almost given up all forms of work.

To achieve my ambition of not doing much – if anything at all – I've recruited my staff team wisely and filled all the posts that report to me with the right mixture of talent and ambition. To make my small part of the Bank tick without much effort from me, all I need to do is occasionally remind them that I'm not just important but I'm crucial to their progress, and then I can relax, and sit and watch paternally over them. Of course, as in all places of work, politics are important, and none less than here. I need to make sure I have appropriate and continual patronage, which I achieve by being on good working terms with the few colleagues that are senior to me. This I do by being properly subservient and making sure that Wollacott receives nothing but good press from both the conferences I attend or at which I present, and from the TV interviews I give.

Whenever an economy somewhere in the world starts to look shaky and the TV companies want an expert, I'm the talking head to whom they turn for the pithy quote. It doesn't matter if it's the UK, Greece or Spain – I've got words for them all. The market holds its collective breath in anticipation. As ever, the Chancellor is walking a tightrope. The Greeks will have to spread the *taramasalata* thinly for the next three years. Even smaller tapas bites for the Spanish from now on.

I would like to think that I'm recognised occasionally by those who watch the news on Sky or the BBC but no one has ever stopped me in the street and asked me for an opinion. Maybe now, with these clever programme-recording machines, no one watches the news on TV anymore. I look keenly at old ladies on the high street, expecting to be consulted about their mortgage options. Once I stared at one intently – willing a question from her through mind-control techniques – but she pointed me out to a Mall security guard. I left quickly in a different direction.

My conference and minor celebrity status does mean I travel often, which I enjoy, and I also get a small clothes allowance for being on TV which only stretches these days to a pair of smart white Y-fronts and striped socks – neither of which get much coverage. The other key skill I regularly employ to keep my life easy, which is often mistaken as a sign of being a real smart-aleck, is my near-perfect memory. I have perfect recall of events, names, documents and conversations. Often it's a blessing, but more frequently it's a curse, because I'm always being called and consulted by nearly everyone in the office as a substitute for a Google search. It was only when I heard that my office nickname was Google that I started to refuse these requests for help. I think it had become a hobby for some. What shall we do today? Why not see what Google knows? Even new recruits were sent to me on their first days with fatuous questions.

I like to be seen as a man of the people, so this morning

I sat reading my daily news digest at the spare desk in the open-plan team office with its views on to Gutter Lane; I was considering the mass-produced poster of some peaceful island scene, chosen – I should add – by the designers and not myself, that hung on the wall above Jane's head. Despite being large enough for eight desks and the general coming and going of people, the room is always tidy, in line with Wollacott's clean-desk policy. How different from my own office where papers and books are everywhere, in imitation of an absent-minded professor (a comparison I am happy to cultivate) and my deliberate flouting of company policy to demonstrate my importance in that I could live above the law. Finding a seat in my office requires moving one pile of documents to an unused corner of the floor. My large modern pine desk is equally inaccessible and made more crowded by the presence of an incongruously large antique desk light. So as I sat browsing the news digest (a totally boring report), Rick Pangan waved across the room and tapped at his watch, reminding me it was time for our twelve thirty meeting. My ability to waste a morning looking busy without expending a single ounce of energy impressed me yet again. Twelve thirty, and my achievements match almost perfectly my input; both were near zero. Rick and I moved into my office.

Rick is a senior member of my team and one I have to watch out for. He has started to think he should be more senior than I want. I like him very much but I needed to resist all threats to my authority. It isn't that I want any promotion for myself; it's a straightforward case of survival. I've carved out a simple and lucrative niche for myself and I don't want to have to fight to keep it, nor work hard in some other department of the Bank.

'Have you read my thesis, Tommy?' He was settling into the chair with the books balanced precariously on the arm, waving his papers in his left hand.

Jane brought us each a coffee and now poor Rick had even more to balance because the space on the side-table was taken with the latest budget forecast and IMF reports (and – even better – it was just that inch or two too far away to be useful). Everything in my office is designed to make my visitors feel uncomfortable. With me, Jane is always polite but curt; my attitude towards her is likely to worsen after seeing how she looked at Rick and how his eyes followed her out of the room. I decided to keep tabs on that developing relationship. You never know what mileage there is in knowledge. Maybe there's also a little jealousy. I have spent entire train journeys wondering what a night with Jane might be like; I soon figured out it would be much better for me than for her.

Now what about his thesis: *Structural Issues in the Fiscal Management of a Highly Indebted Economy*. It was actually quite an inventive and clever piece, as one would expect from a first-class Oxford man. But as I knew from bitter experience, nothing is ever really new. Only a real genius invents. However bright the rest of us think we are, we're all doomed to the sad epitaph that we merely stand on the shoulders of giants. With Rick perched uncomfortably in his chair, juggling coffee cup and piles of papers, I decided this was another chance to demonstrate my own ability and in doing so keep him in his place but first, I thought, some words of encouragement.

'A fine piece, Rick, and I want you to take it forward and develop some of the ideas. Maybe also a version that's a little less technical, while retaining the economic mystique, that we can put into the Board pack. We need to simplify these things for them. You do understand, don't you?'

With a knowing look and a hint of a wink he understood what was required but his aspirations were greater – he was also looking for a more academic publication and greater peer recognition. So to satisfy that wish, I added: 'And when you've made the changes, we can, of course, move to get it published, and that version will require all the citations etcetera, but …' I hesitated at the 'but' because now I had to put him back into the pack. I sat back in my chair, closed my eyes and brought my hands to my chin as if praying. I need a sense of drama for what I had to say next. '… but sadly, Rick, I'm not sure all the ideas are totally original. I think I've read these theories before.'

Rick knew not to question or hold out for any hope of reprieve. He knew I had remembered something. With a deep sense of resignation, he sank into his seat.

'Tell me,' he said, catching the papers that were about to topple.

I went into my deep near-Rodinesque thinking pose.

'Let me think.'

I liked these moments, testing my memory. Sometimes I think it works like a computer: my neurons fire up, electrons whizz around my brain, and I make the connections.

'It was a conference in 1996 in—' I pause for effect. 'In Berlin. There was a Professor Hudolei.'

While Rick watches, I walk myself back to the conference venue. He's seen this performance before.

'Ugly building that conference centre. Third day, as I remember.' In my mind I can see the conference agenda. 'He was the third presenter and put forward very similar views to those you expressed. Now let me think some more.' In my mind I moved forward nine months to the printed conference proceedings. Mentally I flicked through the pages. I could see them all laid out for me to re-read. 'Pages 137 to 145 – I think you'll find your references and citations there.'

I opened my eyes and settled back in my chair and looked at Rick. Mission accomplished with just the right balance. My reputation fully in place and Rick in awe and back to work: a good morning. He left the room and I searched the internet to check I had got it right. Satisfied with my success, I realised I'd missed lunch again. I hadn't so much as missed it, but just forgotten to eat, and I sat in my room with nothing much else to do. I really didn't want to be working; I wanted to release my thoughts and let them roam. I often do silly mental exercises to see where its limits are. I check that the neurons and the filing systems that connect everything in there are working properly. I marvel at the way things cross-check. To test myself again, I took myself back to the conference in Berlin and went through all the speakers and through all their papers. I could recall them all.

I once tried to see if I could forget something I'd previously remembered. It was not easy because first, of course, I had to remember something so that I might later forget it, and in recalling it for such a special purpose meant it was in fact better remembered than most other facts, so I never managed to forget anything, and then I realised the sad irony of the task: I would always remember that I'd set the task and in order to know if I'd been successful I would have to realise what it was I had forgotten – which of course meant I had to remember it again.

To waste some more of the Bank's time I thought some more about the fat-tax I dreamed up earlier that morning and considered writing yet another letter to *Marie Claire*. This time I would go as far as to check whether it got published. After all *Marie Claire* specialises in emaciated models. It should be right up their street; I knocked up a first draft.

Dear Editor

Following a conversation with her Majesty Queen Elizabeth II, Defender of the Faith etc., etc., we have agreed that she will tell her Government to initiate a new tax based on an obesity index. As you are a leading member of the Fourth Estate, we are informing you in advance so that you can take the necessary steps in your upcoming photojournalism.

We look forward to your full cooperation in this matter.

Yours, etc.

Tommy

P.S. To help you take this matter seriously we would remind you that the legal penalty for treason is still hanging.

Actually I couldn't be sure that hanging was still the penalty for treason but I liked the effect it would have on whoever opened the letter. I found an envelope and searched for an address before putting it in my jacket pocket to post later on. I may waste the Bank's time but I do have real scruples about physical theft such as using the mail system for private correspondence. I removed the envelope and used a marker pen to scrub out the Bank's name and address before replacing it in my pocket.

Mid-afternoon drifted into late afternoon, and I began to look forward to my dinner. It had never been the dinner in particular that appealed, but the chance of having an evening away from my thoughts about my disastrous relationship with Jenny. Even that was not totally true; it was more about having an evening where I could do just what I wanted without the approbation of a wife. That's the case for most men, and, I presume, most women. The only difference is that men misuse and abuse the situation when they are off the leash in a way women rarely even consider, yet alone implement because ... well, because – as women know – men are no more than little boys who are a little taller and have learnt how to think with the bulge in their trousers rather than the grey matter between their ears. I know I'm as bad as any man and sometimes I do misbehave, but it's the exhilaration of not having to report my whereabouts that is most exciting. But the cause and effect are so out of kilter. Women don't trust men so they keep the leash pulled tight, and when it's suddenly released, like the apocryphal convent girl, we go wild.

For its senior executives and visiting customers, Wollacott maintains a number of accommodations in the City. Simple one-bedroom, one-kitchen, one-lounge affairs – they're a blessing, saving a trip to a hotel. They're busy most nights of the week and even occasionally during the days, but I had better not go into those activities too much. I've used the flats for an evening when I've been for dinner but never, sadly, for any assignations. It's rumoured that Philpott from Gilts once took his secretary there and the occupants from other flats in the block complained at the excessive noise they made through the night. After that, there were security cameras at the entrance to every flat, and Philpott's reputation soared.

It was just after five when I dropped in at one of the flats to shower and by six I was heading off to my dinner meeting. I was early. Dinner wasn't until seven thirty with a reception from six forty-five. I hated those pre-dinner cocktail conversations. We're just like penguins in our dinner suits and the conversations are boring.

'Ah, you're in fixed interest at Blinks. You've had a good year?' Raise the tone at the end of a sentence to make it into a question. My companion had had a good year, but my question makes him wonder if I know something that may change all that.

'The fundamentals were with us, but we were ahead of the curve and beat budget by twenty.'

'Okay, but let's see how this year pans out. There's a lot of pent-up inflation.' And with that you tap him on the shoulder, turn to leave and say, 'I hope it stays lucky for you.'

Even the certain can start to worry. Ask a golfer – who's in the best form of his life – if he breathes in or out at the top of his swing and watch his game collapse.

I thought of phoning Jenny, thought again and rejected the idea. Then I decided that even if I had to pay for the drinks myself a quick pint in a pub was far better than the idle chat and free drinks on offer at the reception. It's far better to slip in slightly late as if straight from the office on conclusion of yet another mega deal.

On this night, I could walk to the dinner from the flat, and on the way there are a number of pubs I could have chosen for my pint. As I passed each, I half looked in through the open doors. I chose a more traditional English pub – not one of the new wine bars that are ruining the old traditions of drinking; they don't know how to look after and tender a pint of good beer. City pubs are busy places straight after work but even by then people were starting to thin out. I had no problem finding a corner table for both me and my double vodka. I really wanted a beer but I knew that my bladder may not cope well over a long drawn-out dinner.

I could see most of the pub from where I sat. There was a group of young men standing at the bar, drinking too much and following every twirling skirt that walked by. Sometimes just their eyes followed the girl; sometimes there was a shouted invitation to spend the night together. Always there was joking among the group.

I wasn't jealous of them and their youth but I did resent them being here. I resented them being loud and having fun, especially because I felt it was misdirected fun. I was jealous, though, when at their most uncouth they attracted a girl into their circle. I assumed that one or all of them had visions of her naked on her back by the end of the evening; or maybe they planned something against the wall down one of the city's many alleyways. Maybe that was her goal as well? I moved my eyes round the pub having decided that whatever their ambitions for the girl in the short dress, all these thoughts were actually mine.

Three attractive girls sat together a few tables away. I could tell by their clothes – trim white blouses, tailored black skirt and black stockings (oh, I hoped they were stockings and not tights) with sensible but expensive black shoes – they were 'Sloanes' and they were drinking white wine. Their heads were bent in close as, I guessed, they gossiped; maybe the centre of their conversation was polo at Windsor this weekend or the behaviour of their directors and bosses. I stopped going down that line of thought. Maybe they are the directors and it's the junior men in the office they're talking about.

'Have you seen that new scrumptious thing in accounts payable? His trousers are so tight I could almost see the line of his cock. I told him to come into my office. He looked so sheepish. In he trailed. "Close the door," I shouted. "Now, young man, this is the arrangement," I said. "If you want to keep your job, you have to keep me happy – and satisfied." And then I sort of looked at him and sat on the corner of my desk and let my skirt ride up a bit. I just pointed at my pussy and said I want that sucked and licked at least once every day. "Can you do that job?" I asked.'

They burst into fits of laughter at their table. I doubted that was their real conversation but it would have been interesting if it had been. I reminded myself to check the internet to see if any men have ever lodged a complaint of sexual harassment.

I topped up the vodka with the last of the can of tonic. Would it all fit in? I paused and smiled and reminded myself to stop turning everything into a sexual innuendo. Would it all fit in! Jenny once said I suffered from a form of AIDS – Advanced Innuendo Detection Syndrome. I thought that was quite funny – particularly from her because she doesn't make many jokes. She probably got it off the radio from Wogan or Jimmy Young. Something else to check – are either of them still alive? But Jenny's joke probably wasn't a joke or a compliment, just a reaction to something I had said in her company. It's just when someone asks me about a female friend and whether, for example, I had come across her on my visit to New York; my mind goes in different directions. Or if I'm asked what I was up to while I was away, I can't resist answering 'Eight inches'. I suppose it's not just the innuendo, but as I said before I am rather well-endowed and it does seem like a good way to let everyone know. After all, I could hardly answer 'Five inches' even if it was true and get the recognition my length and girth deserves.

I leave the Sloanes and look at who else is there. No one

really; just a group of non-descripts not worthy of any further thought (or I'm finally too old and jaded to invent their life stories for them). Maybe, I think, I should apply to be presenter of that TV programme *Who Do You Think You Are?* Instead of tracing back through the celebrity's real life I could just invent it all. That would be quite fun. I was on this train of thought when *she* sat down at my table.

Normally I expect to be consulted with an amiable request like, 'Is this chair free?', although I've never found a satisfactory answer to that request. We all know chairs are free and emancipated. Gosh, that word again. Whoever heard of a chair in slavery? I wonder if chairs had ever been in slavery. Maybe there was a real-life Mr Arm who once owned a chair and the chair took its name from its master and became an Armchair. But today, all chairs are free chairs and there are no demonstrations or marches and no Wilberforce to free them, but still we just sit in them and treat them as subservient. Sometimes we spill drinks on them, or fuck or masturbate in them, but the fact remains, all chairs are free. I've got the same problem with doors that are alarmed. I see the sign often: THIS DOOR IS ALARMED.

Sometimes there's even an exclamation mark. This door is alarmed! Why? I wonder. Who frightened it and is it permanently alarmed or just prone to alarm, with a propensity to be alarmed? And what behaviour can we expect from an alarmed door? Will it suddenly shut, trapping my arm? These sorts of things trouble me deeply. Maybe the door is alarmed because it has just heard that all the chairs are now free and it wants to be liberated too. Perhaps it's just a little paranoid or schizophrenic. Of course, then it would be just plain unhinged, and lying on the floor, and wouldn't be a door at all – but a trap door. Logical thought to be noted. Doors can't be schizophrenic because they would then be unhinged and no longer be doors. *Ipso facto* all doors must by definition be sane, and therefore if the door is alarmed it's a real threat and I should take it seriously. I impress myself with my wonderful powers of reasoning and deduction. I must write a learned psychology paper and put forward my theory of insanity amongst doors.

Some music in the background: the juke box. *Riders on the Storm* by the …. good grief, yes, The Doors. This is going to be precipitous evening. All I need now is for it to rain and I would have precipitous precipitation and my night would be complete. Anyway, the *'she'* that just sat down looked distinctly unhappy and wasn't smiling. As with Jane this morning, I considered discussing free chairs, alarmed doors, music of the seventies and rain, but then she rubbed her eye to take away a tear and I decided on a different approach.

'Are you okay? Can I do anything for you? … Here take this,' I said offering her a clean hanky from my jacket. 'Are you sure you're okay?'

I'm not good at reading women and their moods (which man is?), but there was a depth of despair I couldn't fathom in her eyes. Had she simply been crying from the insults of the youths at the bar I might have been less sympathetic and kept my handkerchief to myself. But this was crying through sadness, or so I thought, that deserved a small sacrifice on my part. So, as I said, what do I know? Being a woman, it was just as likely that she had lost her lipstick or was in the middle of those horrible hormonal imbalances that men all over the world fear. She took the offered hanky, wiped her eyes, took a sip of her drink and promptly broke down into deep sobs and a very loud wailing.

The patrons of the pub, as one, turned towards us. They thought she was with me and that I had caused the disturbance by making her cry. Everyone knows that women don't cry spontaneously, and if they're with a man then they're only crying because that man made them. So my natural reaction, driven by guilt, as I always am with women, was the same as anyone else's in that situation – I assumed that I was the cause but this time I wasn't, and a small part of me wanted to stand on the table and tell everyone that I didn't know who she was and that her tears had nothing to do with me.

But I didn't stand on the table. None of us would, because that would only draw more attention and bring all those people still oblivious to the weeping and sobbing by the woman who was now quite clearly with me into their circle of condemnation. I had few excuses because by now her head was buried deep in my handkerchief but if I had started to protest, I would have said first that I hadn't beaten her, and secondly that I hadn't fucked her best friend after an all-night party of drugs and rock and roll that ended in an embarrassing three-in-a-bed romp. I paused for a moment and wondered wistfully who did have these three-in-a-bed romps so beloved of the tabloid press? No one I knew was owning up to being there.

But back to this woman in front of me. As her bawling started to subside into grunts and snivels, I wanted to shout to those who would listen that I hadn't made her pregnant nor disowned both her and the baby which was due any day now. In the end I did nothing. She stayed sitting down and cried some more and I said nothing to her or the assembled and watching drinkers. Maybe they thought it was just street theatre? These thoughts passed in a nanosecond (or was that a microsecond?), which was of no consequence to the rest of the assembled, so I stood up and moved my chair round next to hers. I put my arm around her shoulders. She looked at me askance. I summoned up my most comforting of vocal tones and spoke gently.

'Here now. Don't cry. Want to talk about this? You're okay now.'

She just buried her head into my shoulder and cried even more. The pub returned to its own matters and I worried about the tear stains on my jacket. How was I going to explain that at dinner? Mind you, there might be a good story there which was certain to impress someone.

Chapter III

She said her name was Tracy. What manner of parents call their child *Tracy*? They must have had a really bad day when they made that decision. I said I was Tommy. She was, at best, ordinary in every respect. Jenny would have called her a 'chav' on account of her high-street clothes that fitted just rather too tightly. I admit a tight T-shirt showing just a hint of nipple is quite acceptable to me, but Jenny has other views. Tracy was wearing tight blue jeans which at least, I thought, showed she was thin – a potential convert to my emaciated Britain, and the stock chavvy trainers completed her attire. Her coat, now thrown over the back of the chair with a large canvas bag, was somewhat between an anorak and a rain coat. All were bought, I guessed, on the high street. Tracy's hair was predominantly blonde, but the roots showed distinct touches of brown. It was longish and – as they say of film stars – big, but unlike Hollywood stars it was hardly combed. Her mascara was running with the tears. All in all, she looked vulnerable.

I wanted to ask how old she was but I was, at least to the best of my limited ability, being a gentleman, and in the circumstances this didn't seem like the right question. I was holding back and being restrained. I looked at her closely because, after all, she was still crying on my dinner suit. I guessed she was probably in her early twenties, maybe late teens, even mid-twenties. What the fuck did it matter? She was older than seventeen and still at least twenty years younger than me. If Jenny walked in on us now, not knowing her age wouldn't make a damn of difference and would not be the first question she'd ask. Even I couldn't talk my way out of this one. As Jenny's indifference had grown over the years, so had my capacity to lie or – as I preferred to call it – be less than honest. Most of the time there was actually nothing to be dishonest about. I had always been more or less faithful, and then only unfaithful with escorts and girls identified from cards in telephone boxes, and that didn't count, did it? I mean, I hadn't fucked my best friend's wife or, for that matter, even lusted after them (which, by the way, I don't see as a virtue but simply a damnation of my friends for their poor choice of wives).

But over time I found the truth had become mundane. I took to inventing stories and adventures about my life to amuse both myself and Jenny. At first they were all for her benefit. I wanted and hoped she would see through them and laugh, but she didn't, so my stories became more obscure, fanciful and risky. I discovered the art of lying effectively was to stay as close as possible to the truth with only minor deviations, and then practise the story and rehearse all the possible questions. After a time even I believed my untruths and, if ever interrogated, my outrage at being questioned was real and palpable. When in reality I once tripped and tore my jacket, while only slightly drunk, while only walking down a pavement, I said instead that I had been mugged and that I had fought a valiant fight but in the process lost my credit cards. That had the added benefit of covering up the fact I'd been to a lap-dancing club, which in itself was alright because I was entertaining Japanese clients who had insisted that we should go there, and in fact, I had recovered all the costs on expenses as client entertaining. I was definitely happier making up a mugging than owning up to a lap dance.

Along the same lines, missed trains became cancelled trains, allowing me to tell about the near-riot at Cannon

Street when hundreds of delayed passengers stormed the barricades that were the station master's office. My day was often disturbed by student marches that always seemed to be just where I was on my way to for a meeting. My drink on the way home from work would turn into a story about being rounded up accidentally by the police as an agitator on the march before being released with a profound apology and the promise of a letter from the Chief Constable himself. If Jenny ever wondered how the police confused a suited business man for an agitator, she never said so. Of course I had pre-empted that question with an aside, namely that the police had told me that marchers go out of their way these days to look respectable so as not to get arrested.

'What were you doing to get arrested? How did they spot you?' is what she did ask.

'I was just trying to cross Whitehall and I had to push my way through the march,' I replied.

'And why did you want to cross Whitehall?' she asked and I could see that her interest was waning and approaching zero.

'Why did the chicken cross the road?' I said and I was right. That was the end of that conversation.

Slowly, Tracy was calming down and I offered to buy her a drink. Her name still irked me. Imagine if I had forgotten what she drank – how could I call her name across a pub? How could I retain any self-respect? Under my breath I tried.

'Tracy?'

I recoiled in horror at the sound of the word and had I not left my coat on the chair she was sitting on I might have left her and the pub right there and then but I had to live with it as much as she did, and anyway it was only a passing inconvenience. I was with Tracy – and her name – for at worst an hour, but she had to live with the name for her whole life. Soon I would be away from all this.

'Now stay here and don't move,' I said as I went to the bar. I wasn't being paternal or domineering, just remembering a previous night at a pub with a woman – a girl from the office. Actually she was a manager in the Bank but I still thought of her as a girl. We were sitting having a quiet drink and she said she was going to the toilet so I watched her walk off to find the ladies' and I thought it would be a kind gesture to buy us both another drink. I was sure she would want the same again. The bar was busy, almost two deep, and when I got back she still hadn't returned. I waited and I waited. I drank half my beer and waited some more.

And then fright took over. Maybe she had collapsed in the toilets? I panicked as I felt a strong sense of responsibility for getting her here, having badgered her at the office for days and days to come and have a drink with me. Still no sign. Alternatively, maybe she hadn't collapsed but she had met an old lover and they were in a cubicle in the toilets having hot lesbian sex. I found that a more acceptable idea and excused and assuaged the growing guilt. Collapsing on me was bad form, but dumping me for an old lover was okay. On the other hand, she may have met an old boyfriend and might be in the gents' toilet having sex with him. Now, we weren't on a date; we were only two work colleagues having a drink, accompanied by a little bit of flirting and peanuts. But that didn't matter. I wasn't going to be stood up for an ex-boyfriend so, leaving my drink and a small note saying I was going to return and please don't take my drink or seat, I pushed my way through to the gents' toilet. I checked every cubicle, but there was no sign of her, or her lover, nor could I hear any of the general chatter around the bar that would have arisen from the sight of a woman in the gent's toilet. Surely if she had been there, there would have been a hubbub around the bar? I asked a barman how many toilets they had in the pub. Okay just the one. Then she must be in the ladies' and collapsed or having wild sex. I imagined her sitting on the cistern, legs all akimbo and her panties hanging precariously round one ankle with her lover's head between her thighs. Damn that was a hot idea. I needed to know.

I thought of tip-toeing into the ladies' to have a look around, but there always seemed to be someone going in and never anyone coming out. I wondered if that was another universal truth, but I put the thought to one side. Of course, had I been Mel Gibson in *What Women Want*, I would have just marched in and undertaken the cubicle-check myself but, being English (and not Australian), I found it far easier (and I still reflect on this) to ask a random woman in her mid-twenties to help me. Well she wasn't exactly random, because she was on her way into the ladies' loo.

'Excuse me,' I said, 'but could you check all the cubicles to see if my girlfriend … well, actually work colleague because I'm married … and don't worry because my wife knows her as well … has either collapsed in a cubicle and is ill, or is having lesbian sex with one of her ex-lovers?'

I had enunciated the question carefully. It was precise and not time-consuming, but for some reason that I still don't quite understand she walked right past me, tut-tutting. After three further goes with three more women I simplified the question. Now I don't want to stereotype anyone but the next woman I approached was, I guessed, from Essex and therefore open to most ideas with no sense of self-importance.

'Please shout "Anna" and if anyone responds, say, "Tommy is outside getting pissed off".' Kindly she did so, and I heard the call for Anna, but there was no reply and no Anna. I returned to my beer and had to recover it from my table which was now occupied by another group who had totally ignored my note. I drank it, put on my coat and went home, deeply worried. My missing friend occupied my thoughts all through the journey and again on my way back to work the next day. I had reached the conclusion that she had been murdered or taken into white slavery, and in my mind's eye it was just a matter of time before the police arrived at my office. The officer would hold out a grainy picture of a middle-aged woman. 'Do you know this woman, sir? It seems you were the last person other than the murderer to see her alive. Maybe you were the last person?' and I'm marched off in handcuffs, protesting my innocence.

I was almost beside myself with worry and didn't even notice that Jane put sugar in my coffee and was trying to apologise. Nine thirty-two and Anna marched into my office.

'What the fuck were you doing last night, dumping me and leaving me? You're a bigger bastard than I thought!'

No amount of explaining of how I accosted nearly every woman entering the toilets to find her seemed to matter to her, nor the fact that I was at the bar when she had come back from those toilets. She thought I had gone – so she left. Identifying this simple misunderstanding might have been enough to pacify her, but then I had to go and add something about the wild lesbian sex and tell her that I had felt jealous and she said simply 'Pervert' and slammed the door as she left my office.

So, anyway, I told Tracy to stay exactly where she was. As I sat back at the table, it was close to decision time. Sit with Tracy or go to the dinner? For most people that would have been an easy choice. One pays your wages and is uncomplicated, the other can only be bad news and is likely to be costly. So I made the easy decision and asked Tracy if she wanted anything and to tell me all her woes. I never saw the film *The Odd Couple* and I couldn't remember who was in it (I thought it was Jack Lemmon and Walter Matthau), so I stopped Tracy mid-sentence to ask her if she knew who starred in *The Odd Couple*. She looked surprised. Well, who wouldn't? She hadn't even heard of the film. I suppose she wasn't even alive when it was made, but I made a note to check out the cast.

'Anyway,' I said to her, 'we must look like the original "odd couple".'

'S'pose so,' she mumbled.

As an academic at heart I pride myself for working from data. I needed some facts. Again I tried to read her face and disentangle the emotions displayed there. Was it sadness or fear or something else? Oh, how I wished I had Mel Gibson's power to read women's minds.

'Tracy, where are you from?' I asked, trying not to curl my lips when having to form that name. My God how I hated it.

'Scunthorpe,' she said. I tried to remember my geography. I knew it was somewhere in north England and maybe on the east coast, but I couldn't decide if it was in Humberside or East Yorkshire or Lincolnshire. Or was that Skegness?

'So what does that make you?' I asked, looking for geographical clarification.

'A Scunt,' she said. Rarely am I lost for words, or quick repartee, especially when there is the opportunity for innuendo. Yet this was one of those moments. At my best I even have time to rehearse my lines, so fast is my brain, before they are delivered. When I travelled Continental Airlines to Boston in business class, because of course the Bank was paying, the middle-aged female cabin crew (who managed to look even frumpier than the women and grannies who work for British Airways) used to ask me before we took off, as they passed me my champagne and assorted nuts, 'Would you like your nuts roasted, sir?'. I was fast enough the first time with 'No, just lightly squeezed, please.' And with each journey I had a new line carefully rehearsed during the endless versions of that moment. 'Aren't you supposed to wait until we take off?' or 'I've heard of branding, but I suppose this is the polite way?' were two lines that I recall.

Deep breath. 'Okay, so you're a Scunt.' I was no longer interested whether this was in Lincolnshire or not. With just a change in label and a new name, she had changed all my perceptions of her. Now I was really interested and I wanted to know more. I pulled my chair an inch or two closer. I took the handkerchief and patted her red and still tearful eyes.

'Is everything alright now? Just a bit of a boyfriend problem, maybe?'

And while I waited for an answer, I was thinking that if she left now I wouldn't change my mind and go to the dinner; I might instead go down to Soho and wander around. That could be fun.

'My boyfriend is trying to kill me and the police are chasing me. You're my only friend now, Tommy. You will help me, won't you? Tell me you'll help me?'

Soho was also now no go. I stopped drinking

Chapter IV

I looked at Tracy.

'So is this boyfriend of yours very big?' I asked, ignoring all the innuendo that usually stopped me asking such questions. I was also going to ask if he was a hard man, but even my sense of decorum overruled that.

'I mean, if he catches us, will he beat me up? Do I stand any chance?'

She looked at me and I didn't need to hear any of her words in reply. He was going to be a tough guy.

'Okay. So how tough is he?'

'Very.'

'Any chance we can reason with him?' I asked.

I had always believed that a few well-reasoned words would overcome any situation and I wondered why it didn't happen more often; the pen is mightier than the sword, after all. This wasn't a new thought; I remember it from when I was kid watching the Sunday afternoon movies. Often they were World War II propaganda films with a squadron of British Spitfire pilots sitting around on a summer's day somewhere in Kent waiting for Jerry, in their masses, to fly in over the coast. The Squadron Leader, sitting on the veranda while the other pilots play croquet in the background, says, 'I say, Tommy.' (I think, by the way, that's where my parents got the idea for my name). 'I say, Tommy,' the Squadron Leader says, 'Do you think the Hun will be over today? Bit of a shame if they do, because it's a fine day for a game of cricket. Maybe if we can bring down eleven of the blighters then, just maybe, they might be able to rustle up a team. What do you think? Think they would have a fast bowler among them? Much better if we could sort out this damn war at Lords or the Oval.' The siren would sound. 'Oh well, off we go again. Toodle-pip, Tommy. See you at tea time and save one of those cream scones for me.' Tommy would never return and there would be a cricket bat propped up on his chair, a pretty crying woman, probably a WAAF in her elegant, tightly fitting, breast-enhancing uniform, forlornly holding a cream scone, and watching doleful black Labrador. Then the shot, as the camera panned away, was a clear message that if Hitler had learned the manners and etiquette of the English and taken up cricket and cream scones then all of this could have been avoided.

Tracy looked at me. 'Do you speak Serbian?' I shook my head. 'No? Well you won't be able to talk to him.'

'Can you speak Serbian?' I asked.

'Nope,' she said rather too abruptly for my liking. 'We don't have much to say to each other.'

Generally I pride myself on my sharpness and a picture was forming quite quickly. Serbian and tough made me think gangsters and Mafia, except of course they are Italian – although Mafia now seems to be a catch-all phrase for any group of gangsters. We have things like the Russian mafia. Maybe they all sit around cafes eating blini rather than spaghetti, but I didn't have time to think about that as this was all getting rather too serious. I needed some background to sharpen the edges.

'Tracy, what exactly do you do when not being chased around London?'

'I suppose you need to know now you're involved.'

'What do you mean involved? All I've done is buy you a drink and talk to you for about half an hour,' I said as I checked my watch. Really thirty minutes, I thought. Well dinner was definitely off now.

'Yeah, whatever,' she said and pulled her chair closer to whisper a confidence, 'but you'll be on every security camera in here. If the police see those they're bound to want to talk to you, so in a way you're very involved.'

I looked around to see where the pub had its security cameras and spotted two that I'd never seen before.

I remembered once reading a woman's magazine that had been left on the train just after Bromley South by a fat woman who was sweating just a little too profusely to be acceptable. I was on that particular train because that day I had decided to go home through Ashford; it was a longer journey, but the carriages were better quality. Also, I thought, it showed an independent spirit and signified that I could decide to travel in one of two different ways; first day one way, and then the other on the second. It made me feel like a rebel, of a minor sort, and I sat proudly in my seat looking at the other commuters. I nearly turned to the gentleman sitting next to me and told him that I didn't have to be on this train – I could be on another train on a totally different line, and I could make these sorts of decisions because … well, just because I could. I decided though, having studied him carefully for almost an hour, that he probably wouldn't understand. With his demeanour, the whole process of discretionary travel would be too revolutionary for him. I imagined him arriving home in a state of overall breakdown, crying on his little wife's shoulders; his life a total wreck. He would have to tell her that his life was now meaningless and he would never be able to go to work again. He could only get on one train, but he had met someone who made commuting decisions. He would then potter in his garden for an eternity waiting for death as all his children wondered what had happened to their dad. Such a responsibility was too much for me, so I didn't say anything.

Actually the whole journey hadn't worked out too well, because I'd forgotten that I'd driven to Faversham that morning, which meant I had to take a taxi from Ashford to collect my car – which cost me twice as much as the original train fare and added a total of ninety extra minutes onto the trip. But I cared not. I had exercised my right to make an independent decision and it meant ninety minutes less of having to sit with Jenny. Later, when I got home and explained my lateness, I asked her if she'd heard the news about the lion that escaped from the Aspinal Zoo. She gave me that blank look she had perfected, and I said:

'Don't you listen to any of the local news? There are armed marksmen all over the place and road blocks. Held up for ninety minutes on the way back from Faversham, I was. I just had to sit there with my door locked and window closed. Terrible affair. Someone really must do something about stuff like that. You would think it was part of the zoo license.'

And with that she turned and went off somewhere else into the house.

So back to the train through Bromley South with the sweating woman on it. I was reading this magazine and it said that our faces aren't at all symmetrical and we're really all terribly lopsided and the effect is made worse by the way we comb our hair. I had always parted my hair on the left, and back home I looked in the mirror but still I couldn't see whether I was symmetrical or not. It worried me so much that one day on my journey home, I stopped off at the large local DIY shop and bought four fully-adjustable shaving-mirrors which I could pull out and push in and swivel and turn into any position I fancied. Looking at myself from every direction, one mirror through another, I could see my head from every angle. That, I thought, would allow me to really judge how asymmetrical I was. I spent that weekend fitting the mirrors to the walls of the guest toilet. That had taken some explaining to Jenny, but I told her I had read it in a magazine – not the one on the train to Ashford – that this is what they're doing in all the best new homes and hotels around the world.

'In fact,' I said, 'the Burj Hotel in Dubai, which is the only seven-star hotel in the world …' I emphasised, '… now has six mirrors in the toilet for the guests to use.'

There, so take that. I stood back and she left me to my DIY. Fitting the final mirror to the back of the door in a position so that it didn't break when the door was opened was troublesome, until I again drove back to the DIY store and bought a door stop so that the mirror couldn't touch the wall when the door was opened. Another coup for common sense, I thought. It worked well, but it meant that the door wouldn't open very far and it was a bit of a squeeze to get in to the toilet. You had to turn sideways and push a bit.

'What will our guests do when they come here?' Jenny had asked.

'Lose weight or use another loo,' I told her. Thankfully she never asked me the most obvious question: why does a toilet need four shaving mirrors or – as in the case of the Burj – six? I had an answer. 'The toilet doesn't need any mirrors. It's the people using them who need the mirrors.' I knew that as soon as I started on this pedantic streak she would quickly lose interest.

But once all of them were installed I was able to stand there and see myself in "surround vision". It was fascinating because I'd never seen myself from the back before. I stood there for hours turning like a slow-motion whirling dervish, observing myself from every direction and aspect, but particularly searching for signs of asymmetry. It was not easy because of my hair being parted on the left, so I rummaged through the basket of miscellaneous products and found some over-congealed hair gel. Squeezing myself back in to the toilet, I re-combed my hair with a central parting, perfectly in line with the bridge of my nose. That solved one problem. Now I could see for sure if I was symmetrical.

After days of careful measurement with a ruler I bought during one lunch hour from WHSmith, I decided that my left eye was a fraction elongated to the left and positioned slightly lower than my right, and my mouth on the right turned up a little more than the left when I smiled. Of course, this period of measurement had real drawbacks. Firstly, it meant I had to spend many evening hours in the guest toilet; secondly, it meant that for over two weeks I walked around the office with my new central hair parting. Jane did a double-take on the first Monday I arrived newly coiffured. She gave me my coffee and was about to ask me something but then just shrugged and returned to her desk.

I contemplated extending the research to try and work out whether it was actually my left eye that was out of place or whether my right eye was just too narrow and too high, but that required access to a massive database of comparative data on faces. It would probably have to cover all ethnic groups and probably require an international survey that I couldn't justify on any basis as worthwhile for the Bank to undertake. It did however get some consideration. For one moment, when speaking to IT about face recognition and its use in ATM security, there was a distinct possibility of launching such a project, but when outline costings for the venture reached hundreds rather than tens of millions of pounds, I abandoned the plan. In the end, I decided it was my left side that was more deformed than my right side with its lopsided smile, which I passed off as an idiosyncrasy, and I was sure my right side was my best side. So here I was in the pub with Tracy, and I turned slightly in my seat to make sure that if I was to be on any security cameras it was my right side that got photographed.

'So tell me, Tracy, what is it you do to make all these people so upset?' I asked. I was really asking about the source of tonight's tears – not her job – but she misunderstood me.

'It's a sort of customer service job.'

'That doesn't sound like something to get you into these kinds of problems. What do you do? Work in a call-centre or in a bank or a shop?'

I doubted it was the last because as she was sitting there I realised she had taken the opportunity to redo her makeup and tidy herself up, and she was starting to look quite pretty. Put her in some decent clothes and she would scrub up quite presentable.

'I suppose you could call it a call centre. I'm on-call and I service customers.'

I had never thought of myself as dense. I knew I was ultra-intelligent, of course, which I could demonstrate in multiple ways, and there was my near-perfect memory and my ability to talk on any subject with little preparation, using a string of long words all of which were completely unknown to my audience. I worked on the basis that if they couldn't understand what I was saying because they didn't understand the vocabulary, then they would assume that the content was of similar erudition. Once I had also tried adding the complexity of really long sentences to my speeches with clauses embedded within other clauses. I researched long sentences and realised I had a lot of scope. In James Joyce's *Ulysses*, Molly Bloom's final soliloquy consists of two huge sentences, one of over eleven thousand words, and a second of nearly thirteen thousand words (beaten only by one of nearly fourteen thousand from the book *The Rotters' Club*).

So once, when I made a whole sentence last ten minutes, I knew I was still in kindergarten compared to the experts. The stratagem worked quite well, though, but I was disappointed by the overall effect and during questioning I needed to add back some clarity. The real problem was that the structure of the sentence needed, as the jargon says, signposting. I needed to help my audiences with the punctuation. Thus I learnt, and adopted, Victor Borge's ideas on phonetic punctuation, and invented a whole range of guttural sounds for each of the punctuation marks, not adapting Mr Borge's phonetics, of course, because he is Danish they needed to be translated and English needed its own versions. Come to think of it, Mr Borge's punctuation is probably the only thing I've ever really forgotten. (I made a mental note of that as well, which reminded me to clear out many of my mental notes as they were getting too complex to remember. They needed to be filed into long-term memory.) With a *'phlatt'* and a *'zhippp'* covering commas and full stops I soon had a complete repertoire of sounds. The additions added a wonderful obscurity to everything I said:

'Rural economies *phlatt* predominantly in the Third

World *phlatt* and then within an African perspective *phlatt* have a propensity *phlatt* when considered against a global recession and increasing *phlatt* and how should I articulate this *ssshhhppp* a predisposition to fraud *ssshhhppp* demonstrating long-term *phlatt* structural fiscal imbalances which lead to societal imbalances that cannot be rectified through traditional monetary or social mechanisms *zhipp.*'

Sadly I was unable to finish this speech as the Chairman announced after I'd been talking for not even ten minutes and was still on my first sentence that the conference was over-running and I had to stop immediately. I wasn't even given the time to say, 'Thank you *zhippp*'

And nor did I consider myself naive. After all, I was a man of the world and until this interruption by Tracy I had been considering a visit to Soho. But I missed the point of Tracy's words.

'Oh, that sounds interesting,' I said. 'And what services do you deliver?'

'Do you really expect me to list them all out here? It's a long list but I'm very versatile and I'm always open to the right proposal. Or should I say, everything is open for the right proposal.' And still I didn't understand.

'I'm sorry, Tracy, you're starting to lose me now. I really have no idea of what you do.'

'Tommy, you're being really dense.' And, although she didn't know it, that was almost the biggest insult she could hurl at me. 'Tommy, I'm a *call girl*! A hooker, a model, a whore, a harlot, a tart! A working girl, a lady of the night, a woman of pleasure, a street walker! Tommy, I'm a *prostitute.*'

'O-k-a-y,' I said slowly. 'You're a...' and suddenly I was lost. Which of her descriptions should I use? Why should I worry? She had gone through as full a lexicon as I could ever muster and certainly without a great deal more thought. Her choice of nouns suddenly made me realise there were both acceptable and unacceptable descriptions of her profession.

'So, you're a model.'

'Oh come on, Tommy. Don't be so naive or such a prude. I'm a whore. Get it?'

My first reaction was to protest. 'No I don't get it. I never go to prostitutes. I'm married. Well, of course that's not quite true because there was Helga in Hamburg and I thought she liked me, well … liked me a lot actually. I was sitting at the bar after a day at work with a small beer, passing time and waiting for another day at work, when this girl next to me ordered a drink, and then, when she came to pay, she discovered her purse had been stolen. So I offered to pay. Well, I was on an expense account, and she said thank you and smiled, and I smiled and she sat next to me, put her hand on my leg and we got on really well and you know how things are, and I thought I was on to a good thing so I invited her to my room to share my miniatures and she said yes, and, well, to cut a long story short, she then demanded two thousand Euros. You know that was difficult to get through expenses.'

I looked up and saw Jenny – well not actually Jenny, but that same look that Jenny gets – on Tracy's face. Boredom.

'You know that scam, don't you, Tracy?'

She nodded. 'Been there, done that,' she said.

'You seem awfully relaxed talking about your job. In fact, really laid back. Oh gosh, I'm sorry – that's totally the wrong expression. I didn't mean it. Laid back. I meant, relaxed.'

'Get a grip, Tommy.'

'Don't you do that?' I said and regretted my words straight away, and she stood up and started gathering her things together to go.

'Look, I'm sorry. Please stop. I will help you. Please, Tracy, sit down and we can get a plan together.' And there I was right in the middle of a mess I didn't understand.

'Tell me then, what's the story? But before you do that, can I just say I hate your name – I mean Tracy. It's such a chavvy name. What were your parents thinking of?'

I could find some excuse for them. Maybe they were huge fans of International Rescue and the Thunderbirds, housed on Tracy Island with the fabulous crew forever saving the world. Could I remember all the names of the Tracy family? Jeff, Virgil, Scott, Alan, and Gordon? There was one more. Where was his name filed? Today I was like the Thunderbirds – saving one of their own, their own little Tracy. No, she had to have a different name although 'Thunderbirds Are Go!' was a good rallying call for this adventure.

'If I'm going to help you, I can't call you Tracy. I've got to call you something else.'

It came to me. John Tracy, of course. 'Did your parents watch *Thunderbirds*?' I asked her absent-mindedly.

'What then?' she looked at me with a massive indifference.

'Until I think of something I'll just call you Scunt. Or, if I'm thinking kind thoughts towards you, I could call you, my little Scunt. Now tell me what's happening?'

I thought that was all rather funny and a tad clever but confident that she would turn up her nose at the idea. Maybe she had another name? Maybe she was also a Peaches or a Jordan and – compared to those names – Scunt wasn't actually too bad.

'Do you know you now need a visa to get into Jordan? She is getting very particular since Peter Andre!' I smiled at my own joke but the expression on Tracy aka Scunt's face was blank.

'So Scunt it is, then?'

She didn't sit down and stood looking at me. 'Whatever. We can't stay here. He – they will find me, and very soon. I know it. We must leave now and I'll tell you everything on the way. We have to go.'

'And where d'you think we should go?' I asked. I felt the whole pub had been watching us as we had our first little tiff but now, like young lovers, we were reconciled.

'You're supposed to be the clever one. You decide but come on – we need to go. We're in danger if we stay here. Oh come on, Tommy,' and with that she gathered all our belongings together, took my hand and pulled me out into the night.

Chapter V

'But I'm dressed for dinner – not for running,' I protested.

Scunt would have none of it. 'We just have to go now. Come on, Tommy, don't hang about. We have to run away.'

So there I was. I was suddenly on the run from both the police and a Serbian pimp and his gang, with a young woman I hadn't even known two hours ago. I didn't know if I should be excited or shit scared. How could I ever explain something like this to Jenny? For once I wouldn't have to make up a story – something was really happening. Tonight I would get Scunt safe, wander back to the flat to sleep, wake up late, shower and change for work, arriving about mid-day. What would Jane do with my coffee in the morning? Send an email to everyone in the office to see if she could resell it? Then maybe I'd get home tomorrow night and say, 'Life is so boring these days. I wish something exciting would happen. Maybe I'll go to Aspinal's and release a lion. What do you think, Jenny?' Yes, that's what I'd do. Tell her nothing about my adventures, and keep it all to myself. Why should she share my excitement?

'Okay, Scunt. We need to get you safe. What do you think – north or south? You will tell me everything won't you, when you've got more time?'

'Of course, Tommy. Look, there's a taxi coming,' and with that she ran into the middle of the road and stood waving frantic arms to make it stop. The black cab had little choice and screeched to a halt, just avoiding carrying her away on its bonnet. She dived into the back. 'Come on Tommy, don't hang about.'

There we sat, in a London cab, while I tried to catch my

breath. Events were moving very quickly and I knew I wasn't in control. We sat there – me on the left with Scunt close to me, but not so close that we could be mistaken for lovers. But the cab didn't move and the driver in the front was impassive behind his glass divide. We looked at each other and then heard the disembodied voice on the cab intercom.

'So are you going to tell me where to go?' We looked at each other again and Scunt shrugged. So it was decision time. North or south? Well I knew the south well and, at best and most generous, the southern suburbs are boring. Jenny and I had once thought about moving to the London suburbs to live with all the other commuters. She said it would be good to have many more friends around us and I might enjoy not having to wake up quite so early, and I would be back home while it was still light. The prospect filled me with horror. There would be rows and rows of Barratt-built homes, in little cul-de-sacs, each with their totally appropriate saloon car parked outside.

For Jenny, it had always been about status and I could imagine her telling me that we had joined the neighbourhood community club and that as part of the rules we had to keep our cars clean if they were parked outside the house, and mow the lawns twice a week at least, and each spring we had to plant daffodils so the cul-de-sac was a sun blast of yellow. I would have to wash the car on Sunday mornings and mow the grass, not just because they needed a clean or a cut, nor because it's what all our neighbours did, but because that's what the neighbourhood community club rules said.

'What would happen if we planted things that came up red instead of yellow?'

'We would be thrown out of the club,' she'd say.

'Would that be bad news?' I would ask in all innocence.

'Well, first I wouldn't be invited for morning coffee or Sunday lunchtime cocktail parties, and second we wouldn't get our copy of the monthly newsletter.'

'Well that wouldn't matter,' I'd say, 'because the only thing in the newsletter would be details of when to plant the daffodils, who was hosting the coffee mornings, and when the next cocktail party was planned, and if we weren't going to be invited then we wouldn't need the newsletter.'

That was a logical masterstroke but Jenny would have just shrugged and I'd know that the intellectual effort of managing the concept had become too much for her. I wondered whether the closeness of a community scheme like that might really be a front for a huge wife-swapping club or even the real-life setting for *The Stepford Wives*. Those Sunday lunchtime cocktail parties might just be a cover. I'd have to check through the old newsletters to see if there was any talk about a bus being hired to take the children to a zoo or amusement park, because clearly they would want all the children to be away while they were doing whatever they were doing. Yes, that's how I would organise it: hire a bus and take the brats away about eleven and not return them until after six. That would give everyone time to change into their party wear. Would they walk to each other's house naked or put coats on first? So many practicalities to consider. And would there be more rules, like you couldn't go with the same swap each month, you had to rotate around the cul-de-sac? Again I would have to look for hidden clues in the newsletter: 'This month house number 7 has been paired with number 16.'

As Jenny and I had driven to inspect the forlorn cul-de-sac, I was actually getting interested in the idea of a move because I knew I could bring a great deal of innovation and management to the wife-swapping organisation, but then I started to think of the pitfalls. No doubt I would have to walk to the station with one or other of the occupants of the cul-de-sac. I could hear myself trying to find small talk. 'Your wife is very flexible and accommodating. How's my wife? I hope she hasn't been complaining about her bad back again? Do you think we should have a BDSM weekend soon?' That would all be too much, so I would have to leave the house at a different time to avoid everybody, and it couldn't be later, so it would have to be earlier and I wouldn't get enough time in bed. That's when I went off the idea of the southern suburbs. I assumed that somehow North London would be different. I didn't know anything about North London but it just seemed to be different. Maybe it was knowing that there were less suburbs and more student flats and council houses. It seemed a far more grounded sort of place. They wouldn't need newsletters to arrange a fuck. I would just go down to the pub, buy a drink and tell Jenny I was going off with some pretty young thing for a quick bang. Don't wait up for me, I would say.

In fact, that was pretty much what I was doing at that very moment, except I doubted that Scunt and I would ever have sex. I was more concerned about surviving the night. The cab was still stationary and Scunt was looking at me.

'North,' I said.

'Need to be more specific mate,' the driver said, 'there's a lot of north from here.'

Again Scunt looked me.

'King's Cross. King's Cross station.' We were going to go north. There are lots of places in the immediate vicinity of Kings Cross.

'About sodding time,' and the taxi pulled away.

'Scunt, I need to know everything, but not right now. Did you say the police are after you as well?' I was whispering in case the driver had the passenger microphone switched on. Suddenly I was thinking about the Jason Bourne films and the one set at Waterloo. Which one was it? *The Bourne Identity* or *The Bourne Ultimatum* – it didn't matter. The CIA tracked him and tapped his phone with no problem at all. Maybe the London police had access to the same technology and were, right at this very moment, sitting in a darkened control room watching our every step through a network of security cameras. We had to act carefully to fool them as best we could. I was getting into this spat. I knew my intellect could outwit any mere plod of a policeman. I knocked on the driver's window.

'We've changed our minds. We want to go to Waterloo.'

'Make your bloody mind up, sir. King's Cross or Waterloo?'

I overlooked the mixture of swearing and courteousness, assuming that Scunt had heard far worse, and replied, 'Take us to Waterloo please, driver.'

Scunt looked at me and I gave her that I'm-a-doctor-trust-me look and said, 'It's okay. I know what I'm doing. Trust me.' and I sank back in the seat to work out the details.

It was less than fifteen minutes to Waterloo and Scunt thankfully stayed quiet while I started to turn on the memory and get myself into gear. All I needed to do was find somewhere to hide her. I was trying to think of places to the north of London; maybe Hemel Hempstead? I had never been there, but I liked the sound of the name.

'If you want to avoid the police then we need to get you

off those cameras. We need to lose you – in a security sense. This is what you'll do, okay?'

This was exciting. I was living out my film fantasy and I really was Jason Bourne. I didn't know how much money we would need but I needed cash so I wouldn't have to pay for anything with credit cards which they could trace in an instant, except of course for Scunt's train ticket which I wanted them to track. I decided that first we needed to be furtive and suspicious so that we were noticed at Waterloo. I wanted to be noticed at Waterloo so they would think we were going south or west. Later we would make a furtive run to King's Cross.

We were at Waterloo and I over-tipped the taxi driver. He was part one of my plan. He would remember us. I took Scunt's hand and almost pulled her around with me. We avoided the centre of the huge station concourse, even though it was now nearly empty from the rush-hour of commuters. As we passed an ATM we stopped and I maxed out the cash allowance from one card, and then another at a second machine, and finally, at a third, I used my company card, so that I had well over a thousand pounds cash on me. Scunt just looked at me. I'm sure I saw admiration on her face, and respect and – yes – even a hint of love. It didn't surprise me because I was taking control, as every man should. I was a dashing knight on a metaphoric white charger and any woman in her right senses would, at that moment, have fallen in love with me. At that moment, in my dinner suit, I was her James Bond. She would be marvelling at my knowledge of how to avoid the police. She would respect my calmness and my intellect. My God, I was handsome and, as I lived my dream, I used the Scottish brogue of my favourite Bond actor, Sean Connery.

'Just stay close to me, Scunt,' I said as we headed off to the ticket office. 'When I buy your ticket, Scunt, make a fuss,' and I gave her no time to answer. The queue for first-class tickets was short, and that fitted my plan. 'One first-class single to Aldershot, please,' I said.

'Just one ticket?' she asked. 'Aren't you coming with me?'

'No I'm not, Scunt. I'm done with you. I'll buy you this ticket and then you're off by yourself and good riddance I might add,' and turning to the young man dispensing tickets, 'Get a move on – we've got a train to catch!' Scunt huffed and puffed around me as I handed over my card.

'Come on, Scunt, let's get you on a train,' and we set off for the platforms. I had to pull her along as we walked towards platform number three. We were definitely noticed. She was almost scraping her shoes as I dragged her along. It was like a mother in a supermarket pulling a small child away from the chocolates or toys. But I was an old man and she a young woman; we could hardly be missed. All the time she was muttering her displeasure.

'I thought you said you would help me and all you do is buy me a friggin' ticket to Aldershot. What do you want me to do – join the friggin' army?'

I stopped her. 'You're not going to Aldershot and nor am I, so just shut up and listen to me.'

'What's wrong with your voice?' she said, 'it sounds like some funny Scottish impression. Are you pretending to be Billy Connolly? Are you alright?'

'Of course I'm alright.' I dropped the Sean Connery and used my Roger Moore, with just a hint of Pierce Brosnan. 'Anyway, as a Scunt you can hardly talk about good accents. Have you ever heard yourself? Stop talking about my accent and listen to me.'

Waterloo was perfect for my plan.

'I want you to go through the barrier and on the inside you can also walk along to other platforms. Go to the far end and then get back on the concourse as late as possible. As you walk, find a place to undo your hair and let it hang loose. Try to look as different as you can. Stay near the edges, then come back onto the concourse to take a taxi to Euston station. I'll meet you there.'

'What on earth are you playing at, Tommy? Why didn't we just go straight there? And why now Euston? Are we playing Monopoly – collecting every station in London?'

'Oh come on, Scunt, think. The taxi driver, all my credit cards, the ticket booth; this way they'll think we're in Waterloo. We've bought a ticket here and they think we've separated. This way they'll be looking for a single girl in Aldershot, and if they do connect us, the taxi driver will send them here. This is what being clever is all about. This is what Jason Bourne would have done.' The look on her face wasn't one that said she was convinced by my ideas.

'Okay, Tommy. If you say so,' she said as she took the ticket and thirty pounds proffered for the taxi. She pulled her hair out of the scrunchie and shook her head as her hair flowed free.

'I said to wait till you're through the barrier. Oh don't worry. Just go and I'll see you in Euston.'

She looked far more attractive with her hair down and I thought at this moment James Bond would have kissed her. She turned slowly to walk away. I wondered what endearment she would throw my way. Probably tell me she loves me or tell me to take care. The world moved into slow motion as she looked back over her shoulder.

'And who the fuck is Jason Bourne?'

Chapter VI

We took our separate taxis and re-met at Euston, one of London's great railway stations, although the grandeur of the past has been renovated into 1980s chic. I saw Scunt and her anorak and I suddenly felt proud of what I was doing. I was saving a damsel in distress. With all my strategic planning I really hadn't had time to think about her and her predicament. There would be time enough for that later.

'I wasn't sure you would come here. Thanks. But where are we going, Tommy? We need to move,' she said and I pulled her off to the ticket office.

'Let's buy some more tickets, but let's be a little low key this time,' I said, trying to add a little levity into the conversation, but she would have none of it and she was pulling me along.

'Know where we're going?' she asked.

'Hemel Hempstead I thought would be good. Nice and suburban. Book into a Travelodge and no one will find us there.'

We reached the window and I got a more than withering look.

'Fuck off, Tommy. We're supposed to be getting away. Hemel Hempstead isn't getting away. That's like going out for a smart middle-class supper. We need to get *away.*'

We had reached the window and I was about to speak to the teller when Scunt pushed me aside.

'Two singles to Glasgow.'

'Sleeper?' a voice said.

'No. Just ordinary seats,' Scunt said as I watched. 'What time is the train?'

'Twenty-three fifty and gets in at seven thirty. Sure you don't want a sleeper?'

'No. How much?'

'Fifty-five pounds each. That makes one hundred and ten.'

'Give him the money, Tommy,' and I handed over cash from my reserve as she took the tickets.

'Scunt, we're supposed to be low key and you go and make a fuss and tell him my name. Jason Bourne would never have done that. You've got to be more careful.'

She stopped and faced me. 'Tell me, Tommy, who is this Jason Bourne? Is he coming with us all the way? Anyway, we've got half an hour till the train goes. We should get some food. It's terrible on the train.'

At last I thought this woman was showing some good sense. I looked around for a decent restaurant. 'What do you think? Italian or French?' I asked. 'I'm sure they'll do a fast service in a railway station.'

Again Scunt stopped in her tracks and from dismay her face softened and she smiled, just a little smile. 'Tommy, you and Jason Bourne really are useless, aren't you?' and she put her hands round my waist and pulled us into a conspiratorial hug. 'Tommy, we need to buy some sandwiches and drinks. We don't have time for a meal. Come on, let's go to Glasgow,' and she gave me a small peck on the cheek and I felt warm and fluffy inside in a way I hadn't for a long time.

With a carrier bag of assorted sandwiches and soft drinks we settled into our seats on the train to Glasgow. Fuck, Glasgow! What was I doing? I had been going out to a boring dinner or maybe a tour around Soho and now here I was aiding an escaped something or other to the far north.

Nobody in their right mind goes to Glasgow. For that matter, no one in their right mind goes to Hemel Hempstead, but at least that's closer and I could have been back home by tomorrow night. We could have gone anywhere – but we're going to Glasgow. We could have gone to Milton Keynes, although I have to admit you have to be slightly deranged to go there. But why hadn't we gone to Milton Keynes? That would have been a brilliant idea. Even if you have an address, it's impossible to find anywhere in Milton Keynes. It's the most confusing place on God's earth. I should have thought harder about where we could have gone. There are so many sordid and ambiguous little places in England where no one in their right mind would follow us. We could have gone to Hull, for example. What did I hear said about Hull? If God decided to give the world an enema, that's where he would insert the tube? And then there was that line from the Beautiful South song: *When you feel like London and look like Hull.* No one would follow us there. Even our Serbian would think twice. *Ya ne sobirayus Hull.* Of course I can't speak Serbian, but I knew it in Russian.

'Scunt. *Ya ne sobirayus Hull.*' I wish I had one of those big furry hats and I would look just like a Russian. 'Scunt. *Ya ne sobirayus Hull.*' I practised again with a heavy Russian accent.

Scunt looked up at me from her gaze at the passing countryside, mainly hidden in the dark of the night. 'What you going on about, Tommy?'

'I was just saying we're not going to Hull.'

'I know we're not going to Hull. We're going to Glasgow. And what language was that?'

'Russian,' I said rather sheepishly.

'Have a sandwich. Chicken salad. Beef with—' and she

stopped to turn the packing over to read all the contents, 'with lettuce, tomato, horseradish sauce on a seeded rye bread. Or there's tuna. Or there's—'

I stopped her. It was now clear that she had cleaned out the sandwich shop and basically I could have whatever I wanted but I didn't need to know the menu. We probably had enough to start reselling food somewhere near Cumbria to hungry insomniacs. 'BLT?' I asked knowing that somewhere she could provide. She rustled around and drew out a triangular package of deep-filled, one hundred per cent wholesome BLT.

'And anything diet for a drink,' I said before we went through the entire drinks menu. We started to eat.

'So, Scunt. Now would be a good time to tell me what this is all about.' She took a bite of the beef with all its trimmings, put the sandwich down and gathered herself.

'I was seventeen when I left Scunthorpe. I did an extra year after my GCSEs but I hated it so I came down to London and stayed with some friends of my sister – her name's Sharon. It was really cool at first. We went to lots of clubs and had great parties and went to all the festivals whenever we could.'

Always practical, I had to ask. 'What did you do for money?'

'I had done typing at school so I got some temping jobs. It meant I didn't have to work too hard and the guys in the flat always seemed to have some money for booze, so I got by quite well.' She stopped to take another mouthful of sandwich with a finality that suggested the story was finished.

'It's a long way from being a temp and squatting in London to being on the run,' I suggested.

'It wasn't a squat. We paid our rent.'

'Oh, come on Scunt. Get to the interesting bit that has me on a train in the middle of the night to Glasgow. I had much better plans than this.'

'What were you going to do, Tommy, if I hadn't come along? All dressed up in your finery. I like the suit by the way – makes you look very handsome,' she said, feeling the cloth of the lapel between her fingers with that innate skill of women to change the subject of the conversation. I wanted to know about her and she had managed, through a compliment, to make me talk about my plans. I told her about the dinner.

'That sounds as though it would have been really nice. I'm sorry, Tommy, to have dragged you away like this.'

'Scunt,' I said, 'you haven't been to one of these dinners. They're awful. First – they're all men.' I looked as she started to smile.

'Okay, you might like going to do's with all men, but I don't. They all believe they know the answer to every question when in truth they don't even understand the questions most of the time. They pontificate on world matters as if it were a giant Monopoly board and they get paid shed loads of money in amounts measured simply by their arrogance. You just have to sit there during dinner trying to work your way from the outside knife and fork while mass-catering takes its toll. You have to look at the wine bottle and make some comment on the year and the grapes. You have to make small talk and discuss the economy, and then – do you know what the worst thing is? Do you know?'

Scunt looked to me slightly wide-eyed, but not with a look of disinterest, as I once thought Jenny had been interested in my thoughts. 'No, Tommy. Tell me? What's the worst thing?'

'The friggin' speeches after dinner. That's what's worst.' In an attempt to be hip I had even started to ape her language. I hadn't uttered friggin' once in a life-time of swearing. I would always switch from genteel golly-gosh's and gee whiz's to full-on Anglo Saxon fuck and shit. There had never been a half-way house of acceptable swearing.

'That's the worst. The speeches after dinner. They go on and on and on and you have to sit there pretending to be interested.'

'Who gives the speeches, Tommy? Do you?'

'Me? No. God forbid. It's probably the Master of some livery company or other with all his gold chains.'

Scunt had stopped eating and looked at me. 'That sounds quite sexy actually. I like Masters and chains.'

'Scunt, what are you thinking about? This is supposed to be serious.'

'It sounds serious to me. Does he use his gold chains to shackle and whip some beautiful young girl for all you horny men to watch? I'd quite like that job, being naked in front of all those men. It doesn't sound boring at all. Do you get cross because you want to be the one doing the whipping? Tell me, Tommy. Come on, tell me.'

She raised a number of fantastical images that even I hadn't managed to conjure up in my most private (some might say, deranged) moments. Imagine, the dinner over, a chained wench being dragged onto a stage, as willingly as Scunt sounds, and tied up for the pleasure of the guests. Then Master of the Worshipful Company of Barbers would shave every hair off her body, the Blacksmiths would 'brand' her, and the leather-clad Cordwainers would pronounce on the weight of the warp and the weft. The Worshipful Society of Apothecaries would give her aphrodisiacs to drink. The Coopers would lay her over a barrel, the Salters would spice her up, and the Master of the Saddlers would ride her. The Clockmakers and Actuaries – working together – would time how long she resisted for. And the Accountants? What would the Accountants do? Probably moan about how much it was all costing.

'Tommy, come back here to me,' I looked up from my daydream to see Scunt snapping her fingers and reluctantly I re-joined her. I must have been less than a quarter of the way through the list of livery companies.

'No, it's not sexy,' I said, 'unless you call listening to a rather short man, with a belly that shows too many years of over-drinking and over-eating, bore on and on about a subject that has no interest to you, in a tone that would make even the most rebellious and fractious of babies sleep. The speaker will have a hugely inflated sense of his oratory skills and an ambition to do a set at a comedy club. At least there I could heckle. As a speaker he will undoubtedly be hopeless on all fronts and interpret the polite applause as a thunderous reception of his skills.'

Again Scunt seemed to show interest. 'What were you going to do after that? Just go home?'

'I don't know,' I said. 'I was going to stay at the company flat, watch some TV and sleep, I suppose.'

She stared at me as I finished. 'No, you weren't, Tommy. You were thinking of getting a girl in there with you, weren't you? Now tell me the truth. Where were you going to find her?'

I muttered that I might have had those thoughts and that

I might have missed the dinner to go round the streets of Soho, but only after she had delayed me from getting to the dinner at a respectable time. I wondered at her perceptiveness. Was I really so transparent?

'How would you have found her? Would you have phoned an agency or something? Tell me.'

I owned up, but said I hadn't got that far in my plan. I would probably just have gone to the dinner after all, but the thought of illicit sex would have got me through the boredom of the speeches.

'What would your wife say? Would you tell her?'

'Of course I wouldn't, and how did you know I was married?'

'You *look* married. You have that look of *being* married,' she added. 'And if I had been you I would have told her. Anyway, the whore found *you*.' And with that she took another bite of her sandwich and seemed to move just a little closer to me.

'Stand up, Tommy, we need to sleep. It will be early and busy tomorrow.'

'How does standing up help me sleep?' This girl had a logic of her own.

'Get your coat and roll it up as a pillow and come and sit here in the corner by the window.' I was now just obeying. Jason Bourne would never have stood for this, but I did; I rolled up my coat and sat in the corner.

'Now get yourself comfortable.'

I did, and as Scunt stretched out on the other seat with her head in my lap and my hand stroking her hair, she whispered, 'Good night, Tommy. Sweet dreams.' For the first time I thought she looked vulnerable.

Chapter VII

I don't know whether it was the excitement of our race across London, being up since five in the morning, or the openness and ease of Scunt, but I fell into a deep sleep – after making sure she was on the other side of her dreams before me.

'Glasgow. Glasgow Central!' The guttural Scots accent was worse than my alarm clock as the guard roared down the carriage. I had slept as well as one could on a train seat and Scunt was just stirring next to me. With her head in my lap and her mass of hair everywhere, this was an opportunity for a really incriminating photograph – but enough of that. I needed to take stock and prioritise; but I couldn't, because I still didn't know who or what we were running from. It was time to get my brain into gear. First, clearly I was not going to be in the office today. Even if I dumped Scunt, the earliest I could be back in London was mid-afternoon and by the time I had collected my stuff from the flat the day would be done. Second, I couldn't wander around all day in a dinner suit.

Two actions, then. I like being decisive. One: contact the office. Two: buy a change of clothes. What resources did I have? Credit cards with plenty of credit, a heap of cash, a mobile phone and a passport. Life overseas had taught me never to travel anywhere without my passport. On my way to Holland once, it was only at the airport that I worked out I didn't have my passport. I talked my way out of the UK and into Holland on nothing but a business card and a lot of shouting about this being the EU. Coming home, the Dutch were as willing to let me out as the British had been when I left. They must have thought it was going to be someone else's problem when I arrived. It worked out well. As I arrived at Heathrow I marched to the front of a long queue at immigration and asked where someone who travelled without his passport should report. They looked at me, took my business card and just let me through. I had to wait in baggage to catch up with my colleagues. Anyway I don't need my passport to get into Scotland – yet.

Scunt sat up and stretched. 'Morning, Tommy. You need a shave. You look rough.'

A shave. Something else to buy. There's an old rugby club joke about a man never going to bed with an ugly woman but sure as hell waking up with a few. The rugby boot, in this case, was on the other foot. I was no longer the suave, sophisticated, debonair man from the night before; but Scunt had a youthful freshness that was charming me more each moment. The train was slowing and we were in the bowels of Glasgow Central station.

'I've got a plan,' I said.

'I like it when you have a plan. They're always such fun and so impracticable,' she said. 'So what is your plan? No, let me guess? First, we find a nice hotel, and then we check in and have a nice big breakfast. You're so wonderful, Tommy. You have the best plans. Come on. The train's stopped.'

'That wasn't my plan at all,' I said.

'But it would have been if you'd thought about it just a little more – and it's a wonderful plan.' She picked up her bag. 'Now come on, Tommy,' and she started towards the train door. I followed obediently and then she stopped suddenly, causing me to bump into her and I only just avoided stepping on her foot.

'Haven't you forgotten someone?' she said, turning.

'What? Who?'

'Jason? Jason Bourne. Don't tell me you've left him behind,' and she turned, laughed and skipped towards the exit.

'So, Tommy. Which hotel?' she said as we headed off the platform and onto the station concourse.

'I don't know. Thankfully I've never had to be in Glasgow before. Guess we find a tourist centre and ask there,' I said as I started an aimless wandering towards the light of the Scottish outdoors.

This was all a bit of a mess. I was at a commuter station at least an hour or more earlier than I should be, but a station probably four hundred miles away from the right one. I was with a young and increasingly pretty prostitute, whom I called Scunt, who was on the run from a very large Serbian man and the police. Yet, I felt a degree of freedom and cheerfulness that had long been absent from my life. I couldn't weigh up which had the upper hand. Maybe her plan wasn't so bad. Find some good breakfast in a small family hotel, have a wash and then head back to London or Milton Keynes tonight. We would have to book and pay for the night, though. I was sure that Scottish hospitality hadn't taken on board the concept of the love hotels in Japan or Amsterdam, where you booked in for just a couple of hours.

I wondered what happens in those places when the passion extends beyond the one or two hours the room is booked for. Do they just charge you more? Or maybe there's even a special rate whereby you agree that the next couple due in the room can join you; double-occupancy becomes quadruple-occupancy. Or do they count a couple as one, so double-occupancy is really four people? And would they have a special premature ejaculation discount rate, and then you had to leave early? So many issues to consider for the people drawing up the marketing and business plan.

I put these thoughts to one side and moved on to the merits of a home-cooked fried breakfast when Scunt grabbed my hand and shouted something. It suddenly felt like a re-run of last night. All around us people stopped and stared. Had we been spotted? I began plotting our escape. Where were the nearest exits? Should we run or try to board a moving train to make our get-away?

'What?'

'That's where I want to go,' and she pointed at an advert high above us on the street. *Burnet Square*, it said. *More than a Hotel*. 'That's where we're going, Tommy. Look, it's got a spa as well. Oh, how wonderful,' and again she pulled me off, this time to the taxi rank.

I had preconceptions of Glasgow as a coarse and tough city with a mass of poor housing with tenement buildings, chip shops serving deep-fried Mars Bars, street-fighting Scots with the roughest and most impenetrable of accents, and street corners littered by drunks, homeless folk and the generally disadvantaged – which, here, meant everyone. It was meant to be a bleak place of dark corners with John Rebus or Taggart losing an endless battle against an unending wave of crime. I had heard Billy Connolly describe the shipyards of the Clyde and I had seen, only on TV of course, the tribal rivalry that was Celtic against Rangers and the passion they have for turning a football match into a gladiatorial contest between rival fans but my impression had clearly been tainted by friends and acquaintances from Edinburgh – a city I did think was beautiful – who clearly demonstrated their jealousies. As I looked out from the taxi I saw many green spaces and wonderful town houses; and Burnet Square had both. My attempt to live off cash alone and leave the credit card in the wallet was going to be sorely explored. This was not a four-shilling dive.

We headed towards the reception area. This was my territory. I had done this more times than Scunt had had hot dinners, and looking again at her almost painful thinness that was probably true. I've checked into hotels on at least four continents, and I've learnt the art of indifference to the task, which displays experience, savoir faire, and a certain essential disdain for the receptionists themselves. The best approach, especially overseas where the staff have agonisingly poor English, is to slap down a business card and a passport, shout your name and immediately start a conversation on the mobile phone. That way you don't have to talk to them about the beauty of the awful city you happened to have just landed in, or the likelihood of their specialist tourist attraction of vampires careering through the streets after midnight, happening that very night. When you hear them trying to confirm the number of nights' stay, just yell down the phone: 'Hold on, Roger, just got to sort out the receptionist here,' then turn to him or her and say, 'I really don't understand. It's all on the booking form,' while simultaneously holding up the requisite number of fingers. Sign the forms while still on the phone and ask both where the bar is and for the concierge to take your bags to the room. This way you don't have to tip some spotty mule for carrying bags you could easily have carried yourself. Why should Glasgow be any different from any other foreign city? It is after all a foreign city.

'Good morning, sir, madam.' Despite the courtesy of the words, the staff clearly didn't think we belonged in their establishment. I could understand their concern; I was not properly dressed. I knew I should have retied my bow tie. I was about to answer when Scunt started talking.

'Double room for four nights. What's your rate?'

In my world you do not ask this sort of establishment their rate. It's invariable.

'The deluxe is £220 per night, madam, and the suite is £400, which includes service and VAT.'

'Fine. We will take a deluxe room for four nights but we won't pay rack rates. We will pay your internet rates with the special offer of £165. Agreed?'

Of course no one actually knew what rates some geek in marketing had put on the internet, and as residents coming for breakfast were wandering by no one wanted a scene about money. The receptionists looked at each other. Clearly this was in their authority.

'And your names?'

'Mr and Mrs Tommy Scunt,' my newly acquired wife answered, placing our home address somewhere in Berkshire.

'And do sir and madam have any luggage?'

'Not yet,' Scunt answered as we set off to enjoy our breakfast.

There really is no better meal than a full English breakfast. The continental breakfast is just that; something from the continent provided for and suitable for the *effete* of Europe. The Dutch in particular go in for a selection of cold meats and cheese, while the Scandinavians add pickled fish. Now I've got quite a thing about the right time to eat certain foods. It's very apparent, unseen to the continentals, that there's a place and a time for each food. Cold meats and pickled herrings are just fine for lunch or an early evening supper, say around six o'clock. Much later into the evening, towards dinner or even a late supper, they're certainly not the right stuff. In Russia, although not strictly continental, I've been known to have fried fish for breakfast. Again a food not to be taken before midday, although I will permit a little kipper, lightly poached. The French seem to favour croissants, often dipped into a hot chocolate; a pastime I can applaud but only after a full breakfast and, then again, much better mid-morning. However, when the Danish come to adding a sundry range of fruit-topped pastries then I'm sure that afternoon tea has interloped into completely the wrong time zone.

So, with white toast and butter, slightly salted and slightly chilled so you can see it melt into the toast, thick-cut orange marmalade, and a plate of fried eggs, bacon and all the other elements of a full breakfast, I ate well and wanted to shout to the restaurant: 'This is why we fought two bloody wars – to preserve meals like this,' but I didn't. Scunt, despite her tiny frame, was eating as heartily as me. It was close to ten as we finished and I signed the bill off to the room and I looked at my watch. 'I need to phone the office,' I said.

'No you don't, Tommy. They'll manage without you. What we need to do is get some clothes. You're starting to look silly in that dinner suit.'

After taking advice from the concierge on shopping centres, we wandered out with Scunt's arm in mine. We were starting to look like a couple, I thought, but I didn't know what that meant.

Given all we had gone through, our second argument was over the clothes I had to buy. Clearly what I needed was a complete wardrobe and there were major disputes as we headed through the likes of Marks and Spencer. For casual wear I had always favoured classical grey slacks and a blue blazer. It was the look of the polo field and the designated sign of a gentleman; even if not bought at Gieves & Hawkes. Scunt had different ideas, dressed in light-coloured chinos, a yellow jumper and leather jacket, I looked more like a Parisian than I ever wanted.

'You'll have me eating friggin' croissants next,' I said. But she only laughed.

The day-wear I could manage. Actually deep down in my psyche I had always wanted Jenny to do something like this with me, and my reluctance with Scunt was more of an act of defiance than a real show of strength. On the rare occasions I had gone shopping with Jenny, I'd pointed at clothing and said that I would look good in that, and she would shake her head in that way that women do that says 'Over my dead body'. So I had given in and waited for birthdays and Christmas to have my clothes-rack topped up, while other favourite items mysteriously disappeared to make room for them. Once I tried to exercise my rights to choose my own clothes: I chose a pair of blue linen weekend summer trousers with a nice pale white stripe. I was about to head out to a BBQ in them when Jenny had stopped me and asked why I was still in my pyjamas.

'I'm not in my pyjamas. These are my new trousers.'

'They're pyjamas,' she said 'and, if you want to make a fool of yourself, wear them.'

At least I had something to talk about all through the lunch walking around some stranger's garden on a sunny summer Sunday.

'Like the PJs, Tommy,' someone said.

'Late night, last night? Didn't have time to get dressed?'

said another.

'On a promise straight after this do?' another teased.

'Gosh, I didn't know this was a sleep-over.'

I'm sure Jenny must have incited the comments, telling everyone I was in my pyjamas. I thought of her standing at the front gate greeting people as they arrived.

'That's my husband – the one in the pyjamas. Yes, that's him – the one with the asymmetrical face. Please just ignore him. He's not feeling too well today.'

The trouble with Scunt started when she said, 'We'll need at least three days' worth of underwear for you. In fact we had better make it five days. We can't always keep washing.'

'What's all this about five days? I thought we were going back tonight. I can't stay here.'

'Tommy, we can't. They're bound to be watching for me. I have to get away. You've been such a darling. It will only take a few days to get sorted. Oh please, Tommy.'

This wasn't really an argument because Scunt had suddenly found some puppy-dog eyes and I was enjoying myself. I was playing truant, and the last time that had happened was when I was seven and I ran away from primary school one lunch time to go and buy chips down the high street because the school lunch was so awful. I really had lived such a conservative life, I realised. No – the argument came when we went to buy the underwear. Again, this had always been Jenny's domain, and despite all the Calvin Klein adverts in every underground station showing over-proportioned muscular young men in tiny briefs, underpants for me meant white Y-fronts. They're practical, and as I had no intention of walking down an underground station to display my physique there was no reason to deviate. There was no reason to deviate until I met Scunt, that is. The rules were changed. Scunt was choosing. Colours were good. Y-fronts were out. Boxers were okay, but the preference was for tight, shape-hugging shorts.

'I can't wear these,' I said. 'Jenny would go apoplectic if she saw them.'

'Then don't show her, and I need to talk to you about your wife, Jenny,' she said as she put them into the shopping basket, and that was the end of that.

The next disagreement came as we passed the pyjamas and I saw the very ones that had caused me so much embarrassment previously. I told Scunt the story and all she could say was, 'Don't ever wear those or anything else in bed with me. Never ever buy or wear pyjamas while you know me.'

'What do you mean? You never wear pyjamas?'

'Of course not, they're the most evil of inventions.'

'So what should I wear?'

'Just your birthday suit.'

So it was that as Scunt uttered those words that I started to consider my position and our relationship. She had said: *in bed with me*. Did she really envisage us sleeping together? I suppose I had to face up to that as well. We were in a room with only one bed, unless you considered the sofa as a possible place to sleep, and we were booked in for four nights. There was a mixture of excited anticipation and fearful dread; but that was a problem for later in the day. We had finished choosing clothes for me and now it was her turn. As with all women, I was sure that shopping for Scunt was going to be a horror. On rare occasions I had shopped with Jenny, trailing around for endless hours as nothing more than a bag carrier. I often wondered why shopping centres don't have a special man-crèche, like they do for kids. Women could check their men in at the shop entrance to a room where they could be served drinks by young women in bikinis, and then be allowed to watch football and play video games, undisturbed by guilt or pleading to change a light bulb or paint a wall. There would be men-type magazines to read and sofas to sleep on. When the wife finished her shopping she would check her man out again and bore him all the way home about the shoes she had nearly bought and the dress that was just too small (of course, she is never too big) and the fascinating conversation she had with Mrs So-and-So from round the corner.

The real horror for me was when Jenny bumped into a friend who also had a husband in tow. They, the women, would stop and chat while the men just looked at each other. By then, both men have lost the will to live and the only question they have is : "How long have you been married?" You see, marriage is a measure of the number of times you've been shopping. You can discount the first two years because that can be fun. You shop together for lingerie and the wife goes to the changing rooms to try them on and hopefully peeks around the curtains to show you how she looks. In the first two years she always looks sexy. Then, if you're lucky (and the shop is not too careful), you can join her in the changing room and have a bit of fun behind the curtain.

Then come the respite years for most men, who elect to stay home and look after the children. 'Darling,' they say. 'You go shopping and I'll look after the children.' This is a magnanimous gesture, which of course always coincides with the Saturday of a Lords test match or a big football match. The husband stuffs the kids early with baked beans then locks them in their rooms with toys and settles back in front of the game. There may be a price to pay when the wife gets back and there's been a disaster of some sort, but at least he's watched the game. Then the children get older and go to parties and they get a free Saturday afternoon. 'Darling, this is wonderful,' she says. 'It means we can go shopping together again,' she says; and a life of Saturday afternoon purgatory resumes.

Scunt didn't let me peek at her in her new lingerie, but she did try on skirts and tops and came out to show me with a twirl and dance.

'I like it,' or 'I love it,' or 'I hate it,' I would say and she would pull faces of happiness or pretend sadness. She had the quality to see the world like a child, seeing everything for the first time and getting real happiness from simple things, and I thought, not for the first time in our few hours together, there were hidden qualities in Scunt.

Back in the hotel room, Scunt sat on the bed reading the brochure about the spa treatments.

'Can I get a massage, Tommy?'

Even in something fractionally little more than half a day I was so far into this I had almost stopped caring or counting the cost. I had started to think of this time as though it was a holiday.

'Yeah, sure. Why not.'

'Thanks,' she said. 'Are you going to have a shower? I need to get the labels off all these things for you.'

The bathroom was as stately as the bedroom. There was a large white bath with huge ornate taps next to a throne of a toilet. I locked the door. It was more through instinct than need. I knew Scunt would be smirking as I turned the key, but I was going to sit on the toilet. I remember how Jenny, in our very early days together, was happy to wander in and out of the bathroom while I sat there. It was disconcerting and distracting. The longer she stood there talking to me, the less I was able to complete the task – and the longer she would stay and chat. Eventually I took to ensuring I had adequate reading material to take to the toilet, and made it clear that the time I spent in that room was for me. Eventually I would tell Jenny that I was 'going to read' and the euphemism stuck. Today I had nothing to read, but I was not having Scunt walking in on me as I sat there.

The toilet flushed with a rush of what I assumed was Highland spring water and I stepped into the shower. It was a good – even a great – shower. It was both hot and powerful and as I stood there a gush of hot water powered onto my head. I hate those showers were you have to dance a jig to find the jet of water and you're never sure if the shampoo is all out of your hair. I stood there and thought of Scunt and I wished I had not locked the door. If only she would walk in to the bathroom, and into the shower, and into my life. Then I reflected: I wanted her touch – but did I really need her in my life? So I showered, dried and put on the hotel bathrobe to walk back into the bedroom as Scunt was hanging the last of our new clothes in the wardrobe.

'Okay, I'm off for a shower now,' she said gathering up random toiletries.

I wanted to know more about her and why I was in Glasgow. I wondered for a moment whether I should go through her handbag while she was out of the room. Part of me was desperate to know and the other half was scared by what I might find. I had just plucked up enough courage to start to search her bag when she called me.

'Tommy I left the conditioner on the table. It's by the

sofa. Will you bring it here for me?'

She must have known what I was thinking and about to do, and she knew when to interrupt me; female intuition, no doubt, but that was the least of my concerns. When faced with new situations we all have different degrees of panic, and the fear now confronting me was of the worst kind. I had wanted Scunt to interrupt me in the shower and of course, like any man, I wanted to see her naked but on the other hand, the thought scared me. I found the conditioner and pushed at the bathroom door and walked in sideways, eyes closed so I didn't look at her, and with an arm outstretched with the conditioner balanced on the tips of my fingers, I hoped I was heading towards the shower. I was going in roughly the right direction but roughly wasn't good enough and I arrived instead at the bidet. I could hear the shower.

'Are you there, Tommy?'

'Yes.'

'And do you have the conditioner or have you just come in to ogle me?'

'Yes. And no.'

'Oh, Tommy. Don't be such a prude,' and I felt the conditioner being taken from my hands as I fled. I would need another shower I was sweating so much. That word again; I had been the prude. Was that true? Was I really a prude? I had always thought myself open and broad-minded, but maybe I'm a stuffed shirt compared to the modern world. I sat on the bed, trying to compose myself. I'd spent a lot of time trying to compose myself over the last few hours, but without much success, and as I had these thoughts, Scunt came back from her shower and walked into the bedroom, naked except for a turban of towel around her head, drying her hair. My eyes followed her and her lithe body, but mostly I admired how easy and natural she was. She didn't walk sexily or provocatively. She wasn't doing it to excite me, even though that was exactly the effect she was having. All she was doing was walking naked after her shower. She didn't look at me. She just walked over to the dressing table and started on her makeup. I didn't know what to say. Jenny would never walk around so unselfconsciously and nakedness was one of those unwritten signals that tonight was the night for monthly sex.

I had thought that Scunt was going to be skin and bones, but as I looked at her I saw that she was just thin. There were no protruding bones on her hips, just a beautifully rounded shape with a small strip of pubic hair pointing delectably to some hidden treasure. I still didn't know of her life – I mean of her other life – and I didn't know if I was jealous of all those other men, or excited by thought of her having sex with them. She was sitting still putting on her makeup.

'You need to phone Jenny soon,' she said.

'What? Why?'

'If you don't come home even she will get worried, and then they'll all start looking for us again. You can do whatever you need to do about the office, but get Jenny off our backs,' and she carried on looking in the mirror.

'And what do you think I should tell Jenny?' I was getting panicky at that thought.

'Well, you could say you've run away with a pretty young whore called Scunt and we're shacked up in a hotel room in Glasgow and you're watching her do her makeup before she puts on any clothes. Or you might lie. It should be easy for you. Men are good at that when they're sneaking around looking at pussy.'

Scunt was nothing if not direct, and I lay back on my

bed thinking about what I would do. Scunt was right – I had to do something. I reached for the hotel phone and dialled home as Scunt listened carefully.

'Jenny. It's me darling. Look, sorry I can't stay long but I won't be home tonight – maybe not for a couple of days more. The Chairman called me in after he got a call from the FO ... Yes, darling. The Foreign Office. There's a big thing going on with the Ukrainians who are going bust and I've got to fly out on a secret mission ... No, darling, you mustn't tell anyone. Not even anyone at the office. I'm doing this especially for the Chairman and no one else knows ... Yes, it's very exciting ... Yes, darling I might even get a pay rise ... No, I won't be able to phone you. Love you. I've got to go now. There's a private plane waiting ... Bye for now ... Yes. Bye bye. '

Scunt didn't even look at me. 'No wonder I never trust men,' she said.

Chapter VIII

Scunt dressed in her new clothes and without appearing to be too melodramatic, I have to say they transformed her.

'I've booked a hair appointment. I'll be back in about three hours,' she said standing and turning to look at herself in the mirror. 'It's in the hotel so I won't be far away if there's an emergency. Love you, Tommy.' And she skipped her way to the door and was gone. What was I going to do? The excitement was being with Scunt, and now I was just another lonely businessman in a hotel far away from comfort. I picked up the newspaper. A Professor at some university is suggesting a new fat tax in the UK! So someone else had the same idea. Shame. I thought I was unique, but I know my ideas are more far-reaching. So maybe I have a constituency to build on. I flicked though the pages but nothing caught my attention.

I switched on the TV. I'd never watched any daytime TV and soon, with its menu of soaps and antiques, I knew my cultural education had not been impaired. I was bored and didn't know what to do. Maybe a walk would help? But I couldn't even raise enough interest to do that. Then the phone rang. Panic ensued. No one knew we were here but clearly *someone* did because the phone was ringing. Maybe it was the police, checking we were both in the room. Maybe there would be a heavy Serbian accent enunciating a death threat. I let the phone ring and it stopped – only to start again immediately. I had to answer.

'Tommy.' It was Scunt and my heart beat slowed. 'Get dressed and come down here straight away.'

'Why? Is it important?'

'Of course it's friggin' important. If it wasn't why would I have called you?'

'Okay, give me ten,' and the phone went dead.

What could be so important that she needed to see me straight away? More decisions. Which underwear? I looked in the drawer where Scunt had unpacked for us. There, folded neatly were five pairs of pants. Two were red and one of them had something scrawled across the front. I held them up to see what she had bought: Come Here Big Boy. I folded them and put them straight back in the drawer. Without inspecting the others, I went for a familiar white pair of underpants and put them on.

Tailors, as they make the trousers of a suit, ask the question: 'On which side do you dress, sir?' It's an old joke but suddenly it became important. These new pants were best described as 'snug' and held everything in place, unlike the old Y-fronts that are much more liberal in their attention to maintain contact. What would happen if I suddenly became aroused by the sight of a pretty girl? In my old Y-fronts, it's not a problem. My trousers were cut loose and there was space for my dick to explore at those moments. If I was going to wear these new pants, however, I needed to carry around a phial of bromide.

Bromide has a reputation for being an *an*aphrodisiac and was supposed to have been given to soldiers to quell their sexual desire; maybe they should market bromide next to the underpants shelf for middle-aged men to hide their embarrassment. Maybe that was another of Jenny's problem. She was useless at chemistry and easily swayed by clever advertising. Maybe when she bought the salt (she always used much more than me) she had bought a brand high in bromide instead of low in sodium. That would explain a lot, and as I had these thoughts I caught sight of myself in the mirror and my opinion on underpants went from one extreme to the other. Pulled tight across my backside, and there, at the front, a nicely contained bulge that would excite any woman. If I were to have that proverbial accident that my mother always cited as the reason to wear clean underwear, then – in this age of gender equality – probably both the doctor and nurse would be female. I can imagine the doctor looking at my body as they carry me into the overworked and overcrowded accident and emergency department.

'Bring him in here!' she shouts and she cuts away at my shirt and trousers to see the full extent of my injuries. And then she sees the red pants with the provocative and totally appropriate *Come Here Big Boy* logo and the perfectly packaged parcel they contain. The prettiest of the nurses, the one with her uniform pulled tight across her bursting blouse, says 'I'll deal with this one,' and as I start to wake, I see her breasts heaving as she stares in awe at my nether regions. There's another voice.

'Can I help you, Lydia?' I always think that the sexiest nurses would be called Lydia.

'Emma, come and see this,' she says, because if the nurse isn't a Lydia she would certainly be an Emma. And after a short time there's a collection of nurses with heaving breasts staring at me.

'I'm dying,' I shout.

'Shut up,' Lydia says, 'we have much bigger things on our mind,' and as I have these thoughts, the bulge grows and I revert to my opinion to carry bromide.

I found Scunt in the hairdressers. 'You look nice, Tommy.'

'Thank you. What's the problem?'

'There's no problem. I was asking about an appointment for you, and they have a free one. I've booked you in for a haircut and a manicure. Isn't that lucky?'

'Ah, I don't know. Is that lucky?' I never seem to have time to think and that must always be how it is when you're on the run from the police.

My lifelong experience with hairdressers is zero. Jenny goes to the hairdressers and it takes an entire morning and costs a lot. I go to the barbers. At the barbers, the conversation is about football; there are pictures of page-three girls liberally and poorly stuck to the wall. There are only two questions to answer. The first is 'What number?' That refers to how short you want your hair and the gauge of the electric razor. I have a number six but I haven't been to the barbers for a while and my hair is getting long. The second question is: 'What team do you support?' That demands that you've scoured the premises first to determine what scarves and pictures they have on display. From then on in, you can close your eyes and be sure of the outcome. Choose a rival team and you never know what will happen to the hair but this was not a barbers; it was a hairdressers.

An effete Filipino or Chinese boy put a pink gown on me and then, from behind, reached round my waist, his body pushed into mine, to tie it. I riled just ever so slightly at this clear pass at me, but as I've got no objections to homosexuality (although it's not for me), I decided instead to accept the implied compliment.

As I walked with my new companion, we passed Scunt who, from under the clip of the scissors, asked, 'Are you okay, Tommy? You're walking very funnily.'

I didn't tell her it was because of my new underpants.

My hairdresser was a woman. Not much older than Scunt, but heavier and wearing blue jeans, long black boots and a T-shirt emblazoned in garish silver type with the words SEX ADDICT. If my barber ever took to wearing T-shirts, that's what he would have written on his chest (if he could ever be as honest). She ran her hands through my hair, pulling up strands and tut-tutting in a soft and sexy Scottish accent. No harsh Glasgow tones here.

'We have a lot to do. Your wife has told me what to do with all this.' I wanted to concentrate on her easy dismissiveness of the present state of my hair, but the mention of *my wife* completely disorientated me. I nearly shouted, 'What – is Jenny in here?!' and then I looked across at Scunt and realised that at that point she was my wife. It doesn't change, I thought. Once a woman has her claws into you, they're dug in deep, and here was Scunt making decisions for me; this time on my haircut and style. However, whatever men say, they actually like it. It's a bit like having to fill all the cabinet posts in a government with just two people. So long as I could be the Prime Minister with a nominal power of veto, and the Defence Secretary, then I'd be very happy to let my wife have all the other portfolios, particularly on the domestic front. The problem is that she would want to be Prime Minister as well. I'd have to keep telling her to leave me with at least some of the vestiges of power and authority – but when did she ever listen to me?

I wonder, do women ever listen to men? Or for that matter, do men ever listen to women? It would be so much easier if we all spoke the same language. I know it's technically English, but the words seem to have so many different meanings – especially when Jenny does the talking.

She might ask me whether the blue shoes go better with her dress than the red ones, and I'd answer honestly that the blue are the best. Then she'd ask me what's wrong with the red pair. She'd leave in a huff and come back in wearing the red shoes – but a different dress, complaining that I don't support her. It's Mel Gibson and *What Women Want* all over again. But would it really help to know what she was really saying to me? Maybe our relationship would not have suffered so if instead of buying one new house together we had bought two – next door to each other, with her in one and me in the other.

Mine would be decorated with dark pub-like colours, such as red. I'd buy black satin sheets and have posters of near-naked women in the toilet. I'd leave the toilet seat up without having to go through a checklist every time I went to the loo (brush the pan, spray the room, put the toilet seat down and make sure the guest towel is straight). I'd fill the dishwasher once every three days, leave my discarded clothes on the chair or on the floor, and stock the fridge with beer. Meanwhile Jenny would decorate her house in pastel shades and put out fresh-cut flowers. She'd fill the wardrobe with all her clothes and not squash mine into an ever-decreasing corner. She'd invite her girlfriends around for an early evening supper while I'd go with the husbands for a take-away pizza and a re-run of Manchester United's 8–2 walloping of Arsenal on the huge plasma TV that would be dominating my living room. We might get together some evenings and have a romantic supper. If it were at her house, I'd remember the toilet seat rules. I might even ask if she wanted me to stay over. I'm sure we'd have more (and better) sex as well.

My thoughts were broken by my Scots Lass saying, 'I

think we need to get you washed and get some conditioner on this,' and I was handed back to the Filipino or Chinese boy who took to not only washing my hair but massaging my scalp, temples and shoulders. The barber would have been horrified. I don't think Scots Lass knew what an electric razor was; she was all scissors and combs. I sat with my eyes closed when my hand was taken. I opened my eyes to see another girl kneeling at my feet.

Scots Lass explained. 'It's your manicure.'

There are only so many new experiences a man can absorb in a day and in less than twenty-four hours I had had a life-time's worth, so with resignation I allowed my fingers to be soaked, my cuticles pushed and my nails cut and all the while Scots Lass combed and cut and cut and combed. As Scots Lass nearly finished, Scunt came over and put her hand on my shoulder.

'My handsome man, you look wonderful.' I looked in the mirror and saw a different me, but I also saw a different Scunt. There was a lot less hair than I remembered. She looked like Twiggy from the 1960s with it short. The roots were now all blonde and she looked the proverbial million dollars as we walked out, arm in arm, to have tea. I sat in the tea room with Scunt and thought this would be a good time to pin her down and find out all the details of the escape – who were we escaping from and why? I really did need to know. I scanned the room, trying to find the right words. Maybe: "Scunt, I really must insist" or "Scunt, it would be helpful to know".

'It's not true what they say about black men,' Scunt said. 'It's all a bit of a myth.'

'Pardon?' I looked at Scunt. 'What are you talking about?'

'You were looking at that black man up at the bar. I suppose you were thinking that he had a bigger dick than you. It's not true. There are big white men and small black men. You don't have to be jealous of him, Tommy.'

'I wasn't looking at that man and if I was, I wouldn't be thinking about whether he was bigger in the genitalia department than me. As it happens, if you need to know, I'm very well endowed.'

'I'm sure you are, Tommy. No, don't worry about it. Shall we go for a walk? Please let's go for a walk,' and, of course, with my new-found look and the beautiful Scunt, I couldn't say no and dropped my immediate plan for more information, but I wasn't going to let it go completely. So we walked round the centre of Glasgow and I couldn't find it in me to break the spell by asking why I was in Glasgow. As we walked and pointed at clothes in the shop windows we laughed and, like a child, Scunt would skip away waiting to be called back and when she did she held my hand. When we were back at the hotel we went to the reception and I said 'Hello' to the receptionist and asked her if she'd had a good day, and then I asked for the key politely. It simply wasn't me.

'Would you like a table booked for dinner tonight, Mr and Mrs Scunt?' I shook my head. It still wasn't easy to answer to that name. I had to do something about it. It was okay for Scunt to be called Scunt but I was Tommy, and not Mr Scunt. I sulked in the lift back to our room and slumped in the chair as soon as we were in.

'Now look here, Scunt, we need to talk and get this sorted.'

'Of course we do, Tommy, but first let's have that massage we talked about this morning.'

'Scunt, we've only just got in and you want to go out again. Can't we have a minute's rest?'

'Tommy, of course. I don't want to go out at all. I want you to give me a massage. They have all sorts of massage oils in the bathroom. I'm sure you'll be wonderful,' and off she skipped again to get the oils and I stayed sat in the chair.

'How long does it take to get the oil?' I shouted.

'Just trying to choose the right one.' And she returned back into the room with that same uncomplicated, unembarrassed and relaxed attitude and I saw that she was carrying several bottles of oil and again she was naked.

Now there comes a point in a relationship like this that a man particularly dreads. The first of a man's dreads, of course, I have already skated over. When you start dating a thin girl with the slightly androgynous features of Scunt, there's always the fear that she isn't a she but a *he*. I assume that this is worse in places like Thailand, where the unlikely possibility becomes a probability. While this may be a dream for some men, for me it has been a recurrent nightmare. I've been lying in bed with Jenny some distance away on the other side and I've woken in a sweat as the nightmare unfolds. It goes like this.

Me and my new androgyne are slowly becoming entwined in a deep embrace as clothes are shed, and she stops me from reaching down and says, 'Darling, there's something I need to tell you before we go much further.'

'Anything,' I say as I continue to disrobe her.

'Before we met I used to be a hooker. But no longer. Do you mind?'

I look at her longingly and say, 'My darling, I can forgive anything because you're so beautiful.' But with a hint of jealously I ask, 'I hope I live up to the best of the experiences you've had with all the other men you've met?'

'You don't understand,' she says.

'But I do. I really don't mind.'

She looks at me as she finally gets naked and says, 'I mean I was a hooker for the Truro rugby club.'

And then in my dream I see I've taken on more than I could imagine. A beautiful face, wonderful breasts, a slim waist and there swinging between her legs is a dick to make Ron Jeremy feel inadequate. It's at this point that I wake. The first time I had the dream, I was so shocked that I tried to wake Jenny. I pushed her and prodded her and as she woke I said, 'I've just had sex with a transsexual.' She turned and sleepily said, 'That's very nice dear. Do give her my love,' and rolled back over and went back to sleep. I won't be waking her any more. Well, I already knew from the shower incident that this wasn't the reality with Scunt, or – if it was – then she had a very good surgeon.

The next problem was money. Every man knows that one way or the other he buys sex. Most sex is bought with dinner, wine, shoes or jewellery. Occasionally men just pay and the prostitute is really conducting the perfect business-school, free-market transaction and for that reason I don't know why everyone gets so upset with them. As an economist, I profoundly admire their deep understanding of supply and demand. They should be held up as one of the most efficient business models in existence: their marketing is often effective and direct; they're flexible in their working conditions and times; the relationships they have with their clients is very direct and success is quickly measured; pricing matches local conditions. Scunt was right – she is in the customer service business. But despite all this, men and women still play the game the traditional way. So here I was with Scunt and I remembered the story I had told her about Helga in Hamburg. Was she going to scam me for more money even while we were running away from the Serbian?

She pulled the curtains, dimmed the lights, put the oils on the bedside table and lay face down on the bed.

'Come Tommy, help me relax,' she said. I had no more time to ponder my problems.

Where to go and what to do? Being rational is one of my great strengths. While I would undoubtedly gain much enjoyment from the experience in this transaction, she was the main beneficiary so if we were ever to get to the point of a financial discussion I would express great umbrage and demand payment for my services – however I knew she had neither the funds nor the means to repay me – except of course with sex, and that would be an acceptable quid pro quo in line with, and consistent with, most relationships. So I took a bottle of oil and dripped some on her legs and started to massage.

I've had a few massages in my time; most were therapeutic and some erotic, so I knew the moves, but they had never been practised in reverse. I started, as all had done with me, by working on her feet with an unformed plan to work my way up and when appropriate stop and work on her shoulders and work my way down back to the middle. I didn't have a plan for what I would do in the middle. As I massaged each toe I remembered the rhyme, 'This little piggy went to market, this little piggy stayed at home' and soon I was in a rhythm and relaxed as I saw Scunt seemingly sink deeper into the bed. I was doing a good job. There didn't seem much to massage on a calf. Was I looking at Scunt as a piece of meat? But with both hands I found some flesh and as I started to massage her thigh I started to think about the night and sleeping arrangements. It was not supposed to get that far, but absent-mindedly I looked around, checking out the sofas. Which one should I use? It was a long time since I'd slept on a sofa, I thought, as my hands rubbed the oil along the line of the muscle. Scunt had really lovely legs, long and thin, and I started to work on the other. Both thighs massaged, I moved to start work on her shoulders.

'No Tommy, can you massage my arse as well? I really like that.'

'Don't you think that's a bit intimate? I mean we hardly know each other.'

'Don't be such a prude. Please, Tommy?' and I moved back and as I massaged each buttock Scunt started to move a little, moaned gently and as she arched her back she moved my hand to places I hadn't intended, but worse – my underwear was suddenly far too tight. Then she turned over and putting her arms around my neck she pulled me towards her.

'Oh come here, you silly billy.' She kissed me once and again and finally I gave in and there we stayed.

We ordered food and drinks from room service, we put a note out for breakfast in the room. We didn't argue about which side of the bed we wanted and I didn't complain about not having any pyjamas to wear.

Chapter IX

We woke, still in each other's arms, to the knock of room service and giggled as toast crumbs spread all around us in the bed.

'Tommy, you have a shower first. I have to go out quickly to get some face cream. I forgot it yesterday.' She threw on her jeans and left, leaving me with a kiss on the cheek. I had just finished shaving – only minutes later – when she burst into the bathroom.

'Tommy, quick! Pack! We have to leave. Now! I think I've just seen one of his heavies. One of the big ones. I don't think he saw me but they must know we're here. Don't ask me how. Come on, Tommy. Hurry. We have to go.' Her eyes were welling up with tears.

I looked at her open-mouthed. I was settling in nicely to this life. There was so much I still wanted to do in Glasgow. That museum whose name I could never remember that all the critics in London had said was almost passable; after all, Glasgow had been the European Capital of Culture. There was Billy Connolly as well. He was bound to be playing a gig somewhere close by.

'Oh come on, Scunt,' I said, still trying to wrap a towel around me, 'you must be mistaken. No one knows we're here. Have a shower and we can go for a walk.'

She wasn't listening. In a blind panic, she was instead pulling clothes into plastic bags.

'No!' she said with determination and a real edge. 'We've got to leave. Just get dressed will you?' and she threw a handful of clothes in my direction. 'We will have to hire a car and drive.'

'Where?'

'Anywhere, Tommy. We will just have to drive and see where it takes us.'

Her panic was now overtaking me and I joined her, stuffing previously pristine clothes into plastic bags, and with a quick glance around to ensure we had grabbed it all we almost ran down the corridor to the lifts.

'Stop!' I shouted and we ground to a halt with panic on Scunt's face. 'Should we go round the room removing all our finger prints?' In every spy film I had ever seen the fugitives made sure their presence could not be confirmed. Shouldn't we do the same?

'Don't be so friggin' stupid, Tommy. Just run,' and she was off again to the lift.

Checking out of a hotel is something that should be done with the same disdainful panache as checking in; the same indifference is required. But this time it could not be mustered. With our assorted collection of plastic shopping bags we arrived at the concierge desk and were greeted by a mixture of contempt, indifference and little of the humour I was hoping to muster.

'I'm sorry,' I said, 'but our plans have changed and we need to leave now. Can I have my bill? And we also need to hire a car. Where can we do that?'

'Is there a problem with the room, sir?'

'No. There's no problem, it's just that we have to return to London urgently. For a family emergency,' I said hoping that my excuse would both calm the receptionist and put anyone else off the scent.

'Can we book a car?'

The receptionist pointed to a Hertz car-rental desk.

'Scunt, I'll deal with the car – can you check the bill?'

I shuffled from the reception counter to the car-hire desk, collecting up the plastic bags to carry and pile up again.

'We need to buy some luggage, Scunt,' I shout across the foyer, looking at her in the distance, but she was too busy scouring the whole of the reception area on the lookout for Serbian thugs or undercover policemen. If criminals say they can always spot a policeman, I really don't know how they do it. I looked around. Either everyone or no one looked suspiciously like they were watching us. It made me flustered.

'What sort of car would you like?'

'At this time, I'll settle for anything with a wheel in each corner.' I was on edge. 'Whatever you've got ready, right now. How long will it be?'

'About fourteen foot six inches, sir.'

I didn't need humour from the pimply Scot's boy hardly out of school and quite clearly on a work experience exercise. 'Who would like to learn how to annoy the English?' his career tutor might have said and this boy had managed to get his wand in the air first. He was processing this transaction painfully slowly.

Through all of this, our unmanageable pile of plastic bags was really getting on my nerves. At home, back in Kent, I had as good a collection of luggage as any man could wish for (purchased of course by Jenny). Over the years we collected hard-shelled and soft-covered cases in all colours – including tartan and bright day-glow luminescence – only for them all to be destroyed at some point at various airports. With this varied experience and years of attending conferences with bright pink luggage, I lost all self-consciousness about my luggage. We, the travelling businessmen, are happy to travel with any shade of embarrassment because, of course, we all assume it will be easy to spot on the baggage carousel. We all assume the colour is so awful that it will be unique – no man would ever buy anything quite so hideous but it's a fallacy, of course, because these cases were not bought by men; they were bought by the wives, and Jenny, being a slavish follower of fashion even in the domain of baggage, had bought what every other woman had. As a result, there can be tens if not twenties of pink bags circulating the carrousel, each being chased by a suited and booted businessman trying to check for ownership. The conversation is always the same:

'Your wife buy the luggage?'

'Yeah.'

'Hideous, isn't it?'

'Better than a plastic bag, anyway.'

'Sure is.'

And then we part, still running to keep up with the carousel; and that's the simple truth – however awful the colour, it beats a plastic bag. Not because I'm an environmentalist (although it does disturb me that these things will still be around in one or two million years) but it's inconvenient travelling with a dozen sundry pieces of plastic that don't even stack up neatly. For some people, of course, it's a way of life. Even when they have good luggage, they still manage to have plastic bags as well. I suspect it's genetic and they come from some Romany stock, or maybe they fear that someday they'll end up on the streets with an old pram or baby-stroller and then they'll need their beloved plastic bags. I'm sure their luggage is half empty but so strong is the compunction to have most of their belongings with them that they can't resist carrying some in a plastic bag.

Car deal done, I struggle back to the reception with my plastic pile.

'Was everything up to your expectations?' the pretty girl asks Scunt as she processes the cash I'd given to Scunt.

'You'd better ask Scunt,' I said, not even noticing my own innuendo. I think the look of surprise was more at my companion's name than my little joke.

The spotty Hertz man-boy waved at me; the car was ready but when he asked if he could help me with my luggage, I was having nothing of it. In our hired Ford Focus 1.6 with a GPS navigational system and twin air-bags heading out of Glasgow, I said, 'Scunt, we have to stop and get some luggage for all these bags. I can't go home with them. Worse – I refuse to arrive in England, or wherever we next stop, with them.'

Actually I couldn't imagine going home with all the new clothes and a new haircut, regardless of how they were packaged but that was a totally different line of thought. We had left the hotel and were heading on a sort of northerly route, but without a plan, because that was just the way the main roads had taken us. While the lack of a plan had to be rectified, by then my mind was even more resolutely fixed on obtaining some sensible luggage. I had become obsessive about it.

As if reading my mind Scunt said, 'Where are we going, Tommy?'

'To buy some luggage. Even Serbian heavies wouldn't think of looking for us there.'

'But where?' she asked with her rediscovered innocence.

'I don't know. Wind down your window and we can ask

someone.' Scunt obeyed as we cruised to a halt in front of a bus-stop of sundry middle-aged and elderly folk. It was hard to tell their age because as far as I'm concerned, the indigenous people of Scotland look old so prematurely (unlike old-aged pensioners in the South East who are clearly worthy of their free bus-pass and winter fuel allowance). Here, they all looked middle-aged and old, but could really be just school-children. Scunt sat back as I leaned across to her window and engaged them in conversation.

'Good morning.'

'An' guid morn tae ye.' It was incomprehensible.

Leaning further across so I could hear better, I said 'I need to buy some luggage,' and asked 'Can you give me some directions?'

The man turned to a woman in the queue behind him. 'D'ye hear 'at Mary? Th' cheil wants tae buy some luggage. Can we teel heem whaur he can gie some?'

'Ah hae some in th' loft,' said Mary. 'Ah can seel heem fur puckle shillings.' And they laughed and we didn't have the faintest idea what was going on. 'Nae seriously, mah cheil. Follaw doon th' road fur puckle miles.'

I looked at Scunt and she shrugged her shoulders.

'There's a Morrison's supermarkit. Mebbe they seel luggage. Its th' only place aroond haur an' aw th' way up tae Clydeside.' He was sort of pointing in the direction we were going.

I understood 'Morrison's' and that it was a supermarket. They had bought out Safeway and I tried to remember if there was a Calvinistic streak in the old Mr Morrison that had made him such a good shop-keeper. I decided just to keep driving.

'Thanks a lot.'

'Nae trouble. Yer welcome, ye sassenach rockit!' he said as Scunt wound up the window and we headed down the road leaving the sound of laughter behind us.

'What did they say, Tommy?'

'I haven't the faintest idea but I think they meant just keeping going down here to the supermarket.'

Morrison's was just down the road in the vague direction that our bus-waiting Scots had pointed to. It was mid-week and mid-morning and I parked by a recognisable landmark; in this case a huge letter E on top of a pole. In fact, I could have chosen any letter as the huge car park was almost empty but I had spent too many hours walking around car parks having forgotten where I'd parked and I didn't want that to happen. Maybe it's because I have no real interest in cars that I lose them so easily. To some men the difference between an XL and XXL, or whatever they're called, is so obvious that they can spend a whole evening naming, listing and extolling every feature of each. I'm on dangerous ground here as I don't even know what to look for. For me an engine is the thing that sits under the bonnet, which is usually opened by a lever somewhere near my right knee. In my ignorance, I just assume that whoever made the car is perfectly happy that the engine is big enough to move the car at a reasonable speed.

There are some basic shapes I recognise. There are very small cars with two doors, which are driven either by people in big cities or poor people. There are cars with four doors that are not very big, which are driven by sales representatives and people who can't afford bigger cars. There are executive cars that most people aspire to, which have the disadvantage that they have to be cleaned at least once a week otherwise the social benefit of being seen in such a car is removed and you don't get invited to the monthly swingers meetings in the cul-de-sac. There are the monster cars known as the four-by-fours. They're supposed to be driven across deserts or low veldt land. Clearly I should have worked harder at my geography at school because, based on the sheer numbers of these cars on our roads, these deserts and the veldt must exist in every expensive suburban area in the South East of England. Then there are the sports cars – their purpose is clearly not to transport people but to allow men of all ages to attract women (and preferably young ones) into bed. Having said that, I've noticed more middle-aged women driving sporty Mazda MX5s, those small but perfectly phallus-shaped, two-seated sports cars – the new car of the cougar but for me, the main distinguishing feature of a car is its colour, yet when there are only a few colours in vogue at any one time, and for as long as the awful British weather leaves every car looking the same muddy brown, I'm always losing mine.

I parked under the big letter E and Scunt and I headed to buy some luggage.

'Tommy, have you got a pound coin?'

'What for?'

'For a trolley, Tommy.'

'Do I want to buy a trolley?'

'No. We need to rent a trolley and it costs a pound. You get it back after you've used it.'

Either my attempt at humour was falling very flat, or it was too early in the morning for Scunt.

'I know that, but we're only buying luggage,' I said. 'We can carry that. That's the purpose of luggage. It can be carried or even rolled. We don't need a trolley.'

'You never know,' Scunt said looking dolefully at me, and I gave her a one pound coin.

As I looked around we were, by many, many years, the youngest people in the store. In this observation I was, of course, taking our average age, which seemed a reasonable thing to do. In fact I could have taken any method or approach to the calculation and we would still have been the youngest; this was clearly old-aged-pensioner shopping time. As we get older, I was once told, we need less and less sleep, so this lot had probably been awake since five o'clock and now – six hours later – they were thinking about tea. Maybe they congregated here because it was warm? Maybe the Government should pay the winter fuel allowances to the supermarkets. I didn't have time to dwell on these thoughts, but I did hope that anyone who noticed us saw us as a young in-love couple and not as father and daughter, or pretty young girl and paedophile. In reality, we weren't noticed at all. The short-sightedness of the old and the concentration required by them just to stay alive meant an unhindered shop tour.

I had held out hope that Scunt would be different from other women when shopping in a supermarket. Our first time shopping, in Glasgow for clothes, had been different. Then we were in the flush of a new experience and I had enjoyed it but here she showed her true colours and reverted to type. Men shop with a clear idea of what they want. They go to the right shop to buy what they want and say, 'Thank you, Lord, for making it all so easy,' and return home to their place on the sofa in front of the TV. Women do it all differently. Instead of asking an assistant if they even sold luggage, so we could make a decision to stay or move on, Scunt led us on an unguided tour of the whole shop. Maybe

I'm doing her down. After all, she had been in the car and witnessed the last incomprehensible conversation with the locals, so perhaps she'd decided we'd never understand the answer to any questions we might ask, so would end up doing a full tour anyway. Maybe she thought we would save time.

Fresh vegetables and fruit were predictably the first things we saw as we entered. Scunt saw some peaches and asked, 'Shall I get some for the trip?' And without waiting for an answer a pre-packed, cellophane-wrapped box of six was in the trolley.

'Do we want a lettuce?'

'No, we don't, Scunt,' I said as I pushed the trolley into the next aisle. There was a trend forming. Whenever we travelled Scunt needed to stock up with food as if undoubtedly we would be stranded somewhere and need calorific fuel for many days until discovered and released. Throughout our tour of Morrison's, Scunt put things in the trolley and I patiently returned them to the shelf. While I was putting back a second packet of biscuits, a dismembered voice from another aisle shouted across at me:

'Do you think volume is important?'

Scunt is liberal in the extreme. I had recognised that last night in the bedroom, but this was too much. I would still have flinched and turned as red as a beetroot at her question even if we had been in Ann Summers, a shop famous for its erotic lingerie and sex toys.

I was about to ask Scunt if she knew how many dildos Ann Summers sold each year but thought better of it. Asking the question would do no more than perpetuate the conversation. It's a startling statistic, though. I had read it on the internet not a week earlier while conducting research into

UK shopping habits. The answer is they sell two million Rampant Rabbit dildos each year. Then I thought about asking Scunt if she knew what a Rampant Rabbit was. Of course she would know and I would be wasting my breath. She was probably their number-one customer.

In the UK there are twenty million women in the age range of fifteen to sixty-five. If you think (as I do) that fifteen is too young to need a dildo and you exclude all the religious groups and lesbians (after all, they would only need one between them) then maybe there's a population of no more than eighteen million potential customers. That means one in nine women own a dildo from Ann Summers. But these are their annual sales. So either these one-in-nine women wear out their Rabbits each year and have to buy a replacement or, assuming a dildo lasts for four years before it (or the batteries) corrode, it means that every other woman, that's one in every two of them in the supermarket, owns a Rampant Rabbit purchased from Ann Summers. This fact excludes all purchases from other sellers of sex toys! Simply mind boggling. I thought about asking the women around me, right there and then, but realised that they were all outside my fifteen to sixty-five age group.

Scunt again shouted at me. 'Or do you think something that stops it falling out is better? I think I prefer it smooth and silky. Don't you?'

I marched down the shop aisle.

'Scunt. First we shouldn't be having this conversation here, and second we've only slept together one night. Do you really think I'm a good judge of your needs yet?'

She looked at me with a blank stare and I understood she was impressed by my directness and assertiveness.

'What the frig are you talking about, Tommy? What

shampoo and conditioner do you want me to buy?'

I sulked away.

Then she had me looking at baby clothes.

'Aren't these adorable?' she said holding up a tiny set of jeans.

'Maybe, but you need to have a baby to make the purchase worthwhile,' I said, and Scunt gave me that you're-a-real-spoilsport look.

Finally, after a run past the in-store deli and the fresh bakery, we finally spotted some luggage and I drove the trolley in that direction, almost losing Scunt who had returned to look at the baby clothes one more time. Buying luggage didn't involve any difficult decisions. We didn't need a ten-year warranty – ten days was too long. We didn't need the largest case, which was huge and would probably require changing the model of car to fit it in. Medium would do – the larger one for Scunt and the next size down for me. It was easy, and then Scunt returned from her brooding aisle.

'No, we can't have that one.' Or the next one. They were either too large, or too small, or horrible, or just badly made. Somehow there we were, looking at the inside and outside of every case. If there's one thing I've learnt in life, it's this: at times like these it's best just to agree. Whatever happens, a man will never have the last word or make the decision. It's better to go with the flow, and that's what I did, taking cases off the shelf and putting them back until Scunt had decided. Finally she chose one and after a slight detour to collect sandwiches and soft drinks, it was time to check out. Except it wasn't. As we passed the fresh vegetables again, Scunt looked at the shelves and in the trolley.

'I like those small, sweet cherry tomatoes. Can we buy some?' So off we went again. By then, I had the store layout committed to memory and cleverly managed to take a cut-through that took us wide of the baby clothes aisle.

Then it was checkout time again. Working on the checkout of a supermarket must be one of the worst jobs in the world. You don't have to check the price of anything, you don't have to weigh anything and there are no decisions to be made. Take the can of baked beans in the right hand, move it over the scanner into the left hand and repeat. You might pass from left to right hand, depending the seat you're allocated. I wonder if they position staff by their left- or right-handedness to maximise efficiency. Worse still, checkout staff have to deal day-to-day with the general public. Other shoppers, to you and me, but customers or clients to the staff, who are probably called Customer Service Operatives.

Let's be honest. Dealing with most of the general public on a day-to-day basis, especially the aged inhabitants of Glasgow, is not a great way to spend a day. They, the 'great unwashed' as the Victorian novelist Edward Bulwer-Lytton called them in his 1830 novel *Paul Clifford*, are generally just that – the great unwashed. They're generally loud, obnoxious and often not very bright and of course most of them work for someone else; most have a boss so the *hoi polloi* see the genteel checkout lady as an opportunity to be in charge and throw their weight around. Single handedly, they resurrect the class system and see this as the right occasion to stamp on someone they perceive to be beneath them. The young ones are loud and arrogant; the middle-aged manage the class transformation by behaving like most of the managers they've experienced – they show disdain and say nothing, and reject conversation and contact. They behave as if they're auditioning for the role of the Duke or

Duchess in the next series of Downton Abbey.

I, on the other hand, have a real advantage. I know I'm superior and I've got nothing to prove, hence I take it on myself to engage the checkout staff in conversation, and there was no reason not to follow usual practice on that occasion.

'Good morning,' I said. 'You never know when you need new luggage.'

It seemed like an easy start but I had forgotten I was in a foreign country and I was greeted with indifference. Even the English upper class are clearly lower than any Scots worker. These Scots do have an awful chip on their shoulder when it comes to the English. I mean James I was already James VI of Scotland and he was the one who said 'Yes' to unite the countries and it was us English who invited *them* to join *us*. As the packet of cheese sandwiches was scanned, the middle-aged, slightly plump and short checkout woman managed an aloofness that put me in my place. I said nothing more and just handed over my credit card.

Back in our Ford, I insisted that we should transfer the contents of our plastic bags into our new cases right there and then. I wanted to be rid of them immediately, even if they did display the names of some of the top Glasgow brands. I had seen a recycling bin we could use. Scunt was up for it, so we opened the car's boot door and lay the bigger of the cases on the floor. As I watched Scunt's skimpy, sexy lingerie being folded and repacked, I became quite excited – so much so that I forgot why I was there. The sight of my underpants didn't seem to have the same effect on her. Ten minutes later, we were ready to go.

'Where are we going, Scunt? Any ideas?' I said.

'We need to be on a motorway to get away from here

fast. Where is the nearest motorway? Do you know?' Women's logic again; at the hotel we had no time at all, and again she was saying we must rush, but for shopping there's all the time in the world.

'We could always keep going north, but if we do that there will only be more and more Scots to try and understand.' I was thinking out loud. 'Maybe a bit of east–west would be a good idea. Let's go across country to Edinburgh?'

'That sounds good. Now come on, Tommy. Get a move on.'

We turned south again and soon picked up the M8 motorway in the direction of Edinburgh. Scunt had found a local radio station playing middle-of-the-road pop music which kept her quiet and curled up in the corner of the seat with her eyes closed. It gave me time to think and take stock of things. A lot had happened in less than forty-eight hours and it dawned on me yet again that I had no real understanding of what was going on. Last night, with Scunt, had started to colour my judgement and, to be honest, what had started as a bit of a game and jolly jape had taken on a new level of seriousness. Women do that to men; they ensnare them! That's how Jenny did it, and presumably that's how it is for every man. Before I met Jenny I was easy-going and happy to date occasionally – mainly for the sex back then. Companionship I got from my mates at the pub. The dating game is a ritual, in which neither side quite understands the rules of engagement, yet both want an engagement – the men a physical one and the women a ring. Sex is measured out by women, as far as I can see, in return for signs of love and affection, and then strategically withheld because of some unknown indiscretion, and through this the twine is reeled in and slowly – but surely – he is hooked, caught in the net and landed and what does the guy say? 'Well, at least I don't have to go out trawling for sex anymore. Get married? Then I can have sex whenever I want.' Then what does the man find out, and all too late? That marriage is the fastest route ever invented to celibacy.

I had fancied Jenny from the very first moment I saw her. Like Scunt, she had one of those androgynous looks so beloved of the late seventies. Her blonde hair was fashioned in the Sassoon five-points. Her tight jeans were the same make as mine. She wore tee-shirts and had small breasts. At first the sex was fun and frequent. At the time I thought we sort of 'drifted' into marriage but with hindsight I now see I was trapped. One moment I was living by myself in a smart bachelor pad in Pimlico in London. I had a motorbike, and the breathalyser had not yet been invented. After a night out, I undressed as I walked through the door, either because of my lust for the girl I was with or the simple need to get to bed quickly and recover in time to start again the next day. Either way, there was always a trail of clothes at the door and often it stayed there until the need to tidy – either because a female visitor was to be impressed, or a trip to the launderette was required. The pad's décor was interesting and the collection of furniture, eclectic. The sculpture made from empty beer cans behind the sofa was decidedly art nouveau, the permanent ironing board in the lounge was no more than a mere inconvenience, and the collection of unwashed plates was a task better left for a time when there really was nothing else better to do.

Within six months of meeting Jenny, she became a permanent fixture in my flat (and I still don't actually remember inviting her to move in). But the beer cans went.

Magazines were hidden in a drawer. The clothes were always in the wardrobe. The smell of beer and cigarettes was replaced by that of the cut roses and daffodils that I always seemed to be buying. The defining moment, I suppose, was when I found myself spending a Saturday morning fitting net curtains across the bedroom window.

'Why am I doing this?' I asked.

'So people can't see you naked as you walk around the bedroom,' was her curt answer.

'But I've got a good body and I'm very well endowed and if they want to spend their time trying to get a glimpse of me, that's their choice. Can I go round and ask them if they'll pay for and fit the curtains – because the cricket starts soon?'

'Oh Tommy, please, just for me,' is what she would have said. No doubt she would have looked at me with those big   if-you-do-this-for-me-you-can-have-a-blow-job-tonight eyes and I would have hung the curtains. That was it. Another woman had domesticated yet another man. I think it's probably harder to train a dog for shooting, than a man for domestic servitude. I have thought this before and have wanted to do something about it. Men are so disadvantaged that they need special classes at an early age to help them through life and work out how to deal with women. As I've aged, I've taken the pacifist route, which means I always say 'Yes' and accept the blame for anything that goes wrong – to avoid any argument, because an argument with a woman only ever has one winner and she will win, not because of any superior intelligence or debating skills, nor because of her persistence. I know many men who are just as stubborn as women. She will always win because she can withhold the one thing men always need – sex. It's as simple as that. And that, I think, is why women hate prostitutes. Not because of their profession or because they take money for sex. It's not a moral or ethical argument based on women's liberation or the oppression of the gender. No. Women hate prostitutes because they're the way that men can finally *win an argument*. Women withhold sex to get what they want, and the hooker is 'traitor to the cause'. She can provide the one thing men need to be able to hold out in any argument – to resist, until they can re-exert what they believe is their natural and normal intellectual dominance. A whore is the fatal flaw in their plan for female dominance.

These thoughts of whores made me look across at Scunt, now sleeping and dreaming as we sped along. You'd think that as she was the cause of me being here, she could at least stay awake to talk to me. I prodded her.

'Is there another word for synonym?' I asked out of the blue.

'Substitute? Or replacement?' she said without opening her eyes. Not bad, I thought, as I hadn't even expected an answer.

'It was meant to be a joke. But a good try – although wrong. I don't think there is a synonym for synonym,' I said rubbing home the point.

'Make me laugh, Tommy,' she said. 'This is all rather frightening.'

I hadn't thought of her being frightened, but then I remembered the tears, panic and emotion when we'd first met and I wanted to clear her head of the demons. There was something I still didn't know – and I meant more than what we were doing here – that I didn't understand. But first things first.

'Place names are interesting,' I said. 'Where have you

been, Scunt?'

'Not many places,' she said, as the Scottish lowlands drifted by. 'I did once go to Germany, though. A punter invited me. A good gig. Over a thousand pounds and he put me up in this really swanky hotel.'

'So where was that?'

'Germany. Aren't you listening to me Tommy?'

'I mean whereabouts in Germany?'

'Oh, some place called Dusseldorf?'

I thought for a moment. 'Did you know that translated into English Dusseldorf means *docile dwarf*?'

She looked at me sideways from her slumped position. 'Really?'

'Yes. That's how it got its name. It's based on a true story about these small people who used to live in that part of Germany. Being small people, they were docile. They didn't get very angry. Well, they couldn't, because being small meant they would always lose a fight. Or so they thought... Then one day a tribe of tall people attacked their city and they had a big fight and the small people won.'

'When was this? Come on, Tommy, you're having me on aren't you?'

'No, I'm not. The tall people came from Munich in about the fourteenth century and they had to go back as losers and if you had got off your back and done some sightseeing—' and I suddenly regretted my words and the innuendo 'then you would have seen a statue of a dwarf in the city centre but of course it's only a very small statue because it's a dwarf. And, I would like to add...' pressing home the point, 'that a dwarf is both the mascot and the emblem of the badge of the Dusseldorf Bundesliga football team.'

Scunt smiled. 'You're funny, Tommy. Thank you. I really like you. Tell me another one.'

It's not easy to be funny on demand. I tried to think of another city. 'Have you heard of Durban?' I asked.

'Is that in Ireland?'

'No, that's Dublin.' And now I wasn't sure if she was teasing me. 'Durban is in South Africa. Do you want to know how that got its name?' She smiled and nodded.

'Durban. It's made up of two words. *Dur* meaning hard as in *durable.*'

'I like hard things, Tommy,' and she reached across and put her hand on my thigh. A deep breath.

'I'm driving, Scunt,' and she smiled.

'So *dur* meaning hard… Mmm… and what else?'

I tried to remember what I was thinking but she was distracting me, 'and *ban* meaning road as in *bahn* as in *autobahn*. So *Dur-ban* means 'hard road'. And that's because the Dutch travellers who arrived there after their sea journey from Holland on their way to the Transvaal said "It's fucking difficult to get here".'

Scunt was becoming animated. 'Tell me a joke.' It seemed that all the jokes I knew were crude or rude. What did it matter that she knew more about sex than I did.

'A man walks into a bookshop and asks the assistant: "Do you have the latest self-help book for men with really small penises?" "I don't think it's in yet," she replies. "Yes, that's the one!" '

I was making her laugh and I felt good about that.

'Did I tell you I was dyslexic?' I said.

'No, Tommy? Really? Are you dyslexic?'

'Yes,' I said, 'I found out when I went to a toga party dressed as a goat.'

I was on a roll and enjoying myself.

'And, did you know I've been a competitor in the Sex Olympics?' I said.

She played the perfect straight man – or is it straight woman? 'And how did you get on?'

'I won a gold medal – I *came* last!'

So we continued. She became more animated as the banter continued and my confidence increased. We hadn't really talked properly until that point. I mean, I still wanted to talk about why we were on this crazy trip, but now we were talking and teasing as I drove and I was enjoying the easy way the conversation went. She continued to laugh at my jokes until we got close to the English border. We had driven all the way beyond Edinburgh and off the motorway, and were heading vaguely west towards Berwick. As we crossed the border, I thought we should have one last dig at the Scots.

'Do you know how to tell which clan a Scotsman belongs to?' I asked, worrying that I might have to explain all about clans.

'No,' Scunt knew a joke was coming. 'Tell me.'

'Well you put your hand under his kilt and if you find a quarter-pounder then he is a McDonald.' It was greeted with the groan it deserved.

After a few miles of silence, I asked her, 'Do you like men?' It was a question that I'd been wanting to ask ever since Scunt had told me what her job was.

'Of course I do, but not the ones that are chasing and following us.'

'I mean, you see men at their worst. Men who treat women as nothing more than objects. How can you like them?'

'Most of them are very sweet,' she said without any embarrassment. 'You know that you don't need to love someone to fuck them, and that's my job. I get attention and I even get presents. I get complimented all the time and, as you know, I'm good at my job.'

'You mean last night was you just *doing your job*?' I was hurt. 'I thought you were doing it because you liked me.'

'I was teasing you, Tommy. Relax. It wasn't work last night. That was for me. Look – we're not different people. We're like everyone else. It's just that our job is sex. Hey, I kissed you didn't I?'

'What does that mean? You kissed me.' I was trying to work out which emotions were starting to rage inside me.

'I never kiss a punter. That's the real sign of affection.'

'So you're saying a kiss is more intimate than sex?' If I sounded incredulous then my tone was spot on. I was incredulous.

'Of course it is. I never kiss a punter. Do you know any hookers, Tommy?'

'Not socially, Scunt. Other than you, I don't know any. At least, not as far as I know. So do you like men?'

'Of course I do, Tommy,' and she fell silent, starting to brood again, 'and we should change that.'

'Change what?' I asked.

'How far is it to Leeds?' she asked, instead of answering my question. 'Can we stay there tonight?

'Sure. That's the way we're heading. Why?' I asked.

'You'll see when we arrive. Now let's be friends again. Please? Tell me, what's the first joke you can remember?' She pretended to flutter her eye-lashes and produced big puppy-dog eyes that would melt an iceberg. I relented.

'Okay. Friends it is. My first joke… Okay. A man goes into a chemist and asks: "Do you have any condoms?" The assistant looks at him and says, "Sorry, sir, we've sold out. Have you tried Boots?" He looked at her and said "Yes, but it keeps coming out of the lace holes".'

'That's awful, Tommy, but funny. I much prefer you as a friend. I've got enough enemies right now.' And we settled down to driving. As on the train, Scunt was in charge of the sandwiches and she kept me fed and watered. She didn't ask what I wanted but unwrapped each packet and gave me a half to eat as we drove. We stopped for petrol and a pee break, but we drove hard. We flew past Newcastle and Durham, two places I would happily have stopped to see. I was feeling tired when the road signs for Leeds indicated the journey's end was in sight.

'What do we do when we get to Leeds?' I asked.

'Follow the signs for Headingley. I'm sure I'll know the way from there. I have some friends there. They'll let us stay with them tonight. We will be safe. I trust them.'

I'm not an expert at architecture, but as we drove into Headingley, just north of the city centre, it looked to be mainly Victorian, but the signs of a modern rebuild were evident as the motorway seemed to carry us right into the middle of the city. Scunt took over with her directions and had us pull up in front of a large three-storey house.

'Stay here for a moment while I go in and check all's clear. Don't move.'

This was not how I normally arrived at friends. Normally I would just wander up to the door, ring the bell and say hello but then again, Jenny would never allow us to arrive anywhere unexpected. Invitations to house guests would be agreed months in advance.

'Don't book anything for such'n'such a date,' she would say and that date would be three months away. 'Paul and Linda are visiting that weekend.' Then, as we headed towards a planned visit, there was a checklist of items to be arranged. We had to stock up with food and wine. The spare room would get an extra clean. The garden would be mowed and trimmed. I never got as far as being sent to bed early to make sure I had a good night's sleep, but I'm sure if Jenny thought she could have got away with it she would have tried.

So maybe this was how it was done in a normal world when you turned up unexpectedly. You didn't knock on the door with your new luggage. Maybe just one of you went to the door and checked if it was all okay. I watched from the car and saw Scunt talking on the doorstep, arms being thrown around her in a big hug. We were welcome, and as Scunt walked back to me, waving for me to get out of the car, I thought I saw her rub away a tear. Presumably a tear of happiness at being back with friends.

I switched off the engine and was grateful that we now had a matching set of luggage. I really couldn't have moved all those plastic bags again. The small front garden had basically been paved over. No gardening! I immediately started to like these folk in Yorkshire. Unlike Jenny, who would spend her time balancing all the luggage on me so that she had free hands to hug and kiss our hosts while I tottered and teetered like a circus juggler, Scunt carried her own luggage. I was liking her more and more.

A large solid, wooden door was opened by a woman about the same age as Scunt. It led on to a large hall with black-and-white chequered floor tiles. Although not opulent, the house was neat and well maintained. Jenny would have liked it and then gone on about how they don't build houses like this anymore. I would have to explain the economics of why it was now impossible to build these big middle-class houses. Scunt and our hostess stood close together with their arms around each other in a conspiratorial hug and a tangible sense of sadness. Scunt must have been explaining our plight.

'Tommy,' Scunt said, 'this is Mandy. Mandy this is Tommy.' And I put my luggage down and stuck out a hand which was taken firmly. It was difficult to take my eyes of her.

'If you're a friend of Tracy's and you're helping her, then you're a friend of mine too,' she said.

'Tracy?' I couldn't think of who she was talking about. 'Oh, you mean Scunt.'

Mandy and Scunt shared a glance and I don't think it was particularly endearing towards me. 'I'll tell you later Mandy,' Scunt said. 'It's just his little joke.'

'There's a lounge on the first floor,' said Mandy. 'You could watch TV. I'll be free in about an hour or so. Sasha and Natalie are working right now, but I'll tell them you're here. Tracy, do you know Sasha?' Scunt shook her head. 'Doesn't matter. I'll tell her you're here. You'll like her. Now off you two go and I'll see you soon.'

As we picked up our luggage and headed towards the stairs, I watched Mandy who was waiting a moment to make sure we were properly on our way but I was finding it difficult not to turn and have one final look at her. Jenny would *not* have liked the way our hostess was dressed. She had beautiful breasts. Just like Scunt's, they didn't droop or sag but they were larger. I can be quite specific about this because Mandy was wearing nothing more than a tiny Gstring, tied high on her hips and swooping down to a tiny piece of translucent material. As she turned to head towards a downstairs room, I saw that there was hardly any back to it; just a tiny single strand. I would tell you the colour if I could but I can't because whatever was there was hidden between the cheeks of her bottom.

'Is this what I think it is?' I asked Scunt as we headed upstairs.

'What do you think it is?' she said.

'A brothel?'

'Yes,' she said indifferently as we plonked our cases down and I looked at a large room with its great Victorian sash windows and modern, probably IKEA, furniture.

'Why did we come here, Scunt?' I wasn't sure this was the best place to hide.

'First, it's safe. Second, we have to sleep somewhere. And third, I want to show you that hookers are just ordinary people with an ordinary job. I want to change some of your prejudices.'

I couldn't argue. They were all good reasons, so I put my case down next to Scunt's and switched on the TV as Scunt sat down next to me on the sofa.

'You're right. I need to broaden my education, but I'm going to have to shut my eyes for a moment. I'm tired after the drive. Is that okay?'

'Of course, Tommy. Thank you so much. Come here.' She pulled me closer. I slipped off my shoes and put my feet on the sofa and my head on her lap. Our roles reversed, she stroked my hair as I fell asleep.

Chapter X

If you define a brothel as an establishment where more than one woman practices the finer arts of sexuality, then I had never been to a brothel, as such, but when I woke up, after my forty winks, I could have been anywhere. Elbow on the sofa, hand on chin, eyes hardly open, I rested my head and listened more than watched. I had managed to recognise the shapes of four pretty young women in jeans and tee-shirts sitting around chatting, and drinking what I presumed was white wine. I'm not sure what I was thinking. I knew what my preconceptions were, but would they be right?

Prostitutes must be brazen, excessively self-confident, oozing sex appeal, and most of all, they must be men-haters. Liking sex, and being able to have sex with anyone, is not the same as liking men. Surely they must acquire a real contempt and loathing for all the men that pass their way? How could they ever have a loving, trusting relationship with a man after seeing maybe four, five or twenty times a day their infidelities and attitudes so brazenly exposed? As if the customers weren't bad enough, then the pimps were surely all men too, and even more loathsome. How could they have any love for men?

I watched and I listened as they sat and chatted. When I went out with colleagues from the Bank or those who worked closely in the same area of expertise as me, we would naturally talk about our common subject – about economic forecasts or world politics. What do four escorts (models, hookers, call them whatever you like) talk about at the end of a day's work? If I was working in a brothel, then I would expect to hear about the depravity and lust. I didn't expect to hear Mandy complaining that the bakery had increased the price of bread. If she said that a price of 'a roll in the bakery' had increased I would have been more interested. I liked the idea of a bakery branching out to sell 'rolls' in competition with the brothel. The innuendo started to fire up my imagination as a pretty young sales assistant asked me how I would like my roll stuffed.

'What do you think about a large sausage?' I might suggest and she would reply along the lines that sausage was her favourite, and then giggle, coyly.

But how would they sort the real shoppers who actually wanted bread from those who wanted a sexy roll in the dough? Old and female would be excluded, but what if they had men serving. A whole new sexual vocabulary would develop. I would be served by a Slavic beauty called Vánocka. Leaning forward so I had sight of heaving breasts she would ask me what I wanted.

'Maybe you just want an ordinary *focaccia*?' pronounced to make my underwear panic. 'Or maybe you just want to see my bloomers or feel my cobs. Or maybe it's not *me* you want at all,' she teases, pouting and trying to look upset.

'Maybe it's Sally Lunns you want. Maybe you want to pumpernickel her? Or maybe you don't like my big baps and you want some *foccacia* from her – Pandoro – over there? You know she does quick bread and has those tablets for self-rising. But don't tell anyone! Come on! Let's see your French stick. As a special today you can even have it unwrapped.' She looks disappointed at her lack of success.

'Maybe you don't like girls at all, in fact. Are you really a bit of a fruit cake? You see Pane Carasau. Yes, that's him – the one singing. The one with the beautiful bannocks; yes, him with the Kentish huffkins. He's an expert with the banana bread and cottage loaf.' She was working the sales-pitch well.

'Maybe you have some little fetish? Black bread? Hardtack? Crêpe? Cornish splits? Sliced? Come on, there must be something we can tease you with?'

I look and consider. 'Crumpet, please. With a Massa Sovada and maybe a *focaccia* to finish?'

'Perfect choice,' she says, and with a wink asks, 'and shall I use the buttery Rowies with the Massa?'

I was brought back to reality. Two of the girls were going on about makeup and, well, everything you would expect from four young women. I closed my eyes and tried to get back to my bread dream but Scunt saw that I was awake.

'Hello. Tommy. You back with us now? We were just thinking about where we would go to eat. What d'you fancy? Indian or Italian? Or should we get a pizza delivered?'

'I don't mind,' I said. 'I'll just go with the flow.'

That reminded me I need a quick pizza. 'Can anyone point me to a bathroom?'

Not long after, the five of us headed off into Headingley and the New Inn, a little pub on the main street. It was a great pub, in as much as it was busy and served cheap and wholesome food – nothing pretentious – and it was lively. I'm not sure quite what I'd expected from my company, but as I sat there I realised we were an ordinary bunch of people having an ordinary night out. We weren't put in a back-room and isolated because of the girls' jobs and it didn't take long before I lost all my inhibitions about being with this crew of younger women and I cared not what people thought of our relationship.

'If thee need any 'elp with some of those, let us know,' a couple of local lads asked me as I stood at the bar buying drinks.

'I can manage just fine, thanks,' I replied and turned to join my new friends. Scunt sat close to me all night and held my hand as we sat at the table. We shared chicken wings and furtive glances. Once I tried to raise the subject of their work, but Scunt leaned to me and told me to wait until later.

'Later I'll show you around and tell you all the secrets,' she said. 'This is relaxation time.'

The evening meandered on pleasantly and we chatted about life. Mandy, Sasha and Ginny all called my Scunt, Tracy. I wasn't used to it and didn't like it.

In chorus they said: 'Her name isn't Scunt! You should find a better name if you don't like Tracy.'

I protested. 'But she comes from Scunthorpe. She is a Scunt. It's a very proper name. Liverpool girls are called Liver Birds, so why not?'

'So every woman you've called darling must come from Darlington? You're going to lose this one, Tommy,' said Scunt. And she was right; my arguments held no sway and they all agreed I was to be fined if I uttered the word Scunt again. I tried to find out the scale of the penalty. They laughed telling me it was severe. I gave in, but the word *Tracy* I couldn't utter and reverted to calling her 'her' and 'she'. We ate, talked and drank, and we laughed and teased each other and it was, well … it was just a really pleasant evening with friends.

'Time for bed,' said Mandy.

'I bet you say that a lot,' I said and again I immediately regretted the innuendo, but she just smiled.

'I think someone's getting frisky,' she said looking at

Scunt and she smiled.

I learnt that none of the girls lived on the premises. They all lived elsewhere and like commuters all around the world they travelled to work, and at the end of each working day they went home again, but Scunt and I were going to stay in the house. On a summer's evening it would have been possible to walk back. It would have been a pleasant walk and a time to walk hand in hand. We could have talked and I might have unravelled a little more of the mystery but tonight it was just a bit too far in the cold, so we taxied back and were soon back inside the house. I was banned by others from uttering the word Scunt but it was my own inhibitions that railed at the brothel.

'I'm sure you want to look around and see all the rooms, but let's do that tomorrow. We'll get Mandy to show us. Anyway, it's been a long time since I was here. I'm tired now, so let's just go to bed.'

Despite my nap it was fine with me. Maybe it was the Yorkshire beer or the chips that had tired me out, so I was happy enough. In the hotel, going to bed with Scunt had been easy. There, we were in one room and we naturally just shared the bed. The massage had just prefaced the inevitable and made sleeping together natural. But here again I was confused. What was going to happen now? I had never slept in a brothel before. I had to get my head clear. We were in any old four-bedroomed house. I tried to convince myself that it wasn't a brothel. Maybe *brothel* should be a verb, not a noun. When Mandy and her friends are in the house, they are *brothelling*. That didn't seem right, though. Yet I refused to think I was sleeping in a brothel; it was just a house.

'We need to make up a bed,' Scunt said. 'Here, give me a hand.'

It had never occurred to me that there might be many beds in a brothel; only rarely – if ever – would anyone sleep in them. None of them was made up with sheets, duvet, pillows or pillow cases.

'How many beds are we going to make up?' I asked, still unsure of my role. I received no more than a quizzical stare from Scunt.

'Just one, idiot. Now here, hold this,' she said, passing me a corner of the duvet. The art of filling a duvet cover I still find mind-boggling. I really think it's genetic. Women can. Men can't. It's just like folding a dry sheet straight off the washing line. Women can fold it into a little square without one piece touching the ground. With men, invariably the sheet has to be rewashed after being trailed across the ground.

We completed our task, cleaned our teeth, said little more. Soon we fell asleep again in each other's arms.

I woke alone in the bed in Headingley. Scunt handed me a cup of coffee.

'Come on, lazy bones. Time to get up. Work starts here soon.'

With your beautiful body, I'm always up, I thought. Then, another inappropriate innuendo: in this house, it's always time for someone to get up. Better not to follow that thought through right now, I decided. I checked my watch on the bedside table. Later than I thought. Half-past nine, but surely too early for work to start.

'What time do they open for business?' and again I wished I had chosen my word more wisely. 'I don't mean the girls, I mean the house. What time does it open?'

'About eleven.'

'What – I mean who – is so horny that they pay for sex

at eleven in the morning? I always thought this business was a night business?'

'Tommy, you've got so much to learn. Most houses close about six or seven at night; it's only independent escorts who work night times. Now, have a shower and get dressed and Mandy will show you around.'

Again I did as I was told. What had happened to me? An order like that from Jenny would have been met with a flat rejection, or a totally opposite reaction. I would have stayed in bed as long as I reasonably could but today I was awake and in the shower in a shake; it was just nine thirty and I'd been in bed for four hours more than on any normal workday. I could get to enjoy this lifestyle. I looked at the coffee Scunt had brought me and, momentarily, thought of Jane back at the office. Would she have bought me a coffee today, on her way into work? What would she have done with it? It was only a passing thought; I couldn't really give a damn. Work was far from my mind, and gaining a new but very distant perspective.

The perspective I met as I headed into the lounge was further from work than anything I could have imagined. None of my business-school training or case studies had prepared me for this work environment. It was not yet mid-morning, Sasha and Ginny had just arrived, and Mandy was already ready for work, wearing one of the smallest bikinis I had ever seen. What could I say and what could I do?

'Morning, Tommy. Sleep well? You going to be working today, Tracy?'

'I'm not sure. Maybe if there's a special client. What do you think, Tommy?'

I went into a panic. This kind of question had never bleeped across my radar before. I'd never come home from work to have Jenny tell me she was a hooker now and ask if I minded. Then again, coupling thoughts about Jenny and sex had become pretty rare.

It wasn't necessarily anything to do with age. I'd heard rumours about one of our friends, Susie, who repressed her sexuality for many years, until suddenly she 'came out', offering special services to local divorced and single men. I suppose she cruised the local supermarket with her melons on display. I even heard she had a regular monthly arrangement with a couple of rich old-age pensioners. One evening down at the pub, my train-platform buddy, Jonathan, was castigating me yet again for walking right past him on the platform that morning, without so much as a gentle wave. Then he gave me a web address where he claimed I would find naked pictures of our friend Susie. Of course when I got home, I checked it out. Indeed these were pictures of a naked middle-aged woman, but they excluded her head, so they could have been of anyone. Well, anyone female – if the anatomically explicit close-ups were anything to go by. I was so keen to prove her provenance that I printed out a colour picture of the genitalia on view and a picture of Susie taken at one of our BBQs. I spent many hours trying to determine if one belonged to the other.

In fact, this became a subject of intense academic interest that took me on a search through a great deal of pornography trying to match pussies and faces. This was soon after I'd finished my studies of facial asymmetry, where I'd found a great deal of the literature on classifying shape and form. So with a great deal of effort, I also became an expert on the many shapes, sizes and colour tones of vaginas. I went to see the Jamie McCartney exhibition of The Great Wall of Vagina, and mused over his plaster casts of vulvas. It went someway to re-emphasise my conjecture that each and every woman could be identified by her own unique vaginal features. Maybe it would replace face images and fingerprints? The new reliable biometric data to stop female illegal immigrants entering a country? A career in security at Heathrow briefly beckoned to me.

I consulted my friend Chris who worked in the intelligence services. She could never quite tell me what she did (and – yes – we do have female spies). It was the old I'll-have-to-shoot-you-if-I-tell-you routine. She had a business card which said Counter Terrorism Intelligence Unit (CTIU), which sounded more like something out of *Twenty-Four*, that American thriller series with Jack Bauer – only that was the *CTU*, but what was a vowel between spies? Anyway, Chris had much better legs than Jack Bauer, and I was always happy to eat a meal in her company. The problem was that Jenny was always with us, so I was left to dream about my romp with a spy. No doubt Jason Bourne would have managed his way past that – and her. I met Chris at the pub one night, and after beating round the subject, I asked her about my idea; there are unique fingerprints and supposedly unique ear prints, and we know that there is retinal scanning, but is it the same with pussies? At this point she looked at me rather like those women at the door outside the toilet in the pub when I lost the deeply offended Anna, and I could see already she was starting to look sceptical. Or was it quizzical?

'I mean,' I went on, 'is there a taxonomy that I could recognise? What do you do if you find a pussy print somewhere? Can you match it back to a particular female?'

'Tommy, have a drink and keep taking the tablets,' was all she said.

But there were no classifications of vaginal shapes that I could find; I even developed my own taxonomy to go along with facial types. Much to my annoyance, I could find no correlation between them, so I had to report to Jonathan – on another night at the pub – that it may have been Susie, or it may not. He shrugged. While I had taken the academic route, he had been more direct and asked her in person. They were now meeting every Tuesday evening and he was paying a trifling fifty pounds for the whole night.

'What does her husband think about it all?' I asked.

'Oh, he seems quite happy. He comes down to the pub with us after I've bonked her.'

But I had to get back to Scunt's question. She was asking me if it was okay for her to work today. 'What do you think, Tommy? You okay with that?'

There were only three answers; no, yes, or I don't care. *No* meant I had a moral objection which was a general or specific indignation. Well, clearly it couldn't be a general objection because not only was I travelling with Scunt, but I was also residing in a brothel. So the answer *No* would have to be because I didn't want her to work that day, and that of course implied that I had some feelings for her. Fucking hell, why do women always put the onus on the man? On the other hand an answer of *Yes* or *I don't care* showed that she meant nothing to me, that we were just free-willed companion travellers. Of course, *Yes* might have meant that I was a truly modern man who allowed his wife to work and if that work was sex, then so be it.

I'm all for the removal of gender stereotypes and I'm clearly okay with prostitution, but could I merge the two thought streams? An uneasy parallel came to mind and my thoughts drifted back to the suburban Sunday lunchtime wife-swapping parties, with all the associated paraphernalia of newsletters and colour-coordinated tulip-filled front gardens. I hadn't minded the idea of wife-swapping because it was with *Jenny*, and my feelings towards her over the years were – at best – neutral. But that Jenny was not the one I married. Would I have been happy when we first married and were deeply in love, to swap and strut my naked self from house to house? Probably, but I wouldn't have been okay with some other sweaty body on top of her. I knew all the goose and gander arguments, but let's be honest – it's just anthropology working as it always has.

Why was I even hesitating to answer Scunt? She was looking at me and waiting for any words of wisdom or advice.

'Come on, Tommy. What do you think?'

'Maybe we should have him working as well?' said Mandy. 'That would solve his dilemma.'

'What! Me working? What do you mean?' There was clearly panic in my voice, and Scunt and Mandy were finding it hard to keep a straight face. I thought it was a joke, but I didn't know the two of them well enough to be sure.

'It's just that many of our clients are bi- and you have a nice arse. You would make a lot of money.'

Now I looked at Scunt. 'Is she being serious? I won't do it!'

Scunt came close and put an arm in mine. 'I know, Tommy. She's joking.'

'Oh. Thank you,' I said, smiling weakly at Mandy.

She came close and then quickly reached down, grabbed my balls and said, 'But if you change your mind, just ask.'

'That wasn't funny,' I said, trying to be serious, but the

point had been conceded and she moved on.

'Please tell me, Tommy. Do you think I should work today or not?'

There are times when rational arguments should be discarded, when you should rely on your emotions and gut responses. There had not been many such moments in my life, but that was not a reason never to start.

'No. I would rather you didn't work.'

'Why, Tommy? Why not?'

'Just no,' I said.

'That's good enough for me. Sorry, Mandy. It's just you and the girls today. Will you show Tommy around now?'

'Of course.'

Scunt made a point of holding my hand and keeping me close as Mandy set off on a tour of her Headingley brothel.

'The kitchen you've seen, of course and this…' Mandy said as she walked back towards the front door, 'is our reception room. This is where our clients wait. We try not to have them waiting long. We encourage them to phone and book ahead but sometimes they stack up.'

I went in to the room first, and the others followed. It was a little like a doctor or dentist's waiting room; chairs around the outside and a small table in the middle. I looked at the magazines laid out and decided it would be a very, very progressive doctor to offer this reading selection. Of course, ever since I was young, I've had access to and have read so-called top-shelf magazines. Some of them try to claim some moral standing (maybe that's not the right term – perhaps respect or reputation?) by putting words between the pictures; but it's all fluff. In the pub and at work I've discussed articles that have appeared in daily newspapers, *Private Eye*, *Punch*, the *Economist* and even the *Spectator*, but I can't recall a single debate over the content of *Playboy* or *Penthouse*. They're mainly American in origin; the continental magazines, without the benefit of a shared language, are all pictures and lack the pretentiousness of the American imports, and, if that is what you liked (and we all did) the pictures were also what you would call *stronger*.

Reaching out to the table casually, I picked up a magazine and flicked through the covers of the rest. Most, I quickly decided, must have been bought on a day trip to the continent as I didn't know where to buy such material in the UK. Then again, I'd never had cause to do so recently because the internet provides a surfeit of opportunities, and trips to the newsagents are no longer required. Whenever I do find myself in a newsagent, I always look upwards at those shelves and wonder who still buys them. Surely a good colour printer would be a better investment if hard copy is required; and hard copy is exactly what it is. At that point, I suddenly became aware of my new underwear, and remembered why Y-fronts are so much better.

'Do you mean they sit in here, waiting?' I asked.

The image intrigued me; two or three men sitting there all waiting for a shag. Surely no one would talk. They would all be too embarrassed to say anything, or even look at each other. I couldn't imagine any conversation, although maybe flicking through the magazines one of them might say: 'Who are you seeing? Oh, Mandy. Yes, she's very good. So flexible, and a nice bum. What was that? Does she do any fetish? I really don't know. Depends what you call fetish, of course. You know – one man's fetish is another man's cup of tea. Ha, ha. Her rope work? Very good too. I'm told she trained with a Japanese guy in Warrington. Oh, hello Ginny. You ready for me now? Okay, bye. Have a good time with

Mandy.'

No, I couldn't see that level of *bonhomie* developing. With that thought, Mandy turned on the side lights and closed the heavy velvet curtains. The room was pitched into a darkness, filled only with small pools of light. I understood why, but it was a shame because there was barely enough light to look at the pictures so thoughtfully provided in the magazines.

Mandy must have read my thoughts. 'We try never to have more than one person waiting in here. We take them into other rooms but, you know, sometimes it does happen. The customers don't like it.'

I didn't think they would.

Then we went upstairs. The first room Mandy showed me was the one Scunt and I had slept in. The duvet had gone again, and a single dark red sheet was stretched over the mattress. Mandy reached out and picked up my watch from the wooden bedside cabinet.

'Guess this is yours?' she said. 'I've put your luggage in our lounge – where you had your little sleep last evening.'

I hadn't even noticed it was gone from the room. And last night I hadn't noticed the large mirror behind the headboard – just an affectation of interior design, of course, because there was no sexual position I could imagine for which it had any possible use, unless you wanted to check your haircut or pimples while in the doggie position.

'This is our vanilla room,' Mandy was saying. 'I suppose it's the one we use most.'

'Vanilla?'

'Yes, Tommy. After this one, all the rooms sort of pick up themes and the next three get a little more exciting. Want to see the others?'

I really was interested, and I wanted to see all there was to see. I nodded my agreement. There was a strange fascination with the idea of Mandy and Ginny having sex every day in these rooms. We moved on. Walking had another distinct advantage; for the second time in a very short time, striding out eased the increasing discomfort inside my underpants.

'Do you all have your own room to work in, or do you share?' I asked as we walked along the corridor.

'We share, of course. It depends on what the punter wants,' Mandy said as she opened the door to the next room. 'This is the mirror room.' The reason for the name was obvious when I peered inside. Every square inch of the walls and the ceiling was covered with mirrors. Standing in the room I saw us in never-ending corridors of repetition. Like a scary fairground attraction. Behind me, I saw the door was painted a deep red.

'Why isn't the door a mirror as well?'

'It used to be, but the first day Sasha used it, she couldn't find the way out. She became frightened and started screaming and the punter didn't know what to do and we thought there was an accident.'

'What sort of accident?' I asked.

Mandy looked at me. 'Like a muscle strain or, worse, a heart attack. That's our big fear. Then we get all the bureaucrats checking us out. A punter dying on us would close us down. Wish we could get everyone to have a health check before they come here. Anyway, we rushed in and found Sasha naked, screaming and lying on the bed on her back, kicking her legs in the air while he just sat there with his head in his hands. We had to give him his money back of course.'

I could imagine secret services around the world wanting to use this room for interrogations. It frightened me.

'I think I would chose the vanilla room,' I mumbled.

'But wait until you see the other two,' Mandy said. 'What do you think, Scunt? Think he'll choose either of them?'

'I'm sure he will. Deep down, they all love the fourth room.'

'Which is?' I asked.

'You'll have to wait until we get there' Scunt said holding onto me more closely and again I felt terribly out of place, but there was nowhere else to go. Men lust after sex and are intrigued by all aspects of it. That's why the largest use of the worldwide web is the consumption of porn. But when you come face-to-face with the detail, even the most hardened of men can be frightened and intimidated. Was it hypocrisy, a lie or a sign of the natural dominance of women? Anyway this was certainly a great deal more interesting than being in the office.

I looked at Mandy, so un-selfconscious in her tiny bikini, and thought of Jane at the office. I wondered how she would fit in here. Maybe she would? Maybe she did? Maybe this was her night-time hobby? But I was pulled out of my thoughts as we entered the next room. All white and set up like a hospital room. A bed, a massage table, a chair that would be more at home in a gynaecologist's consulting room, and cabinets full of medical equipment. Even my wildest imagination couldn't take it all in. Luckily I didn't have to, as we were interrupted by Sasha, pushing us aside with the hoover – solely for the intention of cleaning the floor, it seems. The juxtaposition of the normal and the exotic was confusing.

'Sit in the chair, Tommy,' Mandy shouted above the noise of the hoover. Why not, I thought. As I sat back and made myself comfy, Scunt and Mandy took a leg each and stretched them on to supports which pulled my legs wide apart. I began to feel uneasy.

'Of course, by now the client would be naked, and we could tie him down, if he wanted.'

'Why?' I asked.

'So we can play *properly* with him. But the massage table is more popular these days. Everybody seems to want a body to body massage. They've all heard about tantric sex. Come on, Tracy, let's show him the special room.'

The girls all smiled and I was even more uneasy. I pushed at the next door I was shown. Inside was a dark dungeon with big furniture and whips and other instruments of apparent torture hanging all over the wall. I stepped half in, and then stepped back out again.

'Who goes in there? I mean, it's a torture chamber.'

'Oh, lots of men like to be dominated,' said Mandy. 'Ginny is our expert, but we all have a few of the required skills. So what are you two going to do today?' she asked, nodding at Scunt and me. 'Work starts soon. You can stay here and sit in the lounge, or go and have some lunch and look around Leeds.'

Scunt and I looked at each other. 'Let's go and look around, Tommy. It's a nice day and we don't have much else to do. We can't sit in here all day. Let's go for a drive and get some lunch.'

It was easy to agree as I was feeling uncomfortable and out of place. Later, in our comfortable hired car we drifted north out of Headingley into the West Yorkshire countryside. I didn't know where we were going but it was quiet in the car, which had become a refuge of sorts. Scunt was painting her nails and I had so many questions to ask her still, but none of the right words. In every sense, I wasn't quite sure where we were going. On a practical level, I thought about going across to Ilkley and having a walk on the moor, but I looked at Scunt's shoes. She was not ready for a moorland walk. Maybe Otley? I didn't know the area. Then, we entered a little village called Bramhope, and I saw a nice-looking pub. I wanted to talk again, in more relaxed surroundings. The Fox and Hounds was a stone-built Yorkshire pub with a history, but that didn't really interest me.

'Come on, then. Let's get a drink and some food and relax,' I said.

I still wanted to know why we were on the road, being 'chased' across the British countryside, and I wanted to talk about Scunt's friends and their work. No – it wasn't just her friends' work. It was also Scunt's work.

'What's wrong, Tommy? You've been grumpy all the way here. Are you missing your office and your job? Don't you want to be here with me anymore?' Trust Scunt to ask the impossible question. I thought about it.

'Actually, Scunt, I'm really enjoying myself but I'm trying to understand your job. I thought I knew what was happening. But now I don't. Can we talk about it?'

'Of course – just get me a white wine and I'll answer any questions.' And again I did just what I was told.

'What's the problem, Tommy?' she asked as we found a comfortable bench seat.

I had no idea where to start because I didn't know exactly what was bothering me. 'I suppose I didn't know what to expect,' I started. 'And you were right – it was, I mean, it *is* an education. They're just three ordinary girls whose job – and it is a job, isn't it –' Scunt smiled and nodded, 'is just such a personal one that it attracts attention. I suppose it's because sex and love are so intertwined in most people's thoughts that one without the other seems so alien.'

'But you've been with prostitutes before. Why are you surprised? Weren't they all just ordinary girls as well?'

Of course they were. I remembered how I'd been ready to head off into Soho and find myself someone I was willing to pay. Why was I so upset now? I tried to answer Scunt's question. 'It's because I've never associated a hooker with a personal life. When we were in the hotel, were you comparing me with all your clients?'

'Look, Tommy. It's just a job. I like sex. I'm good at sex but I manage to keep my personal life separate from my job. Think of it as just a job. Nothing more. I don't always like my customers but most are very sweet and kind. Do you like all the people you work with?'

'Of course not.'

'But you still work with them. It's the same with us.'

I had to ask: 'But can you have a personal loving relationship and still do your job? I mean, can you go home and cook the supper and make love to your man having had sex all day?'

'Of course I can. Don't be so silly. It's not *my* problem but the man's. I can do the job I do because I've got a high sex drive. You'd probably have more sex with me than ever with Jenny. The question is: would you want to come home to a wife who had been having sex all day with other men?'

It was my problem again. My prejudice and my sense of guilt. She was right and I shook my head in response to her last question.

'But what about all the girls who are trafficked into the business. That can't be right. Surely?'

'Absolutely right. Me, Mandy and the others do this job because it's what we want to do. It's our decision how best to use our skills to make money. We've got no time for men who exploit and use disadvantaged women against their will. That's why we work as a collective – no pimp! They're the real villains.'

Her phone rang just as I was beginning to see the light and feel a lot better.

'Hi, Mandy. We're in—' She looked at me. 'Where are we, Tommy?'

'Bramhope.'

'We're in Bramhope. No, we didn't go far. About thirty minutes, I suppose.' She went quiet for a minute. 'Go on, then. Tell me,' and she listened to Mandy for a couple more minutes while I looked at my wine.

'I think that's a brilliant idea,' she said. 'We'll be back for four thirty,' looking at me for reassurance. I nodded.

'What was all that about?'

Scunt looked at me and just smiled. A plan had been hatched and I wasn't to know about it, but I felt a lot better and the atmosphere was considerably improved.

'So what's the overall plan, then? I mean, we – especially me – can't stay holed up in a brothel in Leeds indefinitely. We need to resolve this quickly and I need to get back to work. And you can't keep running for ever. We need to get a resolution for you.'

Scunt looked at her glass and ran her finger round the rim. At last she spoke. 'We'll keep moving for a week.'

'A week! I can't do that, Scunt. I've got responsibilities.'

'Of course you do, and right now I'm your biggest responsibility. We'll move for a week and shake everyone off the trail. Then I'll move and start again somewhere else.'

'But the police will still catch up with you.'

'Maybe. But I'll just have to be someone else. At least then it will be only the police.'

'Let's just take it a day at a time, then,' I conceded. 'But I'm not promising a whole week.'

She smiled and pouted and simpered and I knew that it would be a whole week.

We arrived back at Headingley early, just after four, and were greeted by Mandy still in her ultra-small bikini, and Ginny in a long leather catsuit, cut very low with her breasts almost exposed.

'Cup of tea?' Ginny asked, as we settled into the sofas in the sitting-room. If the initial impact of the catsuit hadn't been enough, the sight of her bare bottom as she turned to go into the kitchen clawed at my underwear.

'Have you told him?' Mandy was asking Scunt.

'Nope. I thought we would get him ready and then tell him. I like surprises, and so does Tommy.'

They both looked at me and laughed. Suddenly I had a great sense of unease as it dawned on me that I was the plan. As Ginny walked back into the room with a tray, Mandy looked me straight in the eyes and said, 'Take your shirt off, Tommy.'

'What?'

'Please just do as you're told for once. You're far too used to giving orders.'

I could have resisted or fought them but I've always been told never to hit women and, anyway, what man could resist three girls jumping on him and removing his shirt. And that was what happened. All three jumped on me as I sat on the sofa and they pulled at my shirt. It was one of my new shirts and I didn't want it to get torn, so not only didn't I resist, I sort of helped them. Unless I was mistaken, we were going to have an orgy right there and then in the lounge.

Orgies, I suppose, figure high in every man's fantasies. At least they did on my morning commute, when I had the luxury of Y-fronts. My thoughts had turned more than once to a mass orgy on the train. The words of Roger McGough had come to mind: 'The bus people, and there were many of them, were shocked and surprised, and amused and annoyed, but when word got around that the world was coming to an end at lunchtime, they put their pride in their pockets with their bus tickets and made love one with the other.' Maybe, I had thought, I could start something like that on the train to London? What would be a good thing to shout to kick things off? In 1967, when McGough had written his poem, an imminent nuclear attack was what caused the frenzy, but would it have the same effect today? I was unsure. We've all become a little blasé about nuclear attacks. I mean I know we all got worked up over Iraq and WMD but they never found them, so we're less concerned. I could shout 'Bill Gates is dead!' which would lead to rejoicing from all those who have suffered at the hands of Microsoft and enjoyed the benefit of Apple. But would it spark an orgy? I doubt it. What revelation would be so cataclysmic that it would seem like the end of the world was imminent?

On my morning train, it's always mainly men. I would have to find something that mattered to the few women on board first – to get them in the mood. Something like: 'Facebook has been closed!' That was better, but still it wasn't quite right. And then I knew. I would tell the young girl sitting next to me that her Facebook account name and password was being sent to her employer under a new European Community directive, and everything that had been hidden was now open for them to see. All those pictures of her flashing at the festival, cavorting with sundry men in sundry places, drunk with her head down the toilet, would be available to everyone. It wouldn't just stop at her boss. Her mum and her granny would be sent a leaflet explaining how to see what their loving child/grand-daughter was doing when she said she was at home washing her hair. If this happened to everyone, the world would be in chaos! Nothing would be secret, and all our private memories – so carefully hidden in protected Facebook accounts – would be laid bare to the world. Now that might just cause the sort of panic I was after; it would seem like the end of the world and drive the carriage into an orgy. But naturally I did nothing. Early morning is not my best time for sex and, late at night, after a day in the office, it all seems so pointless.

But here, in a sitting room in Headingley rather than the early morning or late evening train between Faversham and London, I was about to be engaged in a full sexual romp – an orgy, no less – with three highly skilled girls. As I was wondering how it might work and how the combinations might entwine us, my shirt was off, and I was rolled over and then – clink – my wrists, behind my back, were cuffed.

'Scunt! What's happening?'

'I knew you wouldn't agree if I asked you, so you'll just have to trust me, Tommy. We want you to see what happens here and Mandy came up with this wonderful idea.'

'I know what happens. Remember, I've done this before.'

'But you only have your experiences – not ours. This

way you can be part of it and watch and learn. You were always part of the play. This way you can be the audience.'

'Part of it?! Scunt – no one's going to do anything to me! Please Scunt. You know I'm straight. Please!! I don't want to be fucked by a fat Yorkshireman!'

'Would a thin one be okay, then?' she said laughing.

'You know what I mean. Please, Scunt, undo me.'

'No, Tommy. Just go with it and trust me. You'll be safe, I promise.'

I had spent so many days of my life dreaming of such things, but being confronted by this in reality was not so pleasant. Did I have any choice? Of course I did. I could just sit down and they would never move me from this room, but I did sort of trust Scunt and she was trying to help me understand, so, still afraid, I said: 'Okay. What next?'

'That's better, Tommy. Go with Mandy. You'll enjoy it and you'll be safe. We just wanted to find a way for you to be part of the team and experience what we do every day. Go on, get a move on!'

With my naked chest and hands locked behind my back, I followed Mandy who led me down the stairs. The waiting room was empty and as dark as I remembered it, although a porn film was now running on the TV showing two girls getting to know each other as they became very intimate. Ginny, with her bare bottom, was already there.

'Now, we don't want you saying anything to anyone. You need to be silent.' And with that she strapped a gag – a ball of rubber jamming into my mouth – which she then fixed behind my head. God only knows what I looked like.

'And we don't want you wandering off either.' Taking some rope she tied the handcuff to a large ring on the wall. I was fixed there, unable to speak. There was no way back.

'We also don't want to frighten our customers by making them think you can see them. Discretion is everything.' She pulled out a black mask and pulled it tight over my head. I tried to shout something but it was muffled by the gag. What had I got myself into? What I might have shouted was that I *could* see. It was blurred, but I could see.

'It looks as though you can't see, but it's stretched tight, so you can. So you can watch. Now let's get these off.' Getting on her knees, my shoes, socks and trousers were pulled down.

'Nice underwear. Good choice.' For once I was glad not to have the Y-fronts on. 'But you don't need them.'

She whipped them off and left me, tied and tethered, hooded, gagged and naked but, more importantly to me, vulnerable. I could still make out the TV and hear the squeals of the girls, which meant I was more than a little aroused. There was nothing I could do but wait and what I was waiting for I didn't know. Thankfully I didn't have to wait long. The doorbell rang and I heard Sasha say: 'Wait in here and don't worry about him. He can't see you. We'll be dealing with him later.'

In walked a middle-aged man, clearly straight from work in a business suit and as surprised to see me as I was to see him. What could he do but sit down, pick up a magazine, watch some TV, shuffle on his seat and do everything he could not to look at me. He looked ordinary. I don't know what I expected a customer of a brothel to be like. I suppose he was just like me. I wanted to ask him these questions, but I'm sure he wouldn't answer. I wanted to know if he had a 'Jenny' at home but I couldn't ask. I was gagged. So I just watched him with my immediate embarrassment slowly ebbing, knowing he couldn't really see me. The ordinariness of it all was what struck me first. There was none of the furtive diving into darkened alley ways. He was waiting as patiently to have sex with Mandy, Sasha or Ginny as if he were waiting to see the doctor and that was just how it had been with me. I would be in a hotel room somewhere and trawl through newspapers or search the web and find a phone number. A girl would arrive, I would give her money, she would get undressed, we would talk a bit, fuck for less than an hour, and she would leave. Then I would go back to reading the paper. It was actually normal, even mundane.

Mandy came into the room and knelt in front of her customer and chatted quietly. Occasionally they both looked at me and then he nodded.

'Thank you,' she said and they left together leaving me. I was disappointed at not having any company. The embarrassment of my nakedness had totally gone; it was after all a natural state and I was okay with the way I looked. There was also the fact that I was extraordinarily well endowed, so no problems on that count. I settled into my situation as best I could under the circumstances.

'Come on, Tommy,' came a voice from behind me. 'We have another thrill for you. You're going to sit in with me and that customer. You can watch and listen! Right. Off to the mirror room we go!'

Mandy started to lead me upstairs again. With my impaired vision I stubbed my toe on the stairs and tried, pointlessly, to scream. Mandy continued to drag me along. We passed another customer on his way out with Ginny. Judging from the commotion behind me, he must have nearly fallen down the stairs with the sight of this tied-up, hooded, naked man being led around. She shouted at him. 'Would you like to be him next time? Would you like to be our house slave?' Ginny was clearly drumming up business.

Arriving in the room of mirrors, I was seated. I was tied to the chair. The customer was there already; sitting on the bed, looking every bit as nervous as I felt, despite the comforting words Mandy was whispering in his ear. I watched them both, turning my head to try and hear what they were saying. All small talk. How was he? How were the family and the children? How was work? And with each answer he became more relaxed, and clearly my quiet presence no longer worried him. Mandy sat close to him with her hand on his thigh.

How long they talked for was unclear. I'd lost all sense of time and was, if truth be told, getting a bit bored. Mandy had leaned close and undone his tie and then she stood and undressed. It was a little like a striptease but it didn't take long as she was wearing so little. He undressed too. Then she lay on the bed. He put on a condom. He got on top of her and in a very short time he had finished. While he dressed again Mandy sat, still naked, on the bed, restarting their previous conversation by asking him about his son's football team. They talked some more, then he said thank you and he was gone. Mandy led him out, and I heard the main door to the house close.

I thought about my times with the Mandy's and Scunt's of this world, and started to understand what they had been saying. We all get what we want from the relationship and for all of us it's different, but what we have with a prostitute is a short moment with a comforting person who cares about us and shows that she cares for our specific needs. For that moment we were the centre of attention. We all like to be thought of as special and unique and the prostitute delivers that. I was deep in these thoughts when Ginny arrived.

'Off we go again, Tommy. Round two. Did you enjoy that?' and I was led off, following her bare bottom to the dungeon. 'Now, Tommy, I'm going to have to untie your hands for a moment and re-tie you. You won't try and run away will you?' I shook my head. After all how could I run anyway? I was naked.

I don't know how to describe the device that stood in front of me. It was a cross on its side like a giant letter X. Ginny tied my ankles to it, and then my hands above my head. I was spread-eagled.

'Just wait there. I'll be back soon.'

How on earth was I going to do anything but stay just where I was? I waited in the silence. A new customer followed Ginny into the room. He was clearly more of a manual labourer than an office worker and showed none of the reticence of the first by my presence.

'Strip off those clothes' ordered Ginny, and he obeyed – as he did whatever Ginny asked. And during whatever length of time we were all together, she did all sorts of things to him that looked painful and humiliating. She whipped him and left marks all across his back and thighs. She stuffed all sorts of large things into him and then some even larger things. I winced and all the time he said 'Yes mistress,' or 'As you wish, mistress.'

She flicked a whip at his cock and said, 'What sort of pathetic thing do you think this is?' In that respect she was right. And after a time she had him dress again and she told him to 'Fuck off' and he did just as he was told while Ginny started to tidy up. There had been no sex. He hadn't ejaculated and Ginny had remained fully clothed.

'Tracy, we're done,' she shouted as she carried on her housekeeping tasks. 'What do you want me to do with him now?'

Scunt came in and took off my mask and untied my gag. She looked at me.

'Nice,' she said looking at me still tied. 'Shall I send Ginny away and have my way with you?' She ran her nails down my chest.

Ginny looked up from her tasks and smiled. Then in came Sasha and Mandy, and all four stood in front me.

'I see what you mean, Tracy. He's in good shape.' Honestly, I could have been in better shape at that second.

'Stop this and untie me please?' My voice crackled a bit with dryness.

'He has a nice cock and his body isn't bad at all. Shall we just leave him here and have him whenever we want? Are you sure we couldn't sell him out? After all, we could take all his clothes and he doesn't look like the sort to run off naked and go to the police. I mean, who would believe him if he said he was being held hostage by four pretty women in a brothel. No one would listen and he would be taken off to a nut-house.'

'What do you think I am – a commodity?'

'Do you think of women as a commodity – to be used?'

'No, of course not,' I said and I started to see where they were going. All my preconceptions were demolished.

'Okay, Tommy. Let's get you untied and dressed,' said Scunt as the others went about their business. 'We can all go out tonight, have some fun, and relax.'

And that's just what we did. They were my new friends and I was now one of them. I understood them and their jobs, and I was totally relaxed about all that had happened.

Chapter XI

Having sorted our plan out in Bramhope the previous day, we would now travel for the rest of the week and see what happened. That meant four more days with Scunt. We packed first thing and I wandered out to get some Starbucks coffees; then we waited until all the girls had checked into work so we could say our goodbyes. It was all hugs and kisses, and tears were shed by Scunt and Mandy. Mandy told Scunt she should phone whenever she needed support, help or comfort. It was a kind gesture that I'm sure Scunt appreciated. And for me?

'If you're ever in Leeds again,' Mandy said, 'just make sure you stay with me and if Tracy doesn't keep you, just come back and I'll tie you and keep you all for myself.'

I smiled. She gave me a business card. Maybe she meant it.

'Did she mean what she said?' I asked Scunt as we headed into Leeds to get on to the motorway.

'Probably. They all thought you looked quite hunky, especially when you were naked and tied up. They like the vulnerable look.'

'Well. They all sampled the goods, so to speak, but that's all behind us now.'

As we entered the motorway, Scunt said, 'Where do you want to go next, then? We have to aim for somewhere'.

'What about the seaside? I like the sea. A walk along the beach would be nice.' I was thinking about some of my childhood days in East Anglia. Summer days were tranquil and then in the winter the sea would get big. Best of all, I liked to be by the sea in the winter when the North Sea raged against the shore and I could lean into the wind at crazy angles and not fall over. I would get covered by the spray of breaking waves and arrive home tasting and smelling of dried salt.

'Where is Leek, Tommy?'

'Well I know it's not by the sea. Isn't it in the Midlands somewhere – near Stoke? Why do you ask?'

'If it's close, I'd like to go there next. There's someone else I would like to see again and someone I would like you to meet.'

'Another of your working friends? Scunt, I'm not sure I want to visit every brothel in England.'

'No, it's nothing like that,' she laughed. 'Is Leek close?'

'Yes, as close as anything else.'

'Then let's go to Leek.'

'Okay! Leek it is. Going to tell me why?'

'Nope'

At that point, we were moving westward out of Leeds, heading towards Manchester. Despite the prospect of seeing the sea, the flats of the East of England just hadn't seemed appealing. Maybe, though, we might still end up there; anything was possible with Scunt but for now we were on the motorway and I didn't know where Leek was but I was sure it wasn't the way we were going. The next exit was for Huddersfield and we turned off to check the map. It turned out that Leek wasn't that far away. It was in the middle of nowhere and south of us, so we set the satnav for the cross-country route and headed off again. We were taken through and out of Yorkshire's West Riding, through and round the solid and real working towns and villages of traditional stone buildings with quaint names such as Kirkburton, Shepley, Oxspring, Penistone and Thurgoland to the edge of the Peak

District National Park. We were in Derbyshire. As we drove I could imagine that the winters here could be every bit as exciting as my childhood walks on the seafront. The terrain was rugged and beautiful, already turning into a verdant green. Was Scunt a nature lover at heart, I wondered. Did she also just want to feel the soothing touch of natural beauty? It didn't really seem like her, I thought, as we pressed onto Leek on the Park's southern edge.

Leek is an old town, dominated by Victorian architecture. I presume it was part of the industrial revolution. After all, the towns in the cradle of the industrial revolution were all within fifteen miles of each other. I imagined for a moment James Arkwright looking at Leek as the place to be before he moved on to Comford to build the world's first successful water-powered cotton spinning mill in 1771. This was history in the raw.

Scunt was engrossed in other things. She was checking her phone and playing with the satnav.

'Here we are. All done,' and with that, a disenfranchised voice from the speakers said: *Turn right in 250 meters at the junction.*

'What are we doing, Scunt?'

'Be patient, Tommy. You always want to know too much. Learn to enjoy the journey.'

Enjoy the journey? I had always enjoyed 'the journey'; one train every morning and another one every evening. I was always on a journey but I understood what she meant and maybe she was right. I was always on a journey but I never had a destination – other than making sure I was alive to embark on the next one. I remembered what I'd said during my phonecall home. Just what would Jenny think? If she thought I was somewhere secret in Eastern Europe, she couldn't resist telling someone about it, and how important I was because the Chairman had chosen me. I wondered who she might choose to tell.

'I *have* to tell you. I *have* to tell someone,' she would say on the phone to a passing coffee-morning friend. 'Tommy is on a secret mission.'

Well, that part is true.

'He is doing a secret job for the Chairman. I'm sure it will mean promotion and more money.'

There we go again. Always about the money. And what would I get with my new-found wealth? Certainly not more sex with Jenny. I suppose I would just find new and more expensive hookers.

At the roundabout take the second exit.

'Scunt?'

'Yes.'

'What would you do if you had more money than you could imagine?'

'You mean lots and lots of money?'

'Yes, like if you won the lottery.'

You have arrived at your destination.

A very appropriate answer. The sun was fighting and winning its battle with the clouds to brighten the heathlands of the Peaks. It was tranquil and beautiful in a way that only industrial England could be. I wanted to sing a verse or two from Jerusalem and Blake. I knew what he meant. This was England's green and pleasant land.

We pulled up outside a row of small bungalows, each with a small front garden and sloping drive and views over the hills of the peak-land in the distance. There was a bus-stop close by, little traffic, and an elderly couple walking along the pavement.

'Number 14. Pull up there,' Scunt said. 'I'd buy Granny a new house if I had lots and lots of money,' she blurted out in response to my previously unanswered question. 'Come on, let's go see if she's in.'

We got out of the car and Scunt looked at me, up and down. 'You'll do. None of that Scunt stuff here now! Strictly Tracy!' she said as we marched up to the door and rang the bell.

I can never tell if old people start out small or shrink over time. At hardly an inch over five foot, and with permed white hair, the old lady that opened the door was nervous. Clearly not many people knocked at her door unannounced. She looked at Scunt and then looked at me and then at Scunt again, before a huge regal smile covered her face. Her eyes lit up and she grew at least an inch.

'Tracy?'

'Yes Granny! It's me.'

The minutes that followed were a mixture of happiness and disbelief.

'I can't believe it's you! I haven't seen you for so long!' Followed by, 'I'm so happy – this is wonderful!' which was repeated by both of them for a good ten minutes. I stood there and watched.

'And who is this?' Granny finally asked.

'Oh. Granny, this is Tommy. He's my fiancé. Isn't he wonderful?' and she pulled me into their hug before both of them stepped back to inspect me. Again I was being assessed by Scunt's women folk. This was becoming too frequent. I started to talk because I needed to correct Scunt on the fiancé tag. What was all that about? But Scunt knew what I was about to say.

'Later, Tommy. You can tell Q all about yourself when

we've had some tea.'

'Q?'

'Yes. Sometimes I call Granny 'Q'. It's short for QM which stands for Queen Mother. Doesn't she look just like the Queen Mother?' I saw the resemblance.

'Now come in you two,' she ordered, flashing that regal smile again. 'What are your plans? I take it you'll stay for tea.'

'Granny, we hoped we might stay the night if that's okay? We'll buy and cook everything for us. Please say we can stay.'

I looked at Q and tried to communicate with her telepathically: *Please say you have house guests arriving or are going out to the bingo tonight.* But she didn't mention either.

'Mr Taylor was going to drop in for tea. But that's okay. I'm sure he'd like to meet you both. No, I'll cancel him. Oh, this is so wonderful. You've made my day – even my week! My year! Of course you can stay. I'll just have to make up the spare room.'

"Tommy, be a darling and go get the luggage while I help Granny with tea,' and Scunt, or Tracy as she strictly was here, turned and left me standing. It had taken Jenny many more than three days to put me in my place, but here I was again – a luggage boy. Was I worried? Not really, as the joy I saw on Q's face at seeing Scunt more than made up for it. At least I didn't have piles of plastic bags to cope with and I put the new luggage in the front bedroom just off the hall to the left. On the right was the lounge, and at the back of the house was Q's bedroom, and a large open plan kitchen and bathroom.

There we sat in the kitchen, around a circular wooden

table. While I had been moving the luggage, they had found some biscuits and small cakes and laid them out on Q's best crockery. The kettle was boiling and Scunt and Q were head to head in chatter. I was left as an observer as they went through the whereabouts and health of the family members. Where were they? How were they? What were they doing? I tried to remember them all as they chatted. What was I doing, trying to remember? I was normally able to remember everything, but that seemed to be in a completely different life. I already knew a little of Scunt's sister. Her father, I gathered, had died some years ago; her mother still lived in Scunthorpe but was now not too well. There were only a few aunts and uncles and cousins. It was not a large family.

As they chatted on, I thought about my own dysfunctional family. To my parents I was a success; a good man with a good job, a large house and married. Marriage, I remember, was the sign of ultimate success. It was the sign of settling down and being normal. Initially both my parents had liked Jenny and I suppose they still do. She was homely and, in my mother's words, 'appropriate' for a man of my standing. My in-laws were another matter; far too conservative and right-wing for my liking, so much so that I'm sure they could be used by the *Daily Telegraph* as an interview panel to faithfully represent all their readers' views. It would save the *Telegraph* a load of money; they'd never have to undertake another survey of their readers' opinions. All they would have to do was ask my in-laws and that would say it all.

Question One: What do you think of immigration?
There are too many foreigners here already.
Question Two: What do you think about the

unemployed and disenfranchised youth?

It's their own fault; they should work harder.

Question Three: What do you think about footballers' salaries?

They earn too much.

Question Four: What do you think about homosexuals?

They should be shot.

The list was endless and entirely predictable. However, I suppose I should actually say a real thank you to them because they firmly cemented my own political views. I had always been left wing in a bolshie, studenty sort of way. It seemed to me that the left were more able to put up with my irreverence. The right seemed to want me to conform so much more than I was able but I had never pinned my colours to any party mast. Because of my in-laws, I finally had a reason to vote Labour. If they wanted to vote Conservative then I had to be in the opposition's camp. I would spend hours amusing myself in their company, extolling the most radical of left-wing views without any compunction. I didn't believe half of my arguments at all, but I gained great comfort winding them up.

'Of course I believe in a total distribution of wealth and more power to the trade unions,' I would say and watch them almost go apoplectic with rage. I would sit passively and quote from Lenin and all the other communist luminaries. Of course, I paid my price on the car journey back when Jenny ranted and raved and shouted that I should pay her parents more respect.

'But surely being totally honest with them is the greatest respect I could pay them? At work I have to lie all day, but with them I can be honest. Do you want me to lie to them just so they'll like me?'

This line of thinking drove her just as wild. 'It's a lie. You don't believe any of this bloody stuff. You're just making it up to annoy them.'

'No, I'm not. It's just that when I'm with them, I see so clearly what I really feel and think. It's liberating!'

'You're a bastard, Tommy. I can never take you back there again. They never want to see you again. From now on, I'll have to go by myself.'

Now that was a real victory because there was nothing I wanted to do less than spend another day in their company, let alone another night in their house. I suppose we're all generally happier with our own families and Q was reminding me of my Granddad – who had a similar bungalow in Essex with the same quiet, careful approach to life. The main difference between them was that he was dead. It dawned on me that there was no one as close to me as Scunt was to Q. I looked across at Q and Scunt; they were still nattering away.

'More tea, Tommy?' Q asked. 'And tell me all about you and Tracy. She hasn't said anything about you. When are you going to be married?'

I looked at Scunt. I drank some tea. Scunt looked at Q and Q looked at me. Someone had to say something. I ventured a few words. 'We haven't decided yet. We so enjoy what we have now and it would be a shame to spoil it with marriage but we say we're engaged so that people know we're serious about each other.' There. That should put that to bed and off the agenda.

'Poppycock,' Q said almost too quietly to be heard as she reached for a digestive biscuit. 'Absolute poppycock.'

'Why's that, Granny?' asked Scunt.

'I'll tell you young people why you need to get married. You all think that life is so short and quick you don't need to make a commitment. Instant gratification, that's what you all want. How can standing in front of all your friends and family making your vows do anything but make your love stronger. And there's one more thing.'

'What's that, Granny?'

'I'm eighty-five now and I want to go to one more wedding before I die. So get a move on! I want you two married before the end of the year. Can you do that for me?'

Scunt reached across the table and tenderly put one hand on mine and the other on Q's joining us together as if in a communion. She looked at me and then nodded at Q.

'Of course we will, Granny. For you, we will get married before the end of the year. Won't we, Tommy?' and I felt her hand press down on mine – daring me to object. I nodded while inwardly hating that I was telling a fib and somehow, even though I hardly knew Q, I really didn't want to lie to her. But it wasn't my fault. Scunt had set it all up. She had told the first lie.

'So, Tracy, how did you and Tommy meet? Was he a customer?'

'Yes, that's right. That's how I met him, just after his wife died.'

'Did you do everything? Where did you start?' Q asked Scunt.

'In the bedroom,' she replied.

'Really? I thought you said you normally started in the kitchen or the lounge.'

'You're really naughty aren't you, Tommy!' said Scunt, winking at me.

Suddenly, their honesty and openness didn't seem so

right.

'Tommy, was she good?' Q had turned her attentions on me. 'Have you recommended her to your friends? I do hope so. She always tells me how talented she is.'

I looked across at Scunt. What could I say? Here was an eighty-five-year-old woman asking me about sex with my new fiancé. Where did she find the courage to tell her old Granny what she does? This was totally beyond my understanding. Nothing like this could ever happen in my family, but Scunt was holding my hand and laughing. She was enjoying my discomfort.

'Granny, Tommy thinks I'm the best interior designer in the world and of course I work for all his friends. I've even heard him say the service I provide is the best he's ever had. Isn't that right, Tommy? You really do think I'm the best, don't you? Tell me. I like it when you tell me.'

I looked at her and I saw the joy on her face and the laughter in her eyes. Her spirit was infectious.

'Let me tell you, Q. Tracy is the best at her job I've ever known and, believe me, I've tried many. Despite her young years she is almost as good as any veteran. She's talented in ways even you couldn't imagine. And you know what, Q – we will get married before the year is out. Won't we, Tracy?'

Scunt held my hand just a little closer. Not harder – just closer.

'Hey you two, why don't you keep talking like all women do and I'll drive to the supermarket and buy some food. In fact, I'll cook tonight. Much better to eat in, don't you think?' I needed to find some fresh air to justify the colour in my cheeks.

Scunt looked at me and smiled. 'I think that's a great

idea. What do you think Granny? It will be good because Tommy is a really talented chef. Aren't you, darling?' I nodded enthusiastically in agreement.

'There are some things I need to talk to Tracy about,' Q said. 'I'm sure there's something she isn't telling me. And I also want to know all about you.' She went on to say how wonderful it was to be so well looked after.

At that I smiled. 'It's a long time since I cooked for such a distinguished audience. Love you both.' I said as I left.

I had told Scunt that I could cook – just a little but she always had to go the next step and add the hyperbole. So now it dawned on me that I was going to have to cook and make it look like I had been doing it all my life. First stop had to be a bookshop to find a good cookery book and recipe. Have you seen how many cook books there are? From Afghanistan to Zimbabwe, every one of the 192 members of the United Nations has its own cuisine and cookbook and for each one, there's a low-fat, gourmand, fish or vegetarian, fast-food, slow-food, child and adult version. And then every celebrity chef adds his or her own opus to the pile too, and so on. I stood there and tried to decide what was easiest.

I used to be able to cook, but Jenny had taken over that task. She wasn't a great chef and she needed books; she would weigh each item in precise detail while staring at the chosen book. Time to invoke my extraordinary memory again. Which book did Jenny use when she was pressed for time and wanted to cheat? I remembered! Nigella Lawson's *Nigella Express*. So I searched her out among the shelves. As I was browsing, something was bothering me and I couldn't figure it out. Was it something Q had said?

Probably not, because she was quite harmless and actually very pleasant. There were things she wanted to speak personally about with Scunt, though. Had she seen something in Scunt's eyes? Women have this uncanny knack with their emotions and understand so many things that are unsaid. What was it that had bothered Q? Was it the reason we were here, or was it about my unsuitability as a fiancé? If that was the cause, then it could be easily resolved. I didn't have time to work it out right then, though, because I needed to focus on finding the perfect recipe. I came across one for smoked trout paté. That seemed appropriate as a starter. I memorised it. What next? Keep it simple and make it traditional? Gammon steaks with parsley for the main, and instant chocolate mousse for afters? I could handle all that and make it look good as well.

As I shopped, another thought started to worry me. It was about telling lies. I was lying and Scunt was lying. Not big lies. Just little lies to amuse each other and amuse Q. We had told Q we were to be married. We said Scunt was an interior designer. All little lies, but definitely not the truth. Of course, this wasn't the first lie I had told and I knew next week back at work in London I would again be economical with the truth. We all lived in that half-way house, where it's never quite a truth or an untruth. I've been asked by colleagues to be their alibi while they went on a one-night tryst. My latest lie had me working in somewhere in Eastern Europe. No wonder we don't trust any politician to tell the whole truth, or even part of the truth; we assume that everyone only tells us what we need to know for their own self-interest. Honesty is a virtue of the past and lives with people like Q and others of her age.

I knew the philosopher Kant had said that lying was

morally wrong and could never be justified. He said that it degrades our moral worth and removes integrity. Of course in the world of philosophers there's always a let-out, so instead I could go with utilitarian ethics that allowed lying to balance the overall benefit or minimise harm to society. But no ethical framework allowed the selfish, self-centred lie that was the core of the financial world I lived in. That started to worry me as I hunted the near-deserted supermarket for gammon steaks, marsh-mallows and dark chocolate. I pushed my trolley to the empty checkouts. I needed to talk about this with Scunt. I was sure she would have an opinion.

As the goods were conveyed and scanned, I asked the middle-aged checkout lady (I could hardly call her a girl): 'Do you ever lie?'

'What?'

'Do you ever lie? I'm doing a survey about lying. I just wondered if you ever lie.'

'What's tha' pet. You mean like not tell the truth?'

I was now confronted by more regional accents. 'Yes. I mean like not tell the truth.'

She turned to a fellow checker-outer. 'Betty. This one's asking if I ever tell lies. Do I?'

'Only when you ask her how old she is,' Betty said to general laughter.

'Now, pet, I wonder why you ask that. Think I'm overcharging you for this gammon?'

'No, of course not. I was just wondering if everyone lies all the time or if there are still a few honest people.'

'That will be thirteen pounds sixty-four pence and I'll tell thee this. The world was a lot better when we could trust each other and a straight word meant something. Folk up north used to tell it right. You can't trust anyone these days.

I blame that Thatcher woman. She changed it all. Isn't that right, Betty?'

And then she and Betty continued their own conversation as I handed over the cash and got my change. At least I had given them something to talk about for the day.

As I cooked that evening, Scunt and Q talked and set the table. I opened a bottle of wine I'd bought and soon we sat for dinner. My cooking was appreciated by one and all but I still felt niggled about telling the truth. For once I needed to get to the bottom of Scunt's story. What actually happened?

'Do you know the Yorkshire man's advice to his son?' Q asked me.

'No,' I had never heard this. Q focused on me:

'Ear all, see all, say nowt. Eyt all, sup all, pay nowt. And if ivver tha does owt fer nowt, do it fer thissen.'

'Tracy can you translate? I didn't understand a word of that.'

''Hear all, see all, say nothing. Eat all, drink all, pay nothing. And if ever you do anything for nothing – do it for yourself.'

Now there was a creed I could start to understand, being so different from my life. Or was it? Wasn't it just another creed for greed and selfishness?

'Is that true? I mean true today?' I asked.

'Parts of it are,' Q answered. 'We could all be so much better but that woman Thatcher changed all that.'

The blame again thrown at poor Margaret's door. Could one person really have had such a profound impact? I remembered we weren't so far from the South Yorkshire coal fields and the heart of the coal strikes. Here, there was much animosity against Thatcher and the Conservative government. Maybe it was just a local phenomenon, but were we really so much more honest in those days and did we share strong feelings with everyone in our communities? Somewhere during the Thatcher era we all seemed to become more selfish and focused on winning individual races and not team races. But not even that was quite true; the sixties and seventies saw even more dramatic events with the core services going on strike for their own self-interest. Something had changed in the last thirty years to make self-interest acceptable when camouflaged by the spirit of enterprise. It was a generation in which bankers, like me, received bonus after bonus, even when we failed. For once I was deeply uncertain about my purpose. But I was saved from deeper reflection as the two women moved back to the safer topic of the family.

'Granny and I made up the spare bed while you were at the shops. Let's wash up and then get some sleep. I'm tired and you must be too. It's been a long day, and you've done so much driving.'

'And a lot of cooking too,' I added, 'but that's easy with my background.' I tried to hide the sarcasm in my voice.

'Yes, darling. And all that cooking. It was wonderful. Thank you.'

And that's what we did. Q said goodnight and another long and interesting day with Scunt spanning a brothel in Leeds to a cosy family dinner had ended and all the time I found myself questioning my life and my views. They were being pushed to the front from the recesses of the past. Scunt didn't know how educational this trip was for me.

Chapter XII

In the morning I woke with Scunt lying next to me. As always, she was naked and I watched as her chest slowly rose and fell with each breath. Her eyes were still closed and I remembered the times long ago that I had just lain in bed, knowing that Jenny was watching me like this. Maybe Scunt knew I was watching her. We develop that sense that just knows when we're being watched but do we also have that sense of knowing when we're loved?

'Get me a cup of tea please, Tommy, and give me a moment to wake up.' I hadn't meant to wake her. It was quiet and, in a way, just like being at home.

But mostly it was different. It had to be different here because to make tea also meant getting dressed. Here there was none of the comfort of pulling on an old, well-worn dressing gown. At home, of course, I wouldn't even have got up. At the weekends, Jenny was always first to wake, to get the day going, and she was the one who had bought the dressing gowns. Why don't women understand that men don't have the same taste in dressing gowns? We don't want what they want. We want to wear short white towelling gowns like the men in porn movies or even Japanese kimonos; not the heavy purple towelling gowns we all actually own. Today, however, I had no gown, and I had to get at least partially dressed. And it was a wise decision because Q was already sitting at the table having breakfast.

'Can I make some tea?' I asked, hoping she would think politeness was a real virtue of mine.

'Don't worry,' Q said, 'it's already in the pot.'

'Thanks. Been awake for long?'

'Of course,' Q said, 'unlike you two I can't hang about. I've already been out and down to the shops for the milk. I wish the milkman still came. It can get very cold in the mornings.'

And as Q talked me through her morning, I was making a tea for Scunt, and not listening very attentively.

'And then Mary was telling me about these big foreign fellows asking around yesterday. Very odd she said it was.'

Suddenly Q had my attention. 'What foreign men? Asking about what?'

'Oh, I didn't listen, Tommy. Just a couple of strangers. Now do you want toast as well?'

Should I tell Scunt about them? If it was the thugs after us then we had to move, but I was quite at home here. Life was different and I was enjoying different.

'Did you tell Tracy?' I asked, as Tracy appeared in the doorway.

'Tell me what? You were taking so long I thought I would come and get my own tea.' She was wearing one of my new shirts bought only two days ago. Was it really only two days? And already she was wearing it? She had only buttoned the last five buttons, leaving it loose at the top so I could see the line of her breasts. It barely covered her bottom and I knew she had no panties on. My heart skipped but I had to tell her. I stayed as calm as I could.

'Q was just saying that there were some big foreign fellows asking around yesterday. I just wondered if you knew?' I tried to remain nonchalant as I handed over her tea.

What little colour there ever was in her normally pale face, drained away. She composed herself. 'No. I hadn't heard. Thanks for the tea – finally,' and she turned up her nose in mock disdain.

'So what are you two going to do today? Go for a walk in the Peaks?' Q asked.

'No, I don't think so Granny. We have to be on the move again. We've got to get back for work. Just some breakfast and we will be on our way. I'm so sorry.'

But not as sorry as me, I thought. On the run again. We had to get this sorted out quickly. We couldn't go on like this and as if on cue, my phone rang. I looked at the caller ID. It was the office. I had totally forgotten about them.

'Just let me take this. I'll be right back,' and I scurried off to the bedroom for a bit of quiet. What had I said to Jane? Had I said anything to her at all about my absence? I answered the phone. It was time to lie.

'Jane. Hi. Can you hear me?' I spoke softly to make it difficult for her. 'Yes, I'm fine. Sorry, but I wanted to let you know but the Chairman called and sent me on an errand. I really can't say any more. All very hush, hush. Just tell the team I'm ill and won't be in again this week. Same answer if anyone else asks, please. I shouldn't really be saying anything to you. But I trust you. I'm sorry but I have to go. Speak later,' and I hung up.

Of course I didn't trust her, but it would do my standing no harm as she told the rest of the team I was away on the Chairman's business and I could always sort it all out later if there was a problem. I didn't like what I was doing. Why not just say I was away on an unscheduled holiday or sorting out some urgent personal business? That would have been so much easier, but it was not good form. I remember one of my visits to Dubai, sitting and waiting to see one of the important local businessmen for a scheduled meeting. He didn't turn up at all and his secretary just said he had urgent family business. Asking around those ex-pats in the know they all said it was quite common. Family always comes first in the Arab world but not in our so-called sophisticated western business world: work comes first and family suffers.

Scunt was finishing off a bowl of cereal and Q was making toast when I returned.

'Are you packed, Tommy? We should go soon.'

'Yep.' I had hardly unpacked. You don't need much to sleep for one night in the nude.

With the cases back in the car we said our goodbyes to Q, remaking our promise to be married before the year was out and telling her she would be our guest of honour.

'Just make sure you do – and before I die.'

'Of course,' Scunt shouted out of an open window as we headed down the road again and I shrugged.

I soon picked up a sign for Stoke where I guessed we could pick up a motorway. We sat in silence for twenty minutes. I had to ask.

'Do you think it was them?'

'I don't know, but we couldn't take a chance, could we Tommy?' she asked, looking for reassurance.

'No, I suppose not. But I'm getting fed up with this. We need to do something positive.'

'Because you're fed up with me?'

I thought for a moment. 'No, not fed up with you but I am fed up with running. You need to tell me everything and we need to make a plan so that you're safe and I can get back to work and my life. We can't keep going on like this.'

She looked at me. "What would Jason do now?'

A good question. 'Jason would turn round, face them, shoot them and then we would both go and live in Goa or Malaysia. But I'm not Jason. We're not Bonnie and Clyde. We're Tommy and Scunt and we do things like trust and believe in justice.'

Even as I said the words they sounded hollow. We needed to be a little more like Jason and get on the offensive in some way. Running was not the answer, but first I needed data. The call from Jane had reminded me of how I operated. I needed data.

'Okay,' I said, 'maybe we don't need to turn ourselves in, but I do need to know all the truth. Will you tell me now?'

Scunt was silent as we drove. Finally she said, 'Right this is what we'll do. We will go somewhere quiet, somewhere not from my past, and we will stay there for two days and I will tell you everything. And then we'll decide what to do. Will that make you happy?'

'That'll be fine. Just tell me where you haven't been before.'

'I've never been to New Zealand. Does that help?'

'No, it doesn't. That just makes me irritable. Be serious for a moment please.'

'Okay, I've never been to university and I've never been to a pop festival. I've never been to…'

I was starting to wonder if we would ever get to an answer.

'Tommy, I really haven't been to lots of places. Help me.'

We were heading south. Where would that take us? Wolverhampton and Birmingham were on the way. I liked the idea of going south. At least that would take me nearer to home. But I knew I didn't like the Midlands. I could never understand what they said there. Actually, that's not true. I could understand them, but the accent made me irritable; their accent is impenetrable. When I was at university I dated a girl from the Midlands. Her accent was so annoying I decided that, despite her best efforts, I couldn't sleep with her. Well, I was okay with sleeping with her, but not with having to listen to her first thing in the morning.

Worcester and Cheltenham were supposed to be delightful, but this was not a touring holiday. Oxford. Now there was a possibility. A university town as well and then I had it.

'I know where we can go,' I said. 'Let's go to Woodstock! Maybe we can rent a small cottage for a couple of days and try and get this all sorted.'

'Whatever you say, Jason,' and she looked at me and smiled and all was on an even keel again. 'But no questions until we get there. We'll just enjoy the ride and you'll make me laugh. Promise?'

'Promise,' I said as Scunt played with the satnav and I pointed our red Ford Focus south on the motorway.

'Why Woodstock, Tommy? Have you been there before?'

'Nope. I've never been there, but you said you've never been to a pop festival. Under the circumstances it's the best I can do to change that.' She smiled at my answer.

'Tell me about some of the places you've been, Tommy. I bet they're really exciting.'

'They're not. They're just other places. Well, buildings are just buildings. It's the people who make a place.'

'Of course. Say which continents you've been to and I'll decide which one we talk about.'

'Well, I've been all over Europe of course, and I've been to the USA but not Canada. Africa and Middle East, too, and quick visits to India and the Far East, but not Australia. Does that help?

'Tell me about the Middle East. Did you fuck women in all the places you went?'

'No, I didn't. As for the Middle East, Dubai is an interesting place if that's the line you want to go down.' We were on a mutually interesting subject and she was perked up at the thought.

'I've seen those women in their long black robes and face masks. Do they wear anything underneath them? That must be really horny walking along the street and shopping and all the time being naked under a simple robe. I would like to do that.'

'What's the difference between being naked under the robe – and by the way it's called an *abaya* – and being naked under a dress?' I knew the answer – there's a big difference. It's like with striptease; the more that's covered, the bigger the thrill. 'Anyway, Scunt, sorry to disappoint you. They wear some of the finest designer clothes under their *abayas*.'

'Have you seen? I mean have you been with an Arab woman?' She turned towards me, waiting for my answer.

'Actually, and contrary to your every opinion of me, I don't go around the world for the sole purpose of screwing every woman I can. I usually go to these places to work.'

She gave me a look of total disbelief and she was probably right. 'I don't believe you, Tommy. I know what you businessmen do in the evenings. Now tell me what you know about Arab women.'

I tried to think of stories I could tell. Whatever our relationship was, I wanted to preserve some decorum and modesty. I thought about when I was her age and had been dating girls. We all played down our own pasts and denied any previous encounters. Maybe that was the second biggest lie after: *Of course I'll still love you in the morning.*

'Well,' I started, 'one night we were taken to an Iranian night club and there was a stage and a live band. We were guests of honour and we had the front table, and it was piled high with fruit and dates and nuts and of course lots of whisky.'

'I thought you couldn't drink there?'

'In hotels you can – and this was part of a hotel. Up on stage, all the girls from the audience were dancing to the band and it was all very provocative. They were wearing really sexy, short dresses. In fact, most wore short skirts and they would dance together and then two or three of them would dance standing behind each other, looking as though they were fucking each other doggie style.'

'And did you get turned on? I bet you did.'

'Well, yes, but that's not the point. When the club closed and these girls got ready to go home, do you know what they did?'

'Tell me. I bet they came to your table and asked to share a taxi.'

'No they didn't! They put on their *abayas* and covered up. It was unreal.'

'You're teasing me aren't you? It must be easy to pick up women in Dubai.'

'Hmm, it must be, because Dubai has the highest ratio of hookers to population anywhere in the world. In every hotel bar, there are hookers. There are girls in their twos and threes just sitting and waiting for you to buy them a drink. And there are clubs, of course, where the two and three become twenty and thirty and more.'

'Well I'm not going to go and work there – too much competition.' She laughed. 'Where do they all come from? Are they all Arab women?'

'Hardly any are Arab. I'm not sure that I saw one.'

'So you did go to the clubs. You're so naughty, Tommy. Where did they come from then?'

'From what I could make out, and this is just from observation, either the Far East or the old Russian Empire.'

'Were they pretty?'

'Like everywhere, Scunt. Some were pretty and some were ugly.'

'And how did you pick them up? Did you have to buy them a drink or something?'

'You know the answer. You're teasing me. Just like everywhere else. We both knew why they were there, so the only questions were how much and how long. This is getting very personal, Scunt. I'm getting embarrassed. Can we talk about the culture or something else?'

'No.' She was emphatic. 'You said the place is about the people, and I want to know about the people. So tell me, which were the best? The Chinese or the Russians. Who gave you the best time?'

I wanted to be polite and move the conversation on. I was getting very red in the face. 'The English, of course.'

'There were English girls working there?'

'No, not that I saw. I just meant you would have been better than all of them.'

'Thank you for the compliment, but I know that. Now don't change the subject. Chinese or Russian? Did you have a Chinese take-away or a hot Russian *borsch*?'

There was going to be no escape and even though I really hadn't done any market research I had to give an answer. Scunt was not going to believe me if I said I didn't know.

'The Chinese were all too submissive for me, but they

were far naughtier. I liked the 'real women' in the Russians. They're so passionate. Always seemed like so much more of a conquest. I liked their sullenness but I'm really not an expert. You've got to believe me.'

'I don't believe you, Tommy. You're just like every other man. As soon as work finishes you're off to hunt for pussy. While the cat's away, you know? But just so you can keep some dignity, tell me what you know about Arab women. What have you heard?'

For some reason I felt on safer ground. 'I heard that they don't shave – their arms or elsewhere – and like all women they get just as horny, but you can't do anything because if the family find out they'll cut your cock off.'

Scunt just laughed and it was infectious and I joined in.

'Now check where we are on the satnav. It seems to have become your expertise.'

We were well on our way. Our conversation had taken us round the boredom that is the M6 in the Midlands. Birmingham had passed to our right, exactly where it should always be, and now on the M40 we were thinking about reaching Woodstock.

'I would like to have been a *real* hippy,' I said and Scunt smiled.

'Why a hippy? What was so special?'

'It was before my time really, but they had an ethos about their lives and their world and they wanted everyone to share it with them. They seemed to have a freedom to do as they wanted, but not in a selfish way. They stood for peace and weren't over-concerned with money. Idealistic, maybe, but we – businessmen, moderates, governments – we all crushed it, and them. The system took over. Self-interest took over.'

'I know, and yes, you would have been a good hippy. Did you do lots of drugs?'

'I think the right phrase should be *many* drugs and no I didn't. Well, not since uni.'

'What did you do there?'

'Smoked a couple of joints.' And to be honest I was rather proud of doing even that.

'A couple? Wow! You were almost a junkie, Tommy,' and she lowered her voice and I knew a serious question was around the corner. 'Tommy, was it hard to come down? I mean hard to quit? What was cold turkey like?' and she burst into laughter.

'That's unfair. I tried them and it wasn't for me, that's all. You know this whole drug thing is very serious and might be the most important thing society has to face right now.'

She looked at me, displaying her serious face – or was it her sarcastic face? I didn't know her well enough yet. 'I absolutely agree,' she said, much to my surprise. 'I mean all these middle-aged, middle-class people who come home from work and drink a bottle of wine each night. I mean it's terrible. Let me tell you, Tommy, at every university around the country it's all the students talk about. They're asking: What are we going to do about the mums and dads and their booze? They light their joints and they almost weep at the moral decay of their elders. It's oh-so sad.'

'Okay, Scunt. You've made your point but you know what I mean; drugs are a real issue. Something has to be done and we need to do something. I mean look at all the crime tied up with drugs. It's got to be stopped. We need to be hard on drugs. You must agree with that?'

'No, I don't. As ever, Tommy, you're talking absolute

bollocks. And I thought you were clever.'

'Okay, smart arse. What's your great plan?' This would show her up, I was sure.

'It's quite simple. You just legalise them all and do what Portugal and Switzerland have done – make it a health problem.'

This wasn't the answer I'd expected. 'Go on then. Tell me how it works.'

'I said it's simple. If you say we have a problem then we have two parts to it. First there are people who take drugs now, and second there are mainly young people who will start to take drugs sometime in the future. We agree the first group needs help, and the second needs it to be more difficult to start. Do you agree with that?'

Of course I had to agree.

'Both problems need solving. The people taking drugs now need money to feed their habits. We all know it's a long and difficult path to get off drugs. We need to help them and treat them as a public health problem that will take decades to resolve. They cause most of the crime by stealing to get money to get drugs. So let anyone who is on drugs now get them free from the national health, on prescription. Then, when they're registered, someone can work on getting them off them. Some will never be able to, so the State will carry on supplying their drugs free of charge.'

I could see where she was going.

'We should legalise weed just like in Holland and Colorado – did you know about Colorado? Tax it like cigarettes, so we can all get a mild fix and everyone's happy. And because those drugs become legal and sort of accepted by the establishment, it won't seem like such a rebellious thing to do, so the *second* group, the ones not yet on drugs, won't be so attracted to them. That'll take away all the profits for the dealers. When you do that, the market for the dealers goes; they'll move on to some other crime that's more profitable, but there aren't many of those, so maybe they'll work – a proper job? Or leave the country.'

As an economist, I could see her argument.

'Generally – if there's no profit, there are no dealers. And with the dealers gone, there won't be another generation of druggies. They won't be able to buy drugs anywhere. Fewer serious druggies, an open no-blame society, and it's win–win. I don't see the problem. It's just all those *Daily Telegraph* readers who are jealous because they missed out on all the fun. You go on about an inclusive society. Well, be inclusive for a moment, and remember – we're not all here to support you oldies.'

'And how do we pay for all this?' I asked, but I knew the answer.

'By the massive reduction in crime and the costs of policing – now the police will be able to do their real job. It'll pay for itself.' Scunt sat back with a satisfied smile.

I don't know what hurt the most. Recognising the simplicity of her free-market, liberal and out-of-the-box approach – or her dig at my age.

'Am I really an oldie, Scunt?'

'No, you're very sweet and really a kid, but sometimes you do get stuck in the box. You think something's bad because someone told you so. You should think everything out for yourself. Stop reading the headlines and leaders in those terrible newspapers. Drugs aren't so bad – it's the industry around the drugs that's bad. Tackle the real problem. You thought prostitutes were bad, but they're not, are they? Prostitutes and prostitution are fine, but there's the industry of pimps and trafficking to deal with. Attack the right problem and it's all so much easier.' She paused for a moment.

'In a really free society we all have the right to live our lives by whatever code we want. If I want to smoke grass and not cigarettes, that's my choice. If I want to pay for sex with someone who wants to sell it – my choice. I think there are only a few basic rules of a functioning society.'

'Which are?' I asked.

'I think there are only two, as I see it. Never do anything that harms another person or that undermines the integrity of the State. Within that, you should be able to do whatever you like but *harm* is the key word.'

It was just a few words, but there was a lot to take in. In my world, the law had developed piecemeal and there was no discernible simple ethos that underpinned it. And here a young woman had set out a basic tenet through which we could judge all actions. It was a new code, a new way of looking at things and initially I didn't fully understand. The whole moral and ethical code reduced to a simple two phrase statement. That couldn't be right.

'So,' I started to frame a reply, 'what happens if what I do *offends* you?'

'Such as? Test the rules.'

'Okay. I walk naked down the street,' I said.

'Offends but does no harm. It's okay.'

'Rob a bank?'

'Undermines the integrity of the State and usually harms an individual or two. Wrong.'

'Don't pay my taxes?'

'Undermines the State. See it's simple, Tommy. Prostitution may offend, but it doesn't harm anyone.

Trafficking harms.'

'Where did you learn all this stuff? Or is that a question for later?'

'Later. And I didn't learn it Tommy. I do what you should do sometimes. I think.'

I wanted to say that she had a lot of time for that, lying on her back all day, but decided it wouldn't be appreciated.

Chapter XIII

Woodstock is little more than a village located to the north of Oxford in some of the most beautiful country God ever created. I remembered a story I once heard. When God was designing the world he was working on France, and when he finished he looked at his work and marvelled at the sullen, warm Mediterranean coast, the rising peaks of the Alps, the long and beautiful Atlantic coast and the forests and hills of the Midi. He decided it really was his best work to date, but it was so good it couldn't be allowed to flourish totally and be an elite and so, to balance affairs, he designed French people.

This small part of England had much of the richness of France, but it also had delightful people who were kind and helpful. So from our initial enquiry at the high-street estate agent, we were sent along to a small general-purpose shop, and from there to a Mrs Blackaby at the hairdressers, who had a small cottage she could rent to us for a couple of days. It was just down and off the high street. I paid in advance and took the keys. We unpacked our new cases, returned to the general store to buy some bits and pieces and then went back to Mrs Blackaby to say it was wonderful.

The cottage was small and not unlike Q's house for size except that it was on two floors. The decoration was slightly faded and the furniture was all pre-IKEA. There were carpets on the floor and no concession to the modern trend of bare floorboards. In places, the carpet was faded and worn, with floorboards looking that looked like they were making a bid for sunlight and freedom. First free chairs, and now free floorboards. The kitchen was functional but small, and the gas cooker, although clean, was well used. We decided to go on a walk after our long drive and set out towards Blenheim Palace. On Park Street, we sat on a wooden bench which was once used, it seemed, as a set of stocks.

'I wonder what I would do to you if you were shackled up in these?' Scunt teased as she gripped my wrist firmly with both hands.

'You had your chance in Leeds,' I reminded her. We laughed as we noticed the disabled parking bay right in front and had the same thought.

'You would be disabled after a day in those. Wasn't Princess Di something to do with Blenheim?' Scunt asked, again demonstrating her ability to change subject on a whim.

'No idea. We could always find out, though.' I did know, but for once I didn't need to be the smarty pants who knew everything. 'I know Churchill was born here, that's all, and he was a Spencer and her father was Earl Spencer. We could go along and ask. Are you really interested?'

'No, not really. I much prefer real things and not all that fancy historical lords and earls stuff.'

I understood what she meant. We walked down the High Street and passed a restaurant, a cake shop, and one or two estate agents and pharmacies, all housed in Cotswold stone buildings far too big and grand for such humble purposes. But as we walked, and whatever we talked about, my thoughts were on the evening ahead, when I was set to hear Scunt's story. I was fearful that it would be mundane and ordinary; maybe even a little sad. We were on an adventure and I needed it to be something slightly outlandish and exceptional. It turns out I was not to be disappointed.

Again I cooked the supper; a simple macaroni cheese. I

love covering it in tomato sauce as it reminds me of childhood meals. When we were done, we sat on the sofa, Scunt's head on my shoulder, watching a poor American film on the TV. She reached for the remote and muted the sound.

'Want to talk?'

'Yes please.'

'Where do you want me to start?'

'Tell me whatever I need to know to understand why I'm here and not at home and work.'

'Okay. What have I told you so far?'

'Absolutely nothing. Just that you came to London when you were seventeen and stayed with your sister, Sharon.'

'No. With Sharon's friends.'

'Okay, Sharon's friends, in a squat, and you did some typing jobs. That's all, other than the bits about your family that Q was talking about. I know nothing more.'

'Right, well. That was my start in London. Then I found a boyfriend and we lived together for a couple of years and then—'

I interrupted. 'Aren't you going to tell me about the boyfriend?'

'No. It was an ordinary young affair. Nothing important. We broke up. I had an ordinary job and got a flat by myself in Stoke Newington. That was where I met Sarah.'

'Do you have a boyfriend now?' This had been concerning me for some time. Was she cheating on someone and was this another lie?

'No,' she said. 'He was my last significant other.'

I was pleased, but it was time to get back to the main subject. 'How old were you then, when you met Sarah?'

'I must have been about twenty-two,' she said, counting out events and anniversaries on her fingers. 'We'd seen each other in the supermarket and said hello, then we met accidently in a pub one night and started talking. We had a few drinks and I said I didn't have a boyfriend right then, and the only thing I missed was sex. I certainly didn't miss having him and his washing around the place.'

'How old was Sarah?'

'Older than me. Twenty-five or so. Anyway, she said she agreed and we laughed about how useless men are and she said she'd found an answer to that problem. She had advertised on all sorts of dating sites, first just to get guys round for the night. She said there was no shortage of takers for NSA sex.'

'NSA?' I was feeling ignorant. I knew most of the fetishes and kinks but I'd never heard of NSA.

'No strings attached, Tommy. Where have you been? Anyway, Sarah said that after a couple of months being inundated with offers from men of all shapes and sizes, she wanted to prioritise them, so she started charging them. Just small amounts to start with. She asked them to give her the money they would normally spend on dinners and booze, which she didn't want, so they could get down to what interested them both. From there, it had become her job *and* her hobby. She moved off dating sites and worked for an agency that took some fancy photos of her in the nude and she advertised on the web. The agency took the bookings and thirty percent. It was a good arrangement. She had lots of regular customers and went to all sorts of nice hotels and places. She asked me if I wanted to do the same. It was easy, really – I hated my job. In fact I hated working, and like she said, this way I could mix my hobby with my work.'

'So it was as simple as that. One day you had an ordinary job and the next day you were a prostitute,' I said.

'Well, yes, I suppose it was. We called ourselves models or escorts, but I knew exactly what I was. The money was supposed to be for companionship – not for anything else that happened between two consenting adults doing what two horny adults normally do. Sometimes the companionship amounted to nothing more than swapping hellos, but I had some good regular clients who bought me presents and took me to dinner.'

'Were you happy?' I asked, although it did seem rather rhetorical.

'Of course. I was very happy and making a lot more money than I ever did in my other job and if a guy wanted two of us, I would go with Sarah. I got to know her rather intimately, if you get my gist,' she added with a smile.

'So where did it all go wrong?'

'The agency we used was called London Elite, run by a middle-aged lady who used to be a model and, how shall I put this, moved into management. Well, she left the agency quite suddenly and we found out it had been taken over by this Serbian bloke. We never knew what happened to Margie; that was her name. We didn't hear from her, but I suspect she hadn't wanted to sell up. Anyway, the new management said they were going to take forty percent and they didn't screen clients like Margie used to. Margie always asked lots of questions before we saw them. She cared about our safety. We could work or not work – she didn't pressure us but the new owner was different.'

I thought I sensed a seriousness and more than a little pain on Scunt's face. I wasn't sure it was right to make her tell me everything, but I had to know if we were going to sort things out. I filled up her wine glass as she continued.

'The guys, our clientele, became kinkier and kinkier. They wanted anal sex and I didn't do that. They wanted to do it without a condom and I didn't do that. Then they complained and told me the agency claimed I did those things.'

I suddenly thought how we had not used a condom during all of our love-making. I had thought about it at one point, but we had never bought condoms. If Scunt was okay with it, then so was I, but now was not the time to talk about it.

'What did you do about it? Is that why we're here?'

'I was finished with them. I still liked my job but I needed to find a new agency or go independent. I thought I could get my own website going, so I went round to the agency one night to tell them I was leaving. It was a room on the first floor of a house in Soho. I was frightened even when I went upstairs to the office. In one room was a middle-aged woman with a computer and a telephone who seemed totally disinterested in me. I reckon she was high on something. There were no windows in the next room. It was dark and horrible with the heavy smell of cigarettes. The Serbian was there. I'd only met him a couple of times and I didn't like him. He had two minders with him. They were big guys, in black tees and jeans, and I remember lots of tattoos on their arms. They were all sitting round a table playing cards, poker maybe, and they were laughing, mainly because they were drunk. There was a bottle of whisky on the table and an empty one on the floor.

'I told the boss I was leaving the agency, then he got angry and said something about never leaving, that he owned me. His accent was difficult to understand but I understood the word "own" so I started swearing, and I was loud. Then I ran at him and tried to hit him. It was probably quite funny to watch because all I could do was swipe at his chest while he swatted me away with a wave of his hands. I kicked some furniture over – a chair or a table or something. There was a lot of shouting, and that was when the minders got involved. One grabbed me and tried to pull me away. He held my arms down as I flayed out, kicking my legs, and the other one pulled out a gun and waved it around. They were all laughing.'

Scunt swallowed deeply before she continued. 'Then the big Serb came up to me and started playing with my breasts, still saying I would never leave. I kicked out and got him properly in the balls, fair and square and hard. He screamed and shouted, and bent forward, holding on to them like he was naked, hiding them. The guy holding me let go, probably to check out his boss, and the other one, with the gun, ran to the boss too. He ran past me and I grabbed his arm and suddenly the gun sort of went off.'

Another pause. This one longer. I waited patiently.

'With the bang, we all sort of stopped and looked at each other and sort of stood around for a fraction of a second. There was an eerie silence. Then there was a scream and it looked like the bullet had hit him somewhere on his leg.'

'Which one was "him"?'

'The boss. And he screamed all sorts of new curses in whatever his language was. There was blood on his trousers and he was hopping around, flapping his hands, not sure if it was his leg or his balls. And in the confusion I took my chance and ran. I raced home and locked all the doors – they knew where I lived. I changed my clothes, grabbed a coat

199

and left. I couldn't go to Sarah's, because they'd find me there, so I went to a pub and picked up a guy and stayed the night with him. I was going to do the same the next night because I still couldn't go home. I went to another pub, and met you.'

'And here we are,' I concluded. 'That's an awful story, Scunt, but at least now I understand. How do you feel?'

'Now? What do I feel? I feel better and I feel safe. Thank you. What do you think we should do?'

'I don't know. I really don't. I wanted to know everything and I needed to know, but somehow I wish I didn't. I was happy when we were just driving around meeting your friends and Q, but now you've made it all real again. It's broken the spell. I really don't know what to do, but let's sleep on it. We have the cottage for two days. We will work something out. By the way, do you have a cat or a dog back at your flat?

'No. Why?'

'There's been enough injury without having a starving pet on our conscience.'

She laughed, and so did I.

'Let's watch a film again,' I said. 'It's been quite a day. We need a little peace.'

Neither of us really watched the film, though. Scunt started to read a paperback she picked up in the kitchen. She was lying on the sofa with me, her head resting on the arm of the sofa and her feet in my lap. After the film was the crime programme CSI, set in Miami or New York. I set the volume so it wouldn't disturb Scunt, but then I couldn't actually make out what anyone was saying. It didn't worry me though; I was too busy thinking about everything she'd told me. While I thought it through, I massaged her feet. I hoped it was as relaxing for her as it was for me. I didn't know. I didn't know Scunt at all. Hers were dainty feet, maybe no more than a size four, maybe even a three. I decided I didn't like large feet, and stopped to look at them closely.

'Don't stop, Tommy. I like that.' Good, it was relaxing for her. I looked at each toe as I massaged it, and the red paint on each nail. Each nail had been beautifully manicured. I remembered how once I had studied Jenny's feet – a long time ago. I had also liked her feet. They were probably slightly larger than Scunt's, and she painted her own nails, and never went for a pedicure. You could see the difference. I tried to remember if Scunt had had a pedicure in Glasgow? It didn't matter. Nail polish is a funny thing really. I was sure I had seen paintings of women with buffed up coloured nails from the middle of the nineteenth century. Something else to check up on.

I looked at Scunt as she read. Generally she didn't wear much make up, which I also liked. 'Scunt?'

It took her a moment to look up from her book, 'Yes?' and she returned to reading.

'When you're working do you put on a lot of makeup?'

'Normally, yep.'

'Okay.'

'Why?'

'I just wondered,' I said as she put her book down in her lap.

'Come on, Tommy, tell me why you asked. I know you have some amazing fact to tell me.'

'Am I so transparent?'

'Yes you are. To me you're more open than this book,' and she pointed at her lap. 'Don't look so hurt. All your little stories and facts are part of the reason I love you. Now what did you have to say?'

'Okay. Anthropologically speaking…' I saw Scunt raise her eyebrows, 'anthropologically speaking, do you know why women wear deep-red lipstick?'

'To attract men?' Scunt offered.

'Of course, but do you know why it attracts men?'

'Because men like the colour?'

'No. Because you're conning men with your lips simulating your pussy lips, all flushed and ready for sex. You're giving off a very powerful come-and-get-me signal, which, I might say, makes it very odd that all the air hostesses of the very proper Middle Eastern airlines wear it.'

'Have you ever had sex with an air hostess, Tommy?'

'Scunt, get back to your book. Really my sex life isn't that interesting. And the answer to your question is, no.'

Scunt returned to her reading and I returned to the TV while massaging her and thinking about what we should do next. I couldn't think of any other outcome than Scunt facing up to the police and the threat of the Serbian boss, and I didn't want either to happen but it wasn't a decision that had to be made tonight. We were here, away from all those pressures for at least another day; it was just another day to enjoy before returning to my other life. I thought about what Scunt had said and abruptly stopped massaging her feet.

'What did you say?'

'What. Tommy? Please let me read.'

'What did you say about all these little stories and facts being part of the reason you love me.'

'Yes, that's right. And please don't stop the massage. It feels so, so good.' Yet again, she returned to her book.

She admitted that she loved me! Genuine? Or a tart with a heart? Whatever, it didn't complicate anything anymore than it was already complicated. First, I had to get both of us out of this. She had been right about that from the outset. She told me in the pub on that first night what she had done, and now I was helping her run from the police. I was an accomplice, which meant it was also my problem. We had settled into a comfortable way of being together. Sure, we both needed space but we also needed to be close to each other. We had learned the art of saying nothing; the art of being quiet in each other's company. It's something that Jenny and I never had. Any silence was filled by the TV or radio because we had nothing to say to each other – not because we wanted to be quiet with each other.

I knew what I should be doing. If I wasn't planning our escape, then I needed to have an answer when Scunt asked me if I loved her (I knew she would). Something else for tomorrow, perhaps even later, but for now I would let my head fill with no more than the crime on CSI, and I knew it would suddenly come to me. Relax, massage, CSI and then bed, and maybe more than a hug from my new lover.

Chapter XIV

Oxford is one of the world's most beautiful cities, but its beauty is only discernible if you can get to see it past the almost impenetrable barrier of its ring road. We toyed with the *Park and Ride* service which would have meant abandoning the car and taking a bus, but the infrequency of the buses and high fares put us off. I wanted to have my car near to where we would shop, and I was willing to pay for that privilege, even if that meant taking the car into the middle of the city. Scunt said to dump it right in the middle of the traffic jam: 'Let's just get out and walk and then let them tow it away,' she added. 'After all, it isn't ours and we could always hire another.'

I tried to explain that this wasn't her brightest idea. I still had some expectation of getting back to a more normal life and I didn't want to have to explain to anyone why I was also being chased by the police for stealing a car.

'Then phone the hire company and tell them it broke down and you had to abandon it in Oxford. Be irate and tell them you're going to sue them for wasting your time and giving you a rubbish car.'

Scunt was ranting now. Clearly waiting in traffic jams was not totally compatible with her lifestyle. I was getting as overheated as the car. Maybe we should have used the *Park and Ride* after all, because driving around looking for a car space must be among the most useless of all pastimes. Everywhere they're forcing cars out of towns, forcing us all to use out-of-town shopping centres, which we know are killing the town centres. Soon they'll start to padlock the town centres and the only people allowed in will be city councillors going to meetings bemoaning the lack of activity in the town. Maybe, with an eye to nostalgia, they'll allow access to anyone riding on horseback or with a horse and cart.

We finally made it to the car park on Westgate, but with even more driving around until we found a space we nearly ran dry of petrol. The conspiracy against the motorist was unabated. Jeremy Clarkson for Prime Minister was my call at that moment.

But the beauty of Oxford with its skyline of the college and chapel spires pushed aside all our immediate problems. I would never tire of walking round the town and colleges, admiring the history, and contemplating all the learning that took place there; but it was clear that Scunt wasn't in for an historical tour.

'Let me at least show you one college.'

'Okay, but it's five shops and one meal for every college,' she retorted.

That seemed like a good exchange and the best deal I was going to get. In Cambridge, the University *is* the town, but not so Oxford. Here the University is *part* of the town, so the town-and-gown rivalries seem not to be as fierce. The weather was balmy and walking around with Scunt on my arm wasn't a chore. In the end, we didn't go into any colleges but we walked past many. Even Scunt grudgingly admitted they were quite beautiful.

'Did you go to university, Tommy?'

'Yes,' I was dreading this question.

'Where?'

'Well, here actually. I went to Jesus.'

'You mean you found God? I didn't have you marked down as a religious nut.'

'No, Scunt. I went to Jesus College. It's just the name of the college. I read PPE.'

'So you went to a monastery instead of university and then you didn't read the Bible? You only read one book – the PPE. I haven't even heard of that one.'

'I hope you're teasing me. PPE stands for philosophy, politics and economics and we say 'read' because it's shorthand for saying "the degree I took".'

'Do you know how elitist that sounds, Tommy? Start connecting and talking like a real person again.'

Fuck it. She was right, but her rant didn't last and we were back shopping soon after that and she was happy while I carried all the worries for both of us. But now she had added one more: I was elitist. Was this arrangement how it's supposed to be? Man worries and woman shops?

As Scunt held up dresses and skirts and pointed at shoes, I was away with my thoughts. What was it the Dalai Lama said when asked what surprised him most about humanity: *Man. He sacrifices his health in order to make money. Then he sacrifices money to recuperate his health. And then he is so anxious about the future that he does not enjoy the present; the result being that he does not believe in the present or the future; he lives as if he is never going to die, and then dies having never really lived.*

I had a rant about this when I first read it. What did a man in a saffron cloak, sitting on top of a mountain, know about the modern world? Man had always gone hunting. At first, for food, and then for money to buy food. That's the way it's always been and even Neolithic man (or was it Palaeolithic man? It doesn't really matter) wanted to be head of the tribe, because he hunted better – or had the biggest cock. Man has always sacrificed everything to be the top dog and in those days he must have been more anxious about the future. At least nowadays a job has some semblance of a future, but our stone-age ancestors never knew if another buffalo was going to pass close enough by the cave to provide food for the tribe.

I had thought that Dalai Lama stuff was such self-evident nonsense that I dismissed it right out of hand. The situation is better today and it will be even better tomorrow; it's called 'progress'. We've always worked to live! But then, over the years, I've thought about it, and I've realised that our ancestors did just enough work to live, then they sat around a lot of fires, enjoying being alive, eating, drinking and singing songs together. In my later years, I began to understand some of the old guru's argument. In this modern world all we do is work in order to work harder. Is there much living left to do? It seemed appropriate to have these thoughts on this day, in one of the great historical centres of learning, where erudition and thinking were considered sufficient ends in themselves.

Scunt was trying on another skirt and a tight white blouse. The skirt was short and she had long, hooped coloured socks that passed well over her knees. Just like in Glasgow, she came out of the changing room and laughed and skipped and pirouetted for me. She looked wonderful and sexy and happy in a way that only children ever seemed to look happy. Her happiness was infectious.

'That's wonderful and very sexy,' I said, and she turned to try on yet another skirt and pondered some more.

The world is now totally full. There are over seven billion of us, and most are doing no more than eking out an existence. The future of work is very uncertain. We can't all go on the game like Scunt, and if we did no one would have any money to pay her – or us. I have to think this through carefully. I could be the pioneer of a new wave. I could be at the leading edge of a new revolution. We need to grow things to eat, so we should make that important – the highest priority. What use is a car or a light bulb to someone dying of starvation? The world does need certain manufactured items, but technology means we need fewer and fewer people to make those things, and the manufacturing companies need services to make them run effectively – advertising, logistics and accounting at least. The rest of us (most of us) are supplying services to those who actually make the things. Thus, most of the work in the world is a giant job-creation scheme and therefore a scam. We're all living in a giant Ponzi scheme.

Of course I know all of this. It's part of the great secret that financial centres the world over try to hide. The financiers and bankers make their money from their system – it's not in their (I mean *my*) interests to blow the whistle. The West needs economic growth and redistributing resources from poorer parts of the world has always been part of the game. Today it has a totally new perspective, and not a comforting one, yet still people seem addicted to the idea of work. We all see worth in worthless jobs, and we promote the ethic of hard work and loyalty for nothing. That Dalai Lama was a far smarter dude than I had first thought. Maybe the purpose of living was to live – not to work our balls off. We could all be paid the same for doing less; after all, most work is useless anyway. We could spend the extra time just living but maybe that wouldn't work. For one thing, the industrial owners would end up taking more and becoming even more objectionable. Perhaps I could resolve that though. If I became President of the World, then I could enforce all sorts of new laws about the maximum amount anyone got paid. Why not make a law whereby the maximum pay within a company could be no more than ten times the minimum pay. That would do it.

No. I think the bigger problem is we don't know how to be happy any more. I saw a generation brought up on electronic gadgetry, which I admit can be fun, but it drove all the children indoors and into lonely self-absorbing pastimes, where relationships are more likely to be virtual than real; in a virtual world, you can hide behind any alias or personal vicissitude. In short, you can lie all the time. but Scunt, in her own way, without thought or reason, had transcended the problem and become a free spirit with a solid ethical base. I had set out on this journey with her believing that being elder meant I was the guardian and teacher. It seemed I was learning more from her. That she was my teacher. As I pondered all this, wishing I was the global President, I watched the world go by. I needed more time to reach some proper conclusions, and I decided (for once) that an article in *Marie Claire* would not suffice. I needed a more influential platform, and that wasn't going to be *Penthouse* or *Playboy*.

I heard Scunt speak: 'Come on, dreamy. Solving the world's problems again? You can leave that for another day. Let's see what we can buy to eat tonight. And I want you to cook for me again, please. You're so talented. Let's have a special meal tonight, with some wine, or maybe champagne.'

'Just wine. I don't know what happens to you when you drink champagne. You may turn into a nymphomaniac!'

'Don't you just hope!'

A passer-by heard our conversation and stopped and looked at us. We ignored her, as Scunt took my hand and we walked out, looking for a food shop. As we walked along the street, Scunt asked me, 'Do you think I'm a nymphomaniac, then? I mean, what is a nymphomaniac anyway?'

'It's a woman who trips you up and is on the floor before you,' I answered far too quickly but I was not quick enough to avoid Scunt's playful kick to my leg.

'No seriously,' she said, 'how would I know if I was one?'

It was not a question I'd ever considered. 'I assume you'd have withdrawal symptoms and get headaches if you didn't have regular sex,' I suggested.

'When it's withdrawn, I do get symptoms – I want it back in!' and she laughed. 'I do like sex, Tommy. Especially with you.'

'You don't have to flatter me, Scunt.'

'I mean it! I mean I like sex every day – but it would be nice to have sex with just one person every day. I don't need lots of different people. You understand that, don't you?' She found those puppy-dog eyes and held my hand just a little tighter.

'I understand… Now what do you want for dinner?'

I thought that strand of the conversation was over, but as we mused over smoked salmon and cream cheese in the supermarket, she continued: 'I mean it's important that we both understand what we like about sex. How often we like sex. What we like to do. What we don't like, and what turns us on.' The other shoppers started to move a little closer to eavesdrop more easily. 'I mean, do you like uniforms and role play? I don't know – so you must tell me. Would you like me to dress up as a nurse for you and give you an examination? It would be a very intimate examination and then—'

I stopped her. 'Not here, Scunt. Everyone's watching us

and listening to us.'

I remembered those films when a crowd would be watching some key scene unravel and would wait dramatically for an answer. I turned towards a woman in her fifties, I guessed, as I reached for a jar of sun-dried tomatoes and half expected her to tell me she thought it all sounded like rather good fun, and sexy, and she wished she could ask her husband those kinds of questions, and I thought, well, why not? According to Scunt's ethics, we could have this conversation right here and now. What did it matter that others listened in? So we did. As we moved from fish to steak and breakfast cereals, we continued.

'I've never done role play before. I can imagine you as a nurse.' Indeed I could; my very own Lydia or Emma.

'I know what I would do,' she said. 'I would call you into my examination room and you'd be embarrassed and say you had a little problem. And I would tell you to undress. "Take everything off," I'd say, and I'd walk around you, examining you very closely. I'd stand in front of you with my stethoscope and hear your heart rate shoot up, and I'd say, "From where I stand I would say you had a big problem".'

We were at the checkout at that point and Scunt didn't stop talking. She described in great detail the examination she intended to conduct on me. The checkout girl was listening to every word. Scunt saw this as well, and pulled her into the conversation.

'Do you ever dress up as a nurse for your boyfriend?'

'No. He likes me as a police woman. He likes it when I arrest him.' She laughed. 'Fifteen pounds thirty-seven pence, please.'

'Pay her, Tommy – otherwise she might arrest you.'

They both laughed.

Scunt looked at me as I was handed the change and then ushered me towards the exit of the shop, so she could have a brief and furtive conversation with the checkout girl. Again they laughed.

'Tommy,' she said when she caught up with me, 'go and have a coffee over there. I just want to go and buy something special for supper. I want to buy you a surprise. I'll be back in quarter of an hour or so.'

She was smiling that naughty smile I had come to recognise (and worry about) as she bounced off, leaving me with the shopping. I sat in the Starbucks with a café latte. I decided we were probably safe from our chasers here. I now knew she hadn't actually killed anyone, and the man she had shot wasn't her boyfriend but a gangster – a thug – so the police wouldn't be overly concerned about trying to find her. I just hoped my preconceptions about how the police worked were right. The Serbian had no idea where we were, so bumping into them again would be a very long shot. Yes, we were safe here and I could relax.

In the past few days, Scunt and I had hardly been apart and now I found myself missing her. I'd lost track of the days completely. There was the night on the train, one in Glasgow and one in Leeds. Then we drove to Q's and spent a night there. One in Woodstock, too. Only four days, and during that time, apart from when I'd gone shopping at Q's place, this was only the second time we'd been apart. I couldn't take it all in. Just four days and I was missing her? I wasn't quite sure what I was missing, though. She had led me into a total mess, my life had been turned upside down, and I was a fugitive! Yet still I missed her. I had promised her I'd get us out of this mess, so I had to concentrate on that, but every time I set out all the issues in my mind, over my café latte, I came back to thinking about her. Blast her! I was in the middle of cursing and swearing at the effect she was having on me when she came back.

'Missed me, darling? Get me a coffee. Anything. The same as you,' and she sat down with an unmarked plastic bag at her feet.

'Get what you wanted?'

'Of course.'

'Going to tell me?'

'No.'

'Okay. Coffee coming up.'

Done with our coffee, we headed back to Woodstock as it started to get dark. It all felt uncommonly domestic. A couple coming home from work, chatting about the day and all that had happened. Is this what it was really like for everyone else? Was I marching out of step by commuting into London? No, of course not; the train was always full of other people, arriving home no earlier than eight, who were gone again by five thirty the next morning. We were just a strong bunch of commuters from Kent.

Over dinner, which I have to say I cooked beautifully, I tried to find a way to talk this through with Scunt. She was the one who had said she loved me, but I wondered if she meant it, or whether it was just a casual term of endearment that meant nothing. Only four days. No one fell in love in four days. But, hold on a minute, I used to believe in love at first sight. I fell for Jenny at first sight, but surely not Scunt? I was so much older. Damn, I was confused.

'I've got a surprise for you, Tommy. Would you like to see it?'

'Is it what you bought today?'

'Yes. Would you like to see it? Clear the dishes and I'll get it,' and she was gone. With the dishes piled up in the kitchen, I sat in the lounge wondering what the heck she was doing.

'Are you ready?' she shouted outside the lounge door.

'Yes, I'm ready.'

'Close your eyes.' A pause. 'Are they closed?'

'Yes, Scunt. They're closed.'

'Don't cheat – I'll tell you when to open them.'

'Okay.' Actually I had no interest in opening them. I liked surprises and I knew that with Scunt the surprise would be fun. I heard the door open.

'Mr Tommy. Are you ready for your appointment? Open your eyes, please, and stand up.'

As I did so, I looked at her. She was beautiful and sexy and a slut and a princess. She was so desirable that any doubts I had about love at first sight were removed. She was dressed in a very sexy nurse costume. Her makeup was going-out-to-a-premier heavy, and she had dark-red painted lips. She had been listening to me. The outfit was short with a deeply plunging neckline. I could see both of her nipples peeking out. Her white stockings didn't quite reach the bottom of the dress, leaving several inches of pale, enticing leg exposed. She was the living vision of the Lydia of my dreams. In fact, she was more than I had ever dreamt.

'Now are you ready for your check up?

All I could do was nod.

'I wanted to say thank you, Tommy. Now, Mr Tommy! Get undressed. Your nurse is here.'

Any thoughts I had of a serious discussion on either our plans or our futures faded in an instant and I gave in to her very personal and very intimate examination.

Chapter XV

Breakfast was finished and washed up, and we had packed. Scunt hurried off to the corner shop to get provisions for the journey, then we were off together to see Mrs Blackaby.

'We had a wonderful time,' we told her as we handed back the key. 'It's so relaxing here. So much to see. We would love to come back some day.'

And, then, there we were again, sitting in the car pointing down the road, engine off, staring straight ahead. I knew what was coming.

'So, Tommy. What's the plan?'

I really had no idea but I waited for the words to form. 'You know, Scunt, I've spent all my life lying. I avoided every problem by dancing round it, and, you know, it's done me quite well. I've got a good job and a nice house, but the reality is that I have no life at all. I guess it's time for another approach.'

'And what's that?'

'I think it's time for a bit of honesty. Time to confront all our demons. We're going back to London, Scunt, and we're going to sort it all out. We're going to be brave. You didn't shoot that man – the thug did. Anything you did was self-defence. We trust in the law and we'll explain truthfully. Scunt, we're going to be strong and brave. Are you with me?'

The words just formed. I didn't know where they came from but I believed in them because they sounded right, and I felt right, too. It was a good moment. Would Scunt agree?

'Tommy, I trust you totally. If you say it's the right thing, then that's what we'll do.'

With my heart beating fast, I started the engine and we headed off back towards Oxford and the M40 motorway towards London. This was not my style. I was not Jason Bourne, but I could make this work. I didn't know exactly how to do it, but somehow it would work. We could reach London in a couple of hours, speeding through the stunning scenery of the Chiltern Hills. I decided we would hand the car back to Hertz, and head back, with our luggage, to Scunt's flat in Stoke Newington, north of the city. We would formulate our next plans there. What the plans would be, I had no idea, but I felt increasingly confident as we drove on.

Returning the car meant we had to drive further into London than we wanted to, and the time it took to get back to the flat took almost as long as the journey to London had. Stoke Newington is not one of London's smartest areas. We were probably only a few miles, less than ten probably, from central London but it could have been a full marathon run, it was all so different. Full of student flats and starter flats; a commuter area for students starting their first jobs. The old houses have been split into multiple units, and they look dark and forbidding. It's a totally multiracial community, but you get the sense that once it was a small village on the outskirts of London. Many such communities were swallowed up by the sprawl that is Greater London.

Scunt had to hunt for the keys to the front door. The paint was peeling off, and I wondered what state her flat would be in. We went up one flight of stairs, pushing away piles of uncollected post on the floor. I prepared myself for the worst. It had been a long time since I'd been a student flat. At least her flat, Flat C, had a properly painted door and a neat, working bell. Just one press was rewarded by a solid traditional '*brrrrrringggg*'. I stopped Scunt momentarily, so we could check whether the door had been damaged or opened forcefully. We didn't want to meet a couple of overgrown thugs when we entered (fighting our way out of anything was a plan I knew would fail). From the dreary outside hall, we entered a large lounge with high ceilings.

'Dump the luggage there and I'll make some tea and show you round,' she said.

Leaving the cases by the front door, I was relieved to see that the flat hadn't been ransacked. I hadn't raised this fear with Scunt, but I had wondered if they'd come and smashed it up out of frustration, or while looking for clues as to where she was. As I looked around, nothing was as I had expected. What had I expected? A squalid and dingy student squat? Something like my old flat in Pimlico, perhaps, but with bras, skirts and panties scattered randomly among magazines and unwashed coffee cups. But it wasn't like that at all. It was tidy, clean, chic and very elegant. It was an oasis in a neglected tenement.

What immediately struck me was the use of light. It was heading towards late afternoon and the sun was low in the sky, throwing golden yellow streaks and dark shadows across the room. The eclectic balance of modern textures and textiles in what was probably an eighteen-fifties building was mesmerising. The design welcomed me in to the room, and offered comfort and relaxation without being fussy or overpowering. If she had architected this herself, then she was a master designer and I wondered if she had ever been the interior designer she teased me about that night at Q's.

I followed her to the kitchen, which was every bit as stylish as the lounge, with a Smeg cooker, dishwasher and fridge. I couldn't help but snigger at the brand name. What a name for a range of white goods – clearly just right for a hooker. This wasn't IKEA, though; this was top-end kitchen design. I poked my head round the door of each of the two bedrooms; they provided no further surprises with their decor. They were both luxurious but differed in style and design. One of them, probably the guest room, had clean lines and was predominantly white. A large double-bed was furnished with crisp, clean white linen. The only colour in the room came from a distressed chest of drawers painted in a dull yellow to match the curtains hanging from a painted wooden pole. The other bedroom was more sumptuous. Heavy curtains in a deep, almost black, shade of red, maybe even purple. All the other colours in the room were shades of this – some lighter and some even darker. It was a place for love. Correction: It was a place to have sex.

'Do you bring your customers here?' The quality of the furnishing alone would justify a high price, I thought.

'No. Never strictly *outcall*. Hotels or the punter's place only,' she shouted as she reached into a cupboard to grab some tea bags. 'I like to keep some anonymity.'

'The milk will have gone off, so d'you want tea or coffee?'

'Black coffee would be good,' I answered. 'This is quite a place, Scunt.'

'Yes, I like it. I feel very relaxed here. You know, Tommy, I can read you like a book. You didn't expect this at all did you? You thought I lived in some little, nasty place. Dirty and small and a bit like a student squat. You're so predictable. Do you really like it?'

'Who wouldn't like it? It's great. But am I really so obvious?'

Scunt nodded, and asked the same old question as she handed me a mug of coffee: 'What's the plan then, Tommy?'

The mug had a motto on it. I held it up to read: *Old hookers don't die. They just stay on their backs for longer.* It made me smile. I had only thought fleetingly about the plan when we drove down from Oxford, and I only had a rough outline of what we might do.

'We need to know what happened when Margie left, and how much control they still have over her. So, the first thing is to find Margie and talk to her. We need to know about our enemy. Can we get in touch with her? Do you think we can find her?'

Scunt hesitated and sipped at her coffee. 'Probably. But I'll have to talk to some people first.'

'Okay. We also need to find out how injured this Serbian brute is. That will tell us how angry he is, and we need to know if he really is chasing you.'

Scunt turned angrily to me. "Of course he is! Why d'you think otherwise?'

It was easier to agree with her. She thought he was, and whatever plan I came up with had to remove her fear.

'Okay. We need to understand just how far he would go to catch you.'

'Then what?'

'Well, then we have to find a way to make him change his mind, and – to be honest – right now I don't know how we can do that.'

Scunt looked at me and shrugged. I knew she wanted a clear-cut plan that could be executed in flash, but that wasn't possible.

'Data first. Then plan. Then action,' I said. 'It has to be this way. Can you find Margie? And you have to give me the address of where you went – where their offices are.'

Scunt wandered off without a word. She was taking it

all in and I was very unsure she would agree. She sat in one of the comfy chairs in the lounge with her feet tucked up under her, her mug held in two hands. After all this time she was hesitating. I couldn't work out why. Surely this is what she wanted? She was the one who needed resolution.

Finally she said, 'Okay let's do it. I'll have to go out to find Margie. It may not be easy but, like I said, I need to talk to some people first. Let me finish my cuppa, then we'll both go to their offices. I need to see what's happening. We can do it this evening, or tomorrow. In fact, I'm going to have a shower now, then I'll go find Margie.'

We sat in silence until she went for her shower. I heard the splashing of water and I sat and looked around me. I wanted to think about her naked in the shower and I wanted to join her, but I knew at this moment she needed to be alone. I couldn't just sit there, though, so I tried to get the music system working, realising after some time it was driven off an iPod. I set it onto shuffle and sat back and listened. It was an eclectic selection from classical to rap and other genres I couldn't name. There was a sprinkling of good old sixties and seventies rock. I knew I didn't really understand Scunt, but the more I didn't know the more I wanted to know. I may have dozed off for a while; it was ages before she returned.

Why do women take so long to get dressed? Scunt took ages. Jenny was just the same. I wouldn't even start to think about taking my shower until she called down and said she'd be ready in five minutes; at that point, I knew we were still at least two changes of clothes away from leaving, and then she would have to tidy everything around the house, fluff the cushions and make sure the kitchen was clean. What was it she was so worried about? Maybe she didn't want any burglars to think we were messy. I often stood waiting, car-keys in hand, watching Jenny in her going-out clothes and wearing her bright yellow rubber washing-up gloves as she stood cleaning the kitchen sink. Time-keeping was not her strong suit. When we had to leave to catch a ferry or plane, I would tell her it left ninety minutes before it actually did; and then we only just arrived on time to catch it.

Scunt wasn't quite so tardy. It was late afternoon and she was ready to leave, dressed in jeans and boots and a jumper. She looked so different from the long-haired, crying girl who accosted me only a few days ago in the pub, and I liked the difference.

'There's a spare key in the coffee cupboard. I'm not sure what time I'll be back. It might take some time. Why don't you buy something to eat for dinner? Just in case I'm late back? Maybe you can make something that can be heated up. Love you.' She kissed me and left. And there I was alone in her flat. I still had time to call the office if I wanted, but even though I rehearsed the conversation I could think of nothing to say; therefore I didn't. I listened to some music but I was restless. Maybe I should have a shower. Ah, but which shower should I use? The one in her room or the one in the guest room? I chose the one she had used. I hunted for a clean towel and stripped down as I rummaged through the toiletries. They were all high class – no sign of a Sainsbury two-for-one offer. She was right. She did surprise me and I hadn't expected anything like this, but I set out to enjoy every moment. A powerful shower and expensive shampoo. As I towelled myself down, I looked in the mirror and hardly recognised myself with my new haircut. Scunt had really turned my life inside out and upside down.

I wanted to sit and think more about the plan. What

would I do if we found them, and what would Margie say? What was it I used to say to my staff? The immediate is the biggest enemy of the important. And so it was now. The most important thing was to work out the plan. The immediate was to go shopping and cook some dinner. The immediate won, so I fetched the spare key and went to find a shop.

There must have been a large supermarket somewhere nearby, but first I came across a parade of small shops. I had decided on a *salade niçoise* and stocked up appropriately. I passed a chemist and wondered if I should also buy some condoms, but we'd gone without them so far and had already tempted fate. I knew these days it's wrong to admit it, but I hate that moment when you have to stop in the middle of a passionate embrace to – in the jargon of the adverts – get fitted. At that moment, everything might go wrong and there might be nothing left to fit the condom on to. It also means that the end is close, that all the hugging, stroking, kissing and massage is over and the real business is about to start, which can be a real disappointment for people who enjoy the first part – the foreplay. Personally, I like the tenderness and the loving bits, and I've often wondered if the actual act of sex is far more satisfying for a woman than for a man. The woman can have multiple orgasms or sleep (whichever way the mood takes her) but the guy just has to keep working with nearly all of the satisfaction coming, literally, at the end. But with every reward, nature – or God, depending on your persuasion – adds a cost. And for women, the potential cost of the potential joy of continual satisfaction is having to be with drunk and brutal men, or even Serbian gangsters.

While making the salad, I returned to thinking about the 'important' issue, but my mind was a total blank. There were simply too many options and outcomes. I carried on preparing the food. Time passed slowly and at nine o'clock I ate while watching TV. I'd heard nothing from Scunt. By eleven I was getting worried and by midnight I was almost frantic, but there was nothing I could do. By one in the morning I thought about going to bed; but which bed? I chose the room with the dark and sexy décor, but I still felt uncomfortable, both with being there and with Scunt's continued absence.

I was restless in my sleep when the lights came on.

'Tommeeee, where are you?' Scunt came flying through the air to land on the bed next to me.

'You're drunk and I was asleep,' I said, lying. 'Was everything okay?' Now I was just worried.

'Give me a hug, I feel so tired,' and she snuggled up close to me and promptly fell asleep.

And there she lay, on the bed still wearing her jacket, jeans and boots and now I had a problem I had never faced before; how to get her into bed. Of course this had never happened with Jenny. Jenny was always very careful and would never get so drunk that she could not get into bed. She might get tipsy, but was always capable of getting undressed and removing her makeup (which might take an eternity) while all the time I lay in bed waiting – and hoping. I was hoping of course that with a little alcohol she might loosen up and we might have some fun. Of course she never did and we never did.

I tried to take off Scunt's boots. As I pulled on them, I pulled her body down the bed. I knew there would be a tipping point when her bottom was so far down the bed that she would fall off. Maybe that was the best way? I tried to be gentle and pulled her slowly, but she slowly slipped off the end of the bed anyway and landed with a thump on the floor. I hoped it would wake her, if only a little, so she could help out but she was still dead to the world. At least I had her sitting on the floor now, with her back against the end of the bed. With a mixture of brute force and leverage, I stood over her with my bottom in her breasts and achieved what at the start seemed an improbable task. The boots came off one by one. Then I managed to remove her jacket and jumper. The jeans, I decided, were better dealt with once she was back on the bed. I don't know how long it took me to get her off the floor, but I was building up a sweat and seemed to be burning many more calories than I would during sex.

With her lying back on the bed, undoing the button and zip of her jeans was easy. Pulling the jeans down was far more difficult, but at last she was down to bra and panties, and finally in the bed rather than on it. What had made me stop there, at her undies? Does it count as a personal violation of a drunk person to strip them totally? But then I imagined her waking in the morning still dressed in her underwear, and I knew she wouldn't be impressed. I pulled the duvet back and removed her last bits of clothing. I looked at her body as she lay there. In all its imperfections, it was perfection. She pulled herself into a fetal position, purred and then snored. I covered her with the duvet again and slipped in alongside her. She turned in her sleep, cuddled close and soon we both were asleep.

Chapter XVI

Scunt had looked beautiful when she had gone out the evening before, but at breakfast she looked very rough and distinctly under the weather. She was very quiet, too, but had she been at all inclined to speak, I'm sure she would have thanked me profusely for supplying all the orange juice she was now drinking. It was no use asking what had happened. She had pulled on a long tee-shirt and sat hunched over her toast.

'You got everything else off me last night – you could have done the same with my makeup.' I looked at her face. Indeed, it had run and smeared making her look like, well, someone who had been out drinking all night.

'Did we have sex last night? Did you fuck me?'

'Of course I didn't. I'm not into necrophilia.'

'Huh.' She returned to her toast and orange juice.

There was no point in making any conversation so I acted as waiter, then I sat in the lounge while she had a very long shower. Finally she came back, still wearing the tee-shirt and I assumed not much else.

'Sorry, Tommy. Was I awful last night? How did I get into bed?'

'With a great deal of difficulty. I had to undress you and the boots were the worst.'

'I don't know how you did that. Even I have problems. Did you think of fucking me?' This time she was smiling.

'No, I didn't but I did look at you lying naked on the bed and thought how beautiful you are.'

'That's the first real compliment you've paid me. Thank you. So shall I tell you everything?'

'Yes, please but tell me first, did you manage to track Margie?'

'Yes. I've got her phone number. I haven't spoken to her yet, but we can do that later this morning.'

'Well done! So now tell me what happened.'

She looked sheepish.

'So?'

'First I phoned Sarah and we agreed to meet and we did and then we met some more girls and we did what girls do.'

'Clearly you all drank, and I hope you didn't pick up any men?'

'No, Tommy. I was faithful to you. Don't be jealous. I don't like jealous men. Just trust me. Anyway, I asked around among the girls and one of them knew someone who knew someone and I phoned her and she had Margie's number.'

'And then?'

'And then I had a good time with my girlfriends. And then I came home.'

I felt irritable because I had been worrying and she had simply been enjoying herself. Shouldn't she have phoned to put me at ease? But why should she? After all, I was just a simple bloke whose life she had turned upside down. No wonder I felt irritable and there was an edge to my voice.

'Okay, then. So will you phone Margie and see if we can meet? Let's do it this morning. Agreed?'

'Agreed. Let's do it now. Want to hand me the phone?'

I waited while she phoned and sat next to her on the sofa as she spoke. 'Hi, Margie, do you remember me? It's Tracy. Yes, that's right – when you were at London Elite. I wonder if you're free this morning because I'd like to meet you if it's possible. No, nothing special. I just want to catch up on old times. That'd be good. Where do you suggest? Islington. Upper Street? Starbucks.'

Scunt looked at me and I nodded. 'Sure that will be fine. Twelve o'clock. No problem. I look forward to seeing you again. Bye,' and she cut the phone.

'That's not far. We can get a cab. Let's leave in an hour and a half or so.'

That'll give us time to catch up on what I missed last night, I thought, and she stood, took my hand and lead me back to the bedroom. I had already forgiven her.

We phoned for a mini cab, eschewing the opportunity to stand outside and wait forever for a passing black cab; they didn't tour these parts looking for fares. Our driver was Indian with a big turban. Because I was sitting behind him, it meant I couldn't see any of what was ahead or where we were going, but he did provide us with the full ethnic experience, touching all our senses. The cab smelt as if he'd finished his last curry not ten minutes before picking us up; I was ready to accept any offer of poppadum and lime pickle. The dashboard was festooned with icons and fur and we had a soundtrack straight from the latest Bollywood hits album. Thankfully it was only occasionally that he joined the music with a low and off-tune hum (I say off-tune because it didn't match the music but the music was, to my ear, mostly off-tune anyway).

I can understand why, throughout the world, we speak different languages, but for the life of me I have no idea why there are so many different tonal variations in music. There's a very good twelve-note chromatic scale, each a semitone apart, and natural harmonics produce chords. I've never understood why anyone thinks anything else is at all harmonious. A week ago I would have taken note of this and undertaken a research project; I'd want to know why Indians found solace in their tones, and why the Chinese and Japanese liked their ting-tong music. I'd be interested to know what Japanese fathers thought about their children learning to play the violin, like Fritz Kreisler, Jascha Heifetz or even Niccolo Paganini. But today, in this taxi sitting next to Scunt, there was no choice; it was Bollywood and I could handle it.

Islington I knew from its reputation for trendy socialists and media sorts, where even a quotable belief that wealth should be shared didn't stop people buying million-pound houses. Islington was where the Labour party leaders held fashionable suppers and plotted the downfall of their own leaders and other commissars; I suppose it ran in a long tradition of Stalin and Nicolae Ceauşescu for the *dacha* and more upmarket palaces. I was pleased to hear that Ceauşescu's palace, supposedly the world's second largest building, was to be turned into a shopping mall. Now that really was bringing Communism to the people. Starbucks, on the other hand, is a monument to American consumerism. Franchised all over the world it was always the same the world over. A never-changing formula offering the same overpriced coffee. That sounded more like a Marxist ideal.

Scunt spotted our destination first. 'Stop there!' she shouted over the music, at our turban. He didn't hear at first and we overshot by a couple of hundred yards, then shuddered to a halt. We decided that the short walk back was a great deal safer than the U-turn he was about to attempt.

Scunt saw Margie sitting in a corner in Starbucks, by the window, thankfully some distance from most listening ears. This was going to be a very conspiratorial conversation.

'I'll have a café latte, please Tommy. Margie, do you

want a coffee?' Margie smiled and shook her head, pointing to the cup already in front of her and I was dispatched. By the time I got back they were deep in conversation and I sank silently into a low armchair next to Scunt, trying to get the gist of what they were saying. I needn't have worried, because they were talking about shoes. That gave me a chance to look at Margie. I had learnt over the week not to make any pre-judgments. To some people Margie was a pimp, but to others she was a marketing executive. What I saw was a slightly plump, well (but casually) dressed woman of a certain age who looked very at home in Islington. Like anyone with a good sense of style and fashion, she had taken teenage trends and adapted and moulded them to her style. She wasn't mutton dressed as lamb, but carried a modern elegance. In no way did she portray her past; maybe not even her present.

'Have you explained to Margie why we wanted to see her?' I asked Scunt.

'You had better introduce me to your man first, Tracy,' Margie said, 'and I assume there must be a purpose to this meeting. I mean, calling me out of the blue and wanting to see me straight away is a bit odd.'

Scunt took over and looking at me she said, 'I'm sorry, Margie. This is Tommy. He's my boyfriend.'

Today I had been downgraded from fiancé.

'I always did see you with a more mature man. You have lived so much of your life already; someone your own age would never keep you amused. I'm very pleased to meet you, Tommy,' and although we had been sitting together for a few minutes already she stuck out a hand, which I shook.

'And I'm very pleased finally to meet you. Scunt – I mean, Tracy – has told me so much about you.'

'I hope it's all good?' and I nodded before Scunt took over the conversation.

'Margie, can you help us with some background about the agency you used to run? Those Serbian bullies have hurt both you and me and now Tommy and I want to see if we can get some revenge, so to speak. We want retribution for the past. And maybe you do also? Can you tell us how they took over the place and anything else that might be helpful?'

We had already decided we weren't going to tell her anything about the previous week because it would probably frighten her off, but I looked at Margie and discerned that she was already uneasy. I needed to try and calm her.

'It's okay. Margie. We're not going to involve you in anything. We just want to know a little about them and their style,' I said.

'Hmm, their style? That's easy. You're right. They're bullies. I had a nice business and they just took it. They came in one day and said they wanted to be partners with me. Of course I said no, but they started calling all my girls. I didn't know that of course – they just used stooges and fixed appointments and got all their details. Then they gave me a simple offer: partnership or ruin. In fact, it wasn't an offer because they took it all anyway and I've lost my business.'

'And what are you doing now?' It wasn't relevant, but I was interested.

'Starting again and waiting for them or someone else to do the same thing to me, I suppose. You see, Tommy, in the old days, before the internet, it was all very different. Advertising was all in newsagents' windows or on cards in telephone boxes.'

I remembered that. Every telephone box in London used

to be festooned with small business cards advertising all sorts of services from young girls to mistresses and a dominatrix or two. Even if you just wanted to use the phone for the purpose it was intended for, you were labelled as a punter by anyone passing by. I even knew someone who collected the cards and made a collage for his living room, causing many a provocative discussion at his dinner parties.

Margie was still talking. 'But with the internet, it became so much easier and safer for the girls. Now they all advertise on the web and they screen punters before they meet them. It was only natural that we'd all start getting together on a single site so that we could get good internet rankings and come top of the list in the search engines. So that's what I did. There used to be a young man who visited me who was into computers and he wrote my first site and I asked my friends to join with me. I invested in the site and sat by the phone and took a share of the proceeds. We all benefited. I didn't make the girls work, I just provided advertising and marketing for a reasonable commission.'

'Isn't that what these bullies are doing as well?' I asked.

'No. It's subtly different. When I ran things, the girls worked when *they* wanted. Now they're being told they have to work. I've heard that if the girls don't work, they threaten to send someone round to help them "make up their minds" and often these threats are delivered and word gets around. It's not the way I like it.'

This took me back to Leeds, and the girls there. When the girls are in control, it was fine. It's when the pimps take over that the problems arise.

'But surely they won't have a business soon? All the girls will leave?' I asked, but I knew the answer to my own question and went on: 'But they can't, because the bullies will come round and enforce. Tell me, how many of the customers are regulars? Can we ruin their reputation?'

'Of course there are regulars, but not that many. The reputation is all in the placing on the search engines and that won't change.'

I thought about it for a moment. Suddenly some issues became clear. 'We can't take on the whole world. We can't force them out of business. If it's not them, then someone else will take their place. I feel desperately sorry for all the girls, but we can't change the world in one step.'

Both Scunt and Margie looked crest-fallen.

'After all this, you aren't giving up are you, Tommy?'

'No. I'm not giving up but any ideas we had of stopping them won't work. We can make their life uncomfortable and get some revenge. I need a bit more time to work up a plan. Margie, do you want to be part of this? I can imagine a million reasons why you'd say no. After all, you've seen them at close quarters, and you're starting a new business, and if this goes tits up you'll lose out twice.'

Margie hesitated before answering. 'Let's see what you come up with then. You look like a bright thing. Come and tell me what you want when you've got a plan and I'll see if I can help.'

They looked at each other, shared a nod, and Scunt said, 'That sounds fair enough. Okay, Tommy. We'll let you have the first run at it, if you're sure we can do something.'

'I'm sure I'll think of something,' I said and I meant it. Suddenly the problem didn't look quite so difficult. I didn't know why, but I thought the tide had turned and we stood a chance. Now I had some data to go on.

We finished our coffees. Scunt and Margie carried on chatting about old times and old friends while I sat back and thought about what we could do. Scunt and I had never really talked about the options. Maybe she had ideas of a Wild West shoot-out and us behaving like gangsters. That was never an option for me, nor would it be an option for her. I had calculated that the police really weren't interested in us, but any escalation would soon change that. We could get the police involved by spilling the beans, but they probably knew anyway and had already decided they couldn't do much, or just couldn't be bothered. And if we did involve the police, then it would involve the girls as well and take away their livelihoods. What we could do, of course, was make the Serbian's life a lot less comfortable. We could attack at the source and ruin their reputation (although I had no idea how to do that) and then we could also take personal revenge on them in some way, but without shooting them. Those were the two strands we had to follow. My plan was beginning to form.

Before we parted company and we promised that we would coordinate with each other and keep Margie in the loop, I explained the direction I was going to take. That seemed to encourage them both. Scunt and I grabbed a passing cab and headed back home. She was quiet during the ride.

'What did you expect to happen?' I asked. 'This was about collecting data. The plan would never become obvious during the meeting. Cheer up, Scunt. We are doing something.'

'If you say so, Tommy,' but her mood didn't improve.

Back at the flat, Scunt sulked for a while and then said out of the blue, 'I'll go and get some food. Can I get you anything?'

'Just point me at your PC and set it up. I want to capture

235

my thoughts.'

Scunt opened and switched on her Apple computer. I noticed it was another piece of top-of-the-range equipment.

'I'm off now,' she shouted as she left. 'I'll be back in an hour or so. Look after yourself, Tommy. I love you and thanks.'

Thanks for what? I hadn't done anything, but I did have the outline of an idea, and maybe sometimes hope is enough encouragement. That's why I like optimists more than pessimists; why the glass is always half full and not half empty (but in both, there's always room for more wine). The optimist gives us continual hope that the world is changing and can be better.

I settled down to write, think and work out what we were going to do. I'd spent a lifetime doing economic analysis and strategic planning and I realised how pathetic it had all been. Of course, in the Bank the decisions people like me made affected real people on the street. It all began on a large scale, painted with a broad brush, but the effects rippled down and had their impact, although the true consequences were often distant in both understanding and time from us; those who made decisions. In contrast, this plan needed an immediacy that was worrying me. This was about girls and women being used in ways they couldn't avoid. The plan, whatever it was, was going to change people's lives – I hoped for the better. I had to get it right first time. This kind of reality was missing in my normal daily life.

With no customers, there would be no income, and this would impact on the girls because they wouldn't be able to work if they wanted to. So we had to find a way to get them more work without the bullies chasing them. That seemed to be the most immediate task and I toyed with the idea for an hour or so. I put revenge on the back burner. By the time Scunt got back, I had an outline of a plan, and I was pleased to see her sprits had lifted considerably.

'Tommy, will you help me put all this away?'

She had bought half the store. There were Tesco's plastic bags everywhere on the kitchen floor. 'How did you get all this up here? There's a ton of stuff here.'

'I got the taxi driver to help me carry it up the stairs.'

I had been so engrossed in my work that I hadn't noticed he had been in the flat. I took that as a good sign. My concentration levels were high. In fact, I couldn't remember a recent time when I had been so focused.

'Did your thinking time go well? Do you know what we're going to do?'

'Nearly done. I've got the bare bones sorted. Now come and give me a hug.'

'Let's have a drink, first. Here, I've bought some wine. Open it for us, will you?' She passed me a bottle of an Italian Barolo. 'Nice wine,' I said tasting it. 'It's body is almost as good as yours.' All I got in return for that was a turned up nose and a silently mouthed 'Yeah, yeah'.

As I explained my plan, Scunt was close beside me on the sofa. She nodded as I talked and asked some questions, which were all answered easily.

'My biggest concern is protecting all the girls who are still working. We'll need Margie's help for that. Do you think she'll help us? It should do her business no harm.'

'Of course she will. She hates those thugs as much as I do and she'll help you find the guy you need. I'm going to enjoy this. You are wonderful, Tommy. Thank you.'

I was drawn between exploiting her warmth and

gratitude, and getting the job done. It would have been easy to pull her closer, kiss her on the neck, and slide down the sofa into a consummating embrace. And a week ago that's what Tommy would have done, if he had thought the likelihood of such an encounter was even possible, but now the important took precedence over the immediate.

'Okay. Then you phone Margie and let me speak to her. There's little else we can do right now except enjoy the wine. Are you going to cook tonight? It would make a nice change.'

'Sure, but what are you going to do about your work? Did you phone them while I was out?'

I hadn't thought about my job and my work all day. It had totally passed me by while I was deep in concentration on the problem. 'No. I haven't phoned them. This is my work for the moment, but it can't be forever. You do understand that, don't you?'

'Why not, Tommy?'

'Well, it just can't be. It just can't.' I really didn't know why, and thankfully Scunt didn't pursue it any further. Instead she phoned Margie. Margie asked me many of the same questions that Scunt had, and she also saw the merits of the proposed solutions and promised to help, not least in finding and putting me in touch with some real experts. We had just finished eating and the phone rang.

'It's for you, Tommy. I'm not sure who it is.'

I took the phone, introduced myself and listened.

'That will be fine. Can we meet tomorrow? I'm in north London in Stoke Newington. Yes, that will be fine. Can we say ten o'clock? Good. It was good to speak, Spike, and we'll meet tomorrow.'

'Was that Margie's expert friend?' Scunt asked.

'Yes. I'm about to enter the murky world of the criminals. Are you going to come with me? I'll write his brief in the morning. Now let's finish the wine.'

Chapter XVII

The meeting was in a café about a mile away. I was there early, and not long after in walked a thin, prepubescent geek in a white t-shirt, baggy blue jeans and trainers, with a spotty face, the hint of a moustache and spiky hair. That must be him. Spike. To show recognition I gave one of those half-hearted waves with an accompanying smile. It was totally ignored and I was left looking like a complete prat trying to pick up a teenaged boy. I returned to my coffee and decided to keep my head down.

I didn't know how I could have got it so wrong. A computer geek called Spike should look exactly like the guy who just walked in (and was now sitting as far away from me as possible), but my expectations were totally wrong. The next potential Spike could kindly be described as a middle-aged medieval monk, with a rim of long brown hair surrounding an otherwise bald pate; he had tastefully resisted the option of a comb-over, but when he turned his head to order a coffee, I couldn't fail to notice he was sporting a pony tail. Like a doughball doll, he was podgy, with a belly overhanging his trouser belt. He was wearing a blue cardigan, brown corduroy trousers and a short-sleeved multipatterned shirt. So this is what criminals look like when they hit middle age. It took me a moment to adjust my approach to the body shape in front me. I'd expected a thin, nervous man and I had rehearsed a number of opening lines on this basis, the best of which I had picked up from the IT man at the Bank: I thought it was supposed to be a thin client? It meant nothing to me, but I was assured it would make a true geek fall over howling with laughter. After my wave at the thin young geek, I thought I should check this was the Spike I was due to meet.

'Hi, you must be Spike?' I ventured, which was actually fairly redundant because he was now the only person sitting in the café other than myself. But we always do that. We visit hospitals and ask patients 'How are you?' when clearly they're in hospital and the answer is going to be 'Not too well'. Or we fall over and scream and someone runs over and says 'You okay?'. Again a fairly obvious answer is likely: 'No, I'm friggin' not'. Once I started a campaign against such unthinking trivia by answering the question 'How are you?' honestly. At conferences I would be introduced by colleagues to a complete stranger who would stick out his hand for shaking and say: 'Tommy, good to meet you. I'm Gerald. How are you?'. Aside from the overfamiliarity of Christian names (I never became sufficiently PC to call them by their first names) it was far too early in our relationship to enquire about my health, therefore often – and particularly with Americans – I would show them up by answering their question. 'An interesting time to ask that question, Gerald.' I might say, putting a hand on their shoulder to show the true intimacy of our new friendship. 'I was at the doctor's only yesterday and after a long and very intrusive examination she has pronounced that my haemorrhoids have nearly disappeared. I have to say – and maybe you'll know this, Gerald – it's alright to be just a little excited by a full rectal examination. I mean if it's done by a female doctor. Don't you agree? As for my other complaint, the new antibiotics have worked just fine and little Lola has nothing to worry about now.'

'Yeah. And you must be Tommy,' Spike said – a statement rather than a question; for that alone I took to him.

Introductions over, I started to explain the problem to Spike. The real issue, I told him, was not that we had anything against what the girls did, but the way they were being used by the bullies. I said we couldn't stop them altogether, or maybe even stop them at all, but we could slow them down.

'How well do you know Margie?' I asked, suddenly worrying that he wasn't necessarily a friend and might somehow let us down.

'I've known her for ages. I did my first job in exchange for a little of her time. It was great for me because I really couldn't afford her and I loved my job. Seemed like win–win for me, if you know what I mean.'

I did, as I had the same thoughts about Scunt. Wasn't I doing much the same?

'I know exactly what you mean, Spike. So d'you think we can do something?

'Of course. It's simple. I'll get some of the Community involved.'

'The Community?'

'Yes. We need to get some of my friends in on this. I'm sure it won't cost you. Lots of them know Margie and some of the girls, and they'll be keen to help out. The Community are the ones you all love to hate, but believe me there are some ethical ones who like to right wrongs and not destroy. They'll be right up for this.'

He stopped to think for a moment and I took the chance to interrupt him. 'This 'community'… I mean are you organised, or is it just a casual group of guys?'

'First off, brother…' he said and I was going off him suddenly. (I hate the affectation brother; it's an appalling Americanism that grates to the core. In fact, I hate everything Americans are doing to our language. The French are doing their best to keep theirs free from over-Anglicisation. From the sixteen hundreds they've had the *Académie Française* as the official authority on the usage, vocabulary and grammar of the French language. Maybe we should have an English Academy with the greater remit over English than the *Oxford English Dictionary*. I'm all for language developing and I like street words, but let's at least not have them formed on the streets of Liverpool, Bethnal Green or Birmingham; much rather Tunbridge Wells, Knightsbridge and Eton.)

As these musings flew through my mind, Spike continued. 'First off, we're not all guys. Some of the best are our sisters.'

I had a vision of a community of interbreeding rednecks. Incest – a game for all the family, as the TV advert used to say.

'We're not a formal group, but some of us meet up at the pub on a Friday night. We commune on the message boards and stay close and share common interests.'

I was having enough trouble with a supposedly normal conversation, and I knew I had to stop him before he got into technojargon. 'What are the chances then, Spike?' I asked.

He thought for a moment, or at least he looked as though he was thinking. 'If those Serbs were sloppy when they set it all up, we might be able to do a lot more than you want. So when do we start?'

'We need to coordinate everything so it becomes a bit of a tsunami of problems for them. Can you tell me when you've got everything lined up and then we can go all together? And you'd better let me know if there're any costs.'

'Will do and don't worry about the money – we'll sort that but have you thought about how you'll cover your tracks, if at all? Sounds to me from what you've said they might just link everything back to your bird. D'you really want them aiming their wrath at both of you again?'

'Shit – I hadn't really considered that. What can we do?'

Spike sat and looked at me pointedly. 'You're supposed to be the brains.'

'But this isn't my specialist subject. Come on. Give me some ideas.'

'Well I suppose we could do a bit more good and go for some other foreign shits as well… so it wouldn't look so obvious they're the real target. And we could tell them who we are.'

'I thought we were talking about how we wouldn't be caught?'

'But if we make up some fancy activist name, we could confuse them.'

This was getting interesting and Spike was opening up all sorts of new ideas and avenues for me. I could start to see some real benefits and opportunities.

'Do you mean like the Collective for Ethical Prostitution?'

'Yeah, but surely we can make it a bit more catchy?'

'Okay. Let me think about that and I'll give you a call this evening with some ideas. Is that okay?'

'Sure, Tommy. And thanks for the coffee,' and with that, he stood up and we parted.

Spike didn't have too many social skills. I'd faced that before. I bet he played computer games and got his kicks that way, being Garth the Great Impaler on some interactive sex site. These guys much prefer their computers to people. Well to be truthful, it's a whole generation who prefer technology and the anonymity and cover it provides. I suppose it's just a continuation of the boffin syndrome – that mad professor with white hair flying who's in love with his science. The modern computer allows us all to be boffins and we all have our own science which panders to the need for 'instant gratification'. Instant gratification. That's a horrible phrase, probably conjured up by the tabloid press to explain away a thousand social ailments. Has the need ever been any different? Mr Neanderthal Man would have liked it just as much as the young do today; and if his son had found the place where bison queued up to be slaughtered so he didn't have to go on a week-long trek for the family dinner, would he have complained about instant gratification?

Instant gratification (in my thoughts I had already adopted the abbreviation IG) and real sex wouldn't be much fun though. Imagine if all Garth the Great Impaler had to do was touch someone for them to have an orgasm. That would be as instant as it could be, and if the skill was commonly shared there would be a lot of orgasms. In the mornings, the tube would be awful with everyone having IG orgasms. Women would be too tired to work and men would be in the bar bragging. I can hear the conversations in Starbucks as Jane collects my morning coffee: *'The District Line was terrible today. A woman coming from Ealing had so many orgasms she collapsed on the train. She really should travel off-peak if she can't cope.'* What a delight it would be for all the frotteurists of the world. Now that really would be instant gratification.

I made my way back to Scunt on the underground, taking care to avoid touching anyone. I didn't want to hear any shouts of 'IG!'. As I looked around the carriage, my thoughts briefly turned to my daily commute from Faversham. For me, that seemed part of a distant past and I felt sad as I saw a faraway look on all the faces. Was it a sadness for me or for them? They all carried that worn look of boredom and resignation to the fates ahead of them. In these circumstances maybe a bit of IG and the comfort of a mass orgasm wouldn't be so bad. Commuting is the equivalent of one of Jenny's headaches, which no amount of aspirin or paracetamol can remove.

'Hi, Scunt. You at home?' I shouted as I came back, but then I saw her sitting at the table and the computer in front of her. As I looked over her shoulder I saw the London Elite site. There were pictures of twenty or thirty girls, all in exotic (or was it erotic?) poses and all with posh names.

'Are you still on there?'

'No.'

I stood behind her and leaned forward and our cheeks were almost touching as we looked at the screen while names such as Jade, Krystal and Mercedes flashed by.

'Close it down, Scunt,' I said.

'Yes. That's exactly what we're going to do.'

I explained to Scunt what had happened in my meeting with Spike and how the first task was to think of a name for our initiative. 'We need a catchy name that sounds as though it could be a real organisation. Get some paper and we'll write down all the possibilities.'

We wrote down lots of words and shuffled them around. I thought it was going to be easy but I had underestimated the task. Was this an omen for what was to come, that this first task was so hard? But we persevered and came up with a couple of options, none of which was particularly inspiring, but they were the best we could do. Finally we came up with: Our Bodies – Our Choice. It wasn't a great acronym but it said what we wanted, and truly it wasn't important. It didn't matter. The life of this new activist group was going to be short and of course it wasn't real. I phoned Spike and told him our decision. His lack of comment told me he wasn't too impressed and I told him if he could think of anything better, then he could spend hours working on it. I also said I thought he had better things to do.

'Any progress on your side?' I asked.

'Quite a lot. It's going to be easy. I can get into their system no problem. The people who did the re-work for Margie left all the old passwords in place. That wasn't very clever but it's saved me a lot of time. I can get into their code and I think I can cause some real mayhem.' The enthusiasm in his voice told me that he was enjoying this task. 'And I've started to round up some of the Community. Once they understand what's at stake and why it's important, it'll be no problem getting support. We'll be ready in a couple of days.'

'What else do you need?'

'Well you could ask Margie the names of any other sites that have been taken over the same way. I mean where the girls have acquired a new "boss". We might as well make sure we go for all the bad boys.'

'Got that. I'll try and let you know tomorrow. That's it?'

'Yep, that's it,' and he cut the phone off quickly, just as I expected.

'Is everything sorted with Spike, Tommy?' Scunt asked. 'Is there anything else we need to do?'

'You could phone Margie and see if she can get the

names of other sites that were hit like hers. We want to spread the confusion.'

'I'll do it now.' Scunt reached across me and grabbed the phone, called Margie, updated her on Spike's progress and elicited a promise of a list by lunchtime the following day.

'Well that's it. There's nothing more to do tonight.'

Scunt looked at me. 'There's always one thing more we can do – every night.'

Chapter XVIII

The next morning Margie delivered on her promise and the details were quickly passed on to Spike. I made some calls and got the information I needed. We were nearly ready and were only waiting for the go-ahead from Spike. I went through my check list with Scunt and she agreed.

'That's the direct attack on their business but I don't know how you're going to get your personal revenge, Scunt. I've thought about lots of different ways and they're all so dangerous. If you're wanting one-to-one revenge, it means you'll have to get one-on-one close to him and probably as soon as he sees you he'll want to shoot you. I haven't worked out how to do it. I'm sorry. I don't think it can be done. You'll have to drop the idea.'

'I know you, Tommy. You'll get ideas. Tell me what you've thought of and let's see if we can decide on something together that'll work. And I'll decide what's dangerous and what isn't.'

I went through all the ideas I'd come up with and Scunt agreed that most were totally impracticable. She laughed at the idea of a kidnapping. 'Even if we did catch him, what the frig would we do with him? Who would want him back?'

She admitted she would gain enormous satisfaction from doing a 'Lorena Bobbitt' on him, but where would she throw his cock after she had cut it off? It took me ten minutes or more to get her back on track outlining my next idea.

'I could do that,' she said.

'Don't be silly. He knows you and it's far too dangerous and we couldn't send anyone else in to do that.'

Scunt sat looking at me taking it all in. I could see that she was weighing up the chances.

'Don't think about it, Scunt. It can't work.'

Still she sat quiet. Then: 'Tommy. I am going to do it. I can make it work.' I tried to interrupt but she stopped me by placing a finger on my lips. 'Tommy. I'm going to do it. Now work out how to make it as safe as possible. It needs to happen before Spike goes to work. Don't argue with me. Just make it safe.'

I wasn't sure I could make the plan safe at all, and there was one obvious drawback. 'Scunt, he will recognise you from the off and then he really will rain down his wrath on us.'

'I don't think he will,' she replied. 'I'm good at disguises. Honestly, really I am. I can make myself look totally different.' She clearly saw my sceptical look. 'Tommy, we will be safe. I know you'll work it all out. I just need to hold on to my courage.'

It was clear I wasn't going to make her change her mind. She stood resolute. 'Okay then. If you're determined, then maybe we need to act tonight. We don't have much time. Spike is straining at his leash, wanting to go. I'll stay here and write the email but first you need to go and buy a new disposable SIM card. Do you have an old phone we can use?'

Scunt nodded. 'I've got an old Nokia. I'll make sure it's charged.'

'And then,' I said, 'we need a car. Can you hire one or borrow one?'

Again she nodded.

'Good, and then you need to go to the chemist and get all the things on the list. Can you do all that?'

I was about to add that I thought the list was complete when the phone rang. It was Spike. They were ready and just needed the precise words from me; they could start tomorrow. The tension was rising. We were at last feeling on the front foot – taking control. Our spirits, although never really low, were suddenly lifted. Scunt raced off to get her coat, kissed me and skipped out of the door while I set to work on the computer.

Neither of the two pieces I had to write were easy. I started with the one for Spike. George Bernard Shaw's quote came to mind: 'I'm sorry this letter is so long – I didn't have time to make it shorter'. But I had to find the time. It had to be just right. I reworked the words. My first version was far too long and would never be read. The second version was too sanctimonious. The third, too legalistic. I was spiralling in on the right words, though, and finally I had all I wanted to say down in seventy-five words. I thought about waiting to show the email to Scunt but decided that speed was of the essence, so I phoned Spike and read the words to him.

'Perfect,' he said 'and I've had someone draw a simple logo. It all looks real and genuine.'

'You can kick off tomorrow morning. Everything's ready here.'

'Good. Thanks,' and the phone went dead.

The next bit of writing was just as difficult but didn't demand the same degree of exactitude. It took very little time. A photograph. I'd forgotten to ask Scunt if she had a camera, but with everything else in the flat I was sure she must have. I finished my tasks and started to make some coffee, and I wondered how Scunt was doing. I didn't have to wait long before she bounced back into the flat.

'Tommy, I'm back. How did you get on?' and I told her

that I'd sent the words to Spike. I showed the email to her. She read it and smiled.

'Fantastic. I like it.'

I showed her the other email and that also got a nod of approval. 'And did you get everything we need?' I asked.

'Yep.'

'Oh, have you got a camera and a cable to attach it to the computer? I forgot to ask before.'

'Of course I do. Are we going to do the pictures now? I suppose we'll have to if we're going to send the email.'

'Do you know how you're going to look? I mean you said you were going in disguise. Maybe you should get ready while I make the tea.'

'Uh-huh. This is exciting, isn't it. I'm so excited Tommy.'

'Scunt, don't get too carried away. This is dangerous. Please be careful.'

'Don't worry, Tommy. It will be alright. I'll be back in a minute. You just make the coffee.'

I made the coffee. I drank the coffee. I knew she would be more than a minute. Women can't do anything in a minute.

'Close your eyes, Tommy.' She was playing the game again and as ever I was happy to indulge her.

'And … open!'

It wasn't Scunt in front of me. The first and clear difference was the curly blonde Marilyn Monroe wig. That alone would have made her unrecognisable. Her makeup was distinctively different, with heavy mascara around her eyes and a big Slavic red-lipsticked mouth. Her clothes were also dramatic. She wobbled on ultra-high shoes, black with a silver stiletto heel, and wore a black basque that pushed her breasts together and made them seem larger, showing just a hint of nipple, black fishnet stockings, and a small, tight red satin thong that hardly provided any modesty. Her whole image had changed and was even sluttier than I had thought possible. It didn't quite match the effect we were after, but it would do. Whatever – it turned me on. Scunt saw the look in my eyes.

'That's for later. This is just for the photograph.'

'Damn. I'd totally forgotten. Let's get going.'

'Can I have my coffee first?' she reminded me. I handed her the cup and had to sit opposite her while she drank it. My new underwear was under massive strain again.

We chose a plain wall as a backdrop, although it didn't really matter. These were not meant to be professional photos, which was good because neither of us knew anything about how to take good photographs. There was a lot of natural light in the room, but we switched on every light that we could. Scunt stood in front of the wall and started posing. First I photographed her leaning forward so I could shoot straight down her cleavage; then standing spread-eagled against the wall; she lay on the sofa next, then sat on a chair with her legs wide apart. We did a Christine Keeler shot using a kitchen chair. She pouted, simmered, laughed and frowned, while all the time I snapped away. Thank God for digital cameras because by the end we had over a hundred shots and throughout it all, between the pouts, she laughed and giggled. The importance of our task was masked by the fun we were having – or was the laughter hiding our fear?

'Okay that's enough. We only need two or three. You can change now while I load these on to the computer. Where's the cable?'

We linked the camera and the computer and Scunt sat

next to me. 'Are you going to change? You're very distracting.'

'No I'm not. I want to see myself.'

Slowly all the photographs appeared. They came to over one megabyte and transferring a hundred or so was taking some time.

'Are you still sure about this, Scunt? There's still plenty of time to back out.'

'I'm sure.'

We ran the photographs on a slide show. To be honest, most were very ordinary because of my appalling skills. With practise and a few lessons I reckoned I might get quite good. A few of them were spot on. Luckily it was the model who made them, and not me. Scunt was very photogenic. We had to choose just three or four, so we made a shortlist of no more than fifteen and it was then just a question of managing Scunt's ego. Any of the fifteen would have sufficed but, being a woman, she saw flaws that no man would see because he would be concentrating on trying to find a glimpse of a nipple or a line or shadow on the thong hinting at hidden delights. Finally we got there and the decision was made.

'Is the phone charged? You need to put the new SIM card in it.' We knew that if that phone rang later it would be the chief bully, the Serbian boss, making an appointment to meet up. The tension was palpable. I checked the email address of London Elite and I prepared the email.

'Fuck!'

'What's wrong, Tommy?'

'We can't send the email from your normal address. We need an alias. We don't want them emailing back here.'

'We can just create a new email address in Hotmail,

can't we?'

'Of course we can. What name do you want?'

That should have been the easy part, but it took another twenty minutes. From the prosaic to crude and at last exotic, names were bandied about. We finally settled on August Bloom. Where it came from I don't know, but it made us both laugh. I went to Hotmail and finally created the email address. We couldn't have the simple form but august-bloom@hotmail.com was available so we took it and were taken straight into the mail system. I copied in the text and added the new phone number.

Hi, I was talking to a friend and she told me you ran the London Elite service. I work at a massage parlour now but I urgently need more money. Could I work for you? Please? I'm very sexy and I've sent you some photographs of me. I could come and show you how good I am if I could work for you. I need the money urgently. I'm twenty-six. Could I come and see you today?

August xxxxx

We attached the photographs.

'There's no way back now, August. Are you sure you want to do this?'

'I'm sure,' she said.

Of course it wasn't a final commitment; we could back out at the very last moment, but it did start the ball rolling downhill and it was likely to gain speed rapidly. We decided that if we didn't get an immediate response we would follow up with a phonecall in an hour. Scunt was still dressed in her basque and looking phenomenally sexy. She looked at me.

'What shall we do while we wait?' I could see the glint

in her eye.

'Not this time, Scunt. We need to concentrate. We can't be distracted. We mustn't miss any phone calls. So we just sat there, looking at the screen and the mobile phone next to it. We were like two fathers waiting for news of the birth of our newborn babies. Scunt hadn't changed and now looked incongruous dressed as she was. She switched on her iPod and chose Elgar's cello concerto in E minor. Even in extreme moments she managed to confuse me.

Although it seemed like forever, actually we didn't have to wait for long. There was a beep on the computer – a message to the August Bloom account. We looked at each other and then rushed to see what it said. 'Call me' and there was a mobile number. It's an odd thing about planning, but no matter how much you prepare for any outcome, you can still be surprised. I'm not sure what we had expected; maybe mention of a time or place to meet, or something that at least showed more enthusiasm. This was so neutral that we both felt let down.

'Guess it means you have to phone him,' I said. 'Are you up for that?'

'Tommy, this is nothing compared to what we've planned, so of course I can do it. Give me the phone.'

I took a deep breath. 'Rehearse what you're going to say first.'

I was still unsure that what we were doing was right, but I handed over the phone and watched as she dialled the number. Scunt closed her eyes. The phone was ringing.

'Hey, this is August. You asked me to call you. I really need this work. I've got no money at all.' She talked quickly, saying all that we had agreed and clearly not giving him the chance to say anything. Was she pushing too hard? I didn't even register the innuendo in my own words. With both hands, I gestured her to slow down and she nodded. He was talking now.

'Please. This is important,' Scunt said. 'I can come and show you how good I am if that would help?'

This was the sales line. This was the close, but would he take it? Would he buy?

'Oh, that's wonderful. I'm so pleased. Should I come tonight? I want to get started straight away.'

Scunt pointed at a pad of paper and a pen on the table which I pushed in front of her. She started to write.

'Okay, I've got that. Wonderful. Ten o'clock tonight. Thank you. Thank you very much.'

She was gushing and sycophantic in the extreme and I wondered if she had gone too far, but at least it seemed she had closed the deal. At last the plan was properly in action now. Scunt couldn't contain her enthusiasm and danced around the room, jumping, skipping and shouting for joy. I was looking at the address she'd written down. It was in Finchley, again North London.

'What are you doing, Tommy?' she said as she began to calm down.

'I want to know where you're going. I want to see the area first, before I let you go.'

'How are you going to do that?'

I opened the computer and searched for Google Street. We found the image of the road with its row of large suburban houses. I could manage that.

'What car have you got?' I'd forgotten about this essential part of the plan.

'I borrowed it from a friend. It's a VW something.'

'Where is it?'

'Just round the corner.'

'Okay. We have to leave about eight. I want to know the area well. Now let's go over the plan again.'

And that's what we did. Then Scunt changed into a silk robe and, from the occasional glance, I saw she was naked underneath and I could see that slowly – like an actress – she was getting into her role. If things went badly she would end up having sex with her nemesis and she would become exactly the sort of person she was fighting for. If his minders were there, on guard, then she couldn't go through with it. She knew it, and I knew it, and neither of us were particularly happy with that possible outcome.

Just after six, she went to have a bath. I heard the water running and then the stillness as she lay there. I thought about going in to talk to her but there was nothing I could say. She needed her own space and I sat in the lounge, moving on from the cello concerto to sea songs. My God, I thought, what have I got myself into? Less than a week ago I was a just another commuter travelling into London, ready to go to a boring dinner after work. How would this week rank in my life of adventures? Somewhere near the top, I thought, but was it just an adventure, a passing moment to tell others about over dinner one day? Or was it a life-changing episode? I suppose I wouldn't know until it was all over.

I turned to the immediate, which was now *also* the important. Was there anything we'd forgotten? I wrote a checklist of everything we had to take. We couldn't afford to forget anything. Then, just before eight, Scunt reappeared. She was dressed just as she had been for the photographs. She looked composed and calm. She had her bag with her and we checked each item in it. Everything was in order.

'Okay. Ready?' I asked.

'I've never been more ready.'

'Better get a coat on. You can't sit in the car like that, let alone walk down the street. Have you got the *A to Z*? Bag all ready?'

'Calm down, Tommy. We've been through the list. We have everything.'

She was in a better state than me. I was sweating. I suppose it's easier when you're in the fight rather than watching it, but I felt very protective towards her, and I was frightened for her.

Any other day I would not just be excited, but almost rampant, as I walked down the street with a beautiful young girl wearing a raincoat tied with a belt, and wearing next to nothing underneath. Instead I was apprehensive. We found the car and Scunt began giving me directions.

'You smell good, Scunt. What is it?'

'*J'adore*. Turn right here.'

'*J'adore*? Appropriate choice,' I said, although I didn't quite know what I meant.

We were in Finchley by nine and we drove around for a while. I wanted to know the area and I wanted to know how to get away from it quickly. I had a passing vision of *Bullit* and Steve McQueen and probably the most famous car chase in the history of cinema. I saw myself weaving in and out of traffic, leaving a trail of disaster behind us as we sped away from the Serbian. Jason Bourne had also had many car chases I could emulate, but I didn't want to resurrect any of those fantasies; I wanted a calm and peaceful evening that finished with Scunt being successful and safe. But we needed to know where we were, and the reconnaissance only took half an hour. Ten o'clock was still thirty minutes away, so we sat in the car, further along the road from her rendezvous, in silence.

'I can't stand this. Come on, Tommy. There's nothing wrong with being half an hour early. Let's go.'

I couldn't disagree with her. The tension could be cut with a proverbial knife.

'You're clear about the plan?'

'Yes, I'm clear about the plan. Don't worry.'

'I'll be outside and I'll stay all night if I have to. I'll be here for you.'

'I know you will, Tommy. Now drive.'

We drove slowly down the road and pulled up one house away from the rendezvous. I wanted Scunt to know where I was and I wanted to be close, but not seen.

'Ready?'

'Yes, ready,' she said.

'Good luck,' I said and she leaned across and kissed my cheek.

'I don't need luck, I need courage,' and she sat still for a moment, took a deep breath, opened the door and got out.

I watched fearfully as she walked through the simple metal gate. The path ran alongside a short driveway, through a reasonably well-kept garden and up to the door of a detached house much like all the others on the road. It must have had four or five bedrooms. It must have cost more than I could afford. Clearly the new-found work paid well. I couldn't imagine that he had bought it – it seemed far too suburban. Maybe he was renting it? Maybe it was a trap? Suddenly I was really worried for Scunt. What had I done?

As I sat in the car I realised that our checklist had been incomplete. I had brought nothing to drink or eat and I might be there for hours and couldn't leave. How would it all play out? If things went to plan, I'd only be there for an hour or

so but it could be a lot longer. I didn't know if I should lock
the doors. If Scunt was in a hurry as she got away, I should
leave them unlocked but then again, if the thugs were
looking for an accomplice of hers, it would be better to have
them locked. Bloody hell. So many decisions, but none of
mine were as bad as those facing Scunt. I looked at my
watch. Just fifteen minutes had passed and I was feeling
cold, but I couldn't start the engine to drive the heater. It
would draw attention to me. I could do nothing but sit there.
I looked up and down road; it was all quiet. I had almost
fallen asleep when the door opened and Scunt appeared from
nowhere and dived into the car.

'Drive!' she shouted at me.

I fumbled with the keys as I started the car. There was
no Jason Bourne initial wheel spin or burning rubber, but our
departure was quick. I looked in the mirror. No one was
following us or chasing us. I tried to look across at Scunt as
we moved away, but could only take quick infrequent
glances as I concentrated on the road. Even so, I could see
by the smile on her face that she had not been harmed. Could
I also read success? She threw her bag and blonde wig on the
back seat. I looked at the clock on the dashboard. She had
been in with him for ninety minutes. As I kicked the car
through the gears I managed a little wheel spin which made
Scunt yelp with delight.

'Wow! That couldn't have gone better. We friggin' did
it, Tommy! I friggin' got him. It all went friggin' perfectly.
You're so clever. It was wonderful. I so love you. Thank
you.'

Scunt was on such a euphoric high there was no way
she could talk in anything other than expletives. I wanted
detail. I wanted to know exactly what happened, but first,

more than any of that, I wanted directions.

'Which way do I turn?'

'Anyway you want, Tommy. I really don't give a fuck.'

The adrenalin was wearing off and Scunt closed her eyes, tiredness took over and soon she was asleep and I was left to myself to find the way home. I stopped only a few times to consult the *A to Z* as I made my way back to Stoke Newington. I was totally frustrated by that point. I wanted to know how it had panned out but clearly that would have to wait until we were at home again.

'Wake up, Scunt, we're home. Come on let's get you indoors.'

She stirred and managed to get her shoes back on, but not her coat. We walked back to the flat with me properly dressed and her in her basque and fishnets, arms interlocked and her head on my shoulders. On the pavement we passed a few people heading to their own homes and they all turned to look at the beautiful half-naked woman on my arm. Whatever their thoughts, none would have any idea of the real storm we had just started.

Chapter XIX

'You'd better wash your hands again before you touch me,' I said and Scunt smiled and went for the third shower since we'd been back. This time, I followed her into the bathroom with a couple of gins.

'Thanks. I need this.' She had finished showering and was drying herself. Her makeup had gone and she was back to her normal, natural beautiful self.

'So what happened? Okay to talk now?'

She sipped at the gin as she sat on the side of the bath. I pulled the lid of the toilet down and sat there.

'The first bit was easy. I knocked at the door and he answered and I told him I was August and I said all the things I had said on the call and he took me into a front room.'

'Did you still have your coat on?' I asked.

'Yes. I sat on the sofa still wearing my coat and he told me all about London Elite and how it worked. It was all about fees and the cut he would take for the marketing. He said I would need better pictures and he would arrange that and take the cost out of the first money I earned. It was all *blah blah* and I was hardly listening, but then he came to the point and said of course all this meant nothing unless I was any good at my job.'

'Ah, the casting-couch line. What's he like? Describe him.'

'Tall. Overweight. Bit of a grease ball. And I couldn't understand him all the time. He has such a thick accent. Anyway I asked him what he meant by "If I was any good at my job" and he said was I good at making men happy? Was

I good at sex? It was then that I stood up and took my coat off. He tried hard to look disinterested but I knew he wasn't.'

'Was he by himself in the house?'

'Yes. He told me that later, but you're jumping ahead of the story, Tommy. Slow down. You want to hear it all, don't you?'

'I do. So how did you feel?'

'Friggin' scared! I still didn't know how it would all pan out but I kept myself together. I figured I would look a little scared being there if I was legitimate, but I was a bit worried he would recognise me. I kept saying to myself: It's alright – don't be scared. Well I stood up and he got excited and I said "Do you think this will make men happy?" Then he asked me what sorts of things I do, like sixty-nines and anal.'

'You don't need to go through the list, Scunt. I think I know it.'

Scunt smiled. 'I'm sure you do, Tommy. Sorry. But it got interesting when he asked if I could do mistress stuff. He said there was a lot of money to be made by a dominant. So I said I could mistress, but no submissive stuff because I thought it was too dangerous, and he just nodded. Then he said he wanted to test me, to see if I was as good as I said I was. I knew what he meant, so I thought I would test him and asked if he would pay me, but he only laughed. Then I said I wasn't sure because I needed the money badly. So he said if I passed the test I could be working within a few days after the new photographs were taken. So I feigned reluctance and said okay.'

'You did really well. I suppose the mistress stuff was a bit of a bonus?'

'Tommy… Let me tell the story. You're so impatient.'

She was right. I was impatient, but more importantly I was relieved that she was alright.

'Anyway … so I had said okay and then I asked him if we were alone because I don't do groups. Again he laughed and said he would convince me another day for parties and groups but he was alone right then. I wanted to know if his minders were going to come back soon, so I asked if he lived by himself because it was such a big house.'

'And?'

'All by himself, he said. He said that sometimes friends stayed over but we were definitely by ourselves then. I was still worried that the minders would come back but I had to take the risk.'

Scunt stopped only to take a deep gulp from her glass. Please don't finish it, I thought. I don't want to have to break the flow to top it up. She rattled the ice around, pulled up her towel and continued talking.

'I asked where we would go and he took me to a bedroom. I said I would give him a proper massage first because I was very good at that and he smiled and said yes because he'd had a busy day. I did as you said and I took my coat with me. I told him to undress and lie on his front and I started on the massage.'

'Were you undressed as well?'

'No. He asked me to get undressed and I said he couldn't see me lying on his front and I would do a striptease for him when he turned over. Anyway I used the massage oils and did his legs first – as you said. I knew he wanted more. I took the rope out of my bag, just as we agreed, and dangled it in front of him. I asked if he wanted to see how good I was at mistress stuff. He was pretty eager so I told him I would tie his hands behind his back, massage him some more, then do a striptease for him and after that he would feel how good I was at sex. He liked that idea. So I tied him up and ordered him to turn over and lie on his back. He was certainly well endowed, Tommy. Actually he was huge.'

'I don't think I need to know that. So what happened next?'

'Well, I started massaging the front of his legs with the oil and then I said I needed to get some more oil. I don't think he heard. His eyes were closed and he was expecting something special. I looked at him at that moment and thought of all the damage he had done and I nearly changed the plan.'

'How?' I was worried enough at the risks she was taking. 'But you didn't, did you?'

'No, but for a moment the anger built up and I was close to doing a Bobbitt – or worse – but I took a deep breath and remembered all you had said. I stayed calm Tommy, you made me calm. You are so wonderful.'

I didn't need compliments at that moment; I wanted to hear the story and know the outcome. 'Well done, Scunt, and so what happened next?'

'Okay, Tommy, so I did as you said and got everything packed back into my bag, checked for my coat and took out the Deep Heat ointment. By the way, I've just tried some. It really does work. My leg warmed up and got really hot. Do athletes really use it before they run?'

'Absolutely. And it's a normal ritual in rugby – they all use muscle ointments. They warm up their muscles beautifully before a game. It's the classic smell of changing rooms… but take me back to the story.'

'So, I squeezed the tube and rubbed loads on my hands

and then I rubbed it all over his cock. I only did it for a few seconds, then his eyes opened and I ran. I could hear him screaming already. It was wonderful. He wasn't tied very tightly, of course. I'm sure he'll have gotten out by now. Tell me again, Tommy, what it feels like? How painful it is.'

'It's totally excruciating! When I did it by accident at the rugby club, it was a tiny amount. I tried to wash it off, but the pain didn't go for ages. He'll still be in pain and he won't be liking you very much. Is that enough revenge for you?'

'Oh, yes. It felt wonderful. Thank you so, so much. I really do love you.' She gave me a big hug.

'You've really washed your hands properly? I don't want to suffer like he did.'

'My hands are clean,' she said, holding them up as if to prove it.

'Are they as clean as your conscience?'

She smiled again.

We woke late the next morning, still exhilarated after our adventure. We checked the August Bloom email account. There was only one message and it was totally abusive and didn't wish Scunt a happy day. There were probably equally rude messages on the phone but we didn't bother to recover them. Then we went to check the London Elite web site. As it opened, a 'pop-up' appeared. It was headed:

Our Bodies – Our Choice.

The right to work as an escort or model is the right of a woman and it's not the right of a man to control her, to tell her when to work, or to take any money she receives for working. This company is controlled by pimps and the women are working under duress. We ask you to boycott this site and company and find a truly independent escort, which will be a better experience for both you and the escort.

It was simple and brilliant. No matter how we tried, we couldn't get onto the site without the pop-up popping up. I tried the phone number and email address of London Elite given on the website and neither worked. To all effect, the business was finished. Scunt had one more call to make. I dialled the number and waited for someone to answer.

'Morning. Is that the *Evening Standard*? Could I speak to the features editor?' and I handed the phone to Scunt. We had rehearsed her script for some time.

'Hi. My name is August Bloom and I'm the spokeswoman for OBOC. You may not have heard of us but it stands for Our bodies–Our Choice. I want you to look at a certain business website and then you'll understand what we're about. This is just one of many companies that needs to be researched by you. If you want to find one of the bullies involved, I can give you an address and a phone number.'

The person on the other end of the phone talked for a while, then Scunt read out the url for the site, and gave the Serb's house address and phone number, plus the email address he used to reply to Scunt's email.

'Have you got all that? Good. No, sorry I'm not going to say any more. I'll phone you if I've got anything else to say,' and she ended the call.

I took the SIM card out and threw it in the bin. It had done its job. Then I phoned Spike and told him I thought he'd done a brilliant job with the pop-up. He told me it was appearing on almost a dozen other sites already. I phoned

Margie and told her she could start to contact the girls in a couple of days and see if they wanted to transfer to a well-run agency which was shared by all those who worked there. And at last we could relax. Scunt had got her personal revenge on the Serbian bully and he now had to fight a financial attack on his business. With any luck, the *Evening Standard* would pick up the story, and maybe it would even lead to a police case.

I thought we'd done a great job but I didn't feel as fulfilled as Scunt. Her life was moving ahead, whereas for me this chapter was closing; I could see myself slowly slipping out of her life and back to where I was a week ago. Well ... maybe not even slowly. It might happen quite quickly and that made me sad.

We went out for lunch. It was a mock French bistro café. To celebrate its French-ness we ordered *croque monsieur*, but the Indian chef had never been over the Channel. The closest he'd probably ever been to France was on the flight in from Mumbai. The food was not very tasty. The coffee, however, was high on caffeine and that was good – not that we needed too much of a kick as the adrenalin was still running high. Scunt couldn't stop talking about her encounter and kept reliving every moment.

All it did was make me more depressed. I had done nothing. I had just sat in the car and fallen asleep while she took all the risks. Spike had broken a thousand laws and wrecked some websites, some businesses and hopefully some villainous lives. It made me think that the frustrations of a Field Marshall must be immense; their roles are dusty and arcane, involving long nights of planning, assessing risks and contingencies, without getting into the actual battle or sharing moments of heroism. Definitely not as satisfying as being in a battle – but much, much safer. It was Friday. The end of a week, and I needed time to regroup. I needed some space to get a grip on what had happened and what was going to happen.

'Scunt, I need to go home now.'

The shock was as great for her as it was for me. The words just spilt out; they were not rehearsed. Scunt hadn't expected them and she spluttered on her *croque monsieur*. Some melted Emmental (or was it Gruyère) fell onto the table.

'Why? You don't have to leave. We're having so much fun.'

I didn't want to disappoint her and I didn't want to say that I had to leave precisely because we were having so much fun. Something told me that without a cause the fun might not be so great, and we would have to face some of the realities of our relationship. I found a mundane excuse.

'I'll be back, but at least I need some more clothes. I've been rotating these for nearly a week now. There are only so many times I can wear my underwear inside out and back to front!' That was another benefit of the new kit she had bought me; back to front Y-fronts just wouldn't have worked. 'I'll go home for the weekend and call you and we can plan next week. Also, I do need to go to work as well.'

I thought she understood, but you can never tell with women. It was a holiday romance and holiday romances always finish. Maybe she was just putting on a show for me. After all I had done for her maybe she felt it was inappropriate to agree and tell me simply to fuck off. She sulked through the rest of lunch. When we were back at the flat, she sat and watched as I put all my dirty clothes into one of the suitcases.

Reluctantly she phoned for a minicab. She stood next to me on the pavement until it arrived. I put my case in the boot and opened the rear door. I didn't know what to say or do. Shake hands and leave with a stiff upper lip? Or get emotional? Scunt made the decision for us. She threw herself at me, wrapped her arms around my neck, kissed me and sobbed into my shoulders. It was a mirror of our first meeting.

'I love you, Tommy. Go now. Just go, but make sure you come back,' and she pushed me into the taxi. I turned as we pulled away and I saw her standing, waving with both hands while occasionally pushing away tears. I felt like a real shit.

'Where to, guv?' was what I interpreted from the same turbaned man from a few days previously.

'London Bridge. British Rail, please.'

I paced the platform. The train to Faversham would arrive in twenty-two minutes. I put my case down and began walking concentric circles around it, each a bit wider than the last. I practised some silly walks, all the time leaning inwards as if there was a gravitational pull from the case. I liked the symmetry of the circles and the metaphor that the case, bought with Scunt, was exerting a pulling force on my body. I stopped when my circling took me so far away that my case might look like a piece of abandoned luggage. In these troubled times of terrorism, I assumed there was a platoon of SAS soldiers positioned at every train station, ready to pounce and explode such items. There might be a shout of 'Get down or take cover!' as a missile grenade was launched and hit its target, leaving my dirty underwear in shreds hanging from the station roof. I liked my new clothes and, dirty or not, they reminded me of my week with Scunt and I didn't want them in tatters, but worse they would probably ask me to pay for the grenade because it was a false alarm. I didn't know the cost of armaments, but the newspapers would have us believe they're very expensive because as a country we can't afford them.

Another thirteen minutes to wait. I sat on my case and tried to work out how far I'd walked. The circumference of a circle was an easy formula. My first circle had a radius of two yards. Let's call that six feet, so a single circle was thirty-six feet, but I got bored with all the other calculations involved in walking a spiral. I had pondered this problem many times while sitting on the toilet. For want of anything better to do, books all finished, I had often wondered if I could find the formula for the length of toilet paper that spiralled around the paper tube. I had never been successful in that. Now eleven minutes. Again I sat on the case. A plan was forming and I started to smile, then I laughed, much to the consternation of those around me.

Time began to pass more quickly. The train pulled in. It was early evening and the exodus from London had speeded up. I was on a commuter train. My case was too large for the rack so I plonked it down, right in the middle of the gap between the seats. I knew how much this would upset the regulars. Then I looked at my fellow commuters; glum, miserable, sad and bored. Next to me was a well-dressed woman trying to read a magazine. I was going to break all the rules.

'Is that interesting?' I asked her. Warily she looked up and then turned to me.

'Not really, but it makes the time pass,' and she returned to reading.

'And are you happy? When was the last time you were really happy?' I looked at our fellow commuters and I could see them smirk with that thank-God-I-didn't-sit-next-to-that-nutter look.

'Please,' I persevered. 'I'm conducting a survey about happiness. I just asked whether you're happy.'

All she did was bury her head deeper into her magazine. I tried to catch the eye of the others, but they all found other things to do. No one wanted to engage with me on this topic. Well, if they weren't going to engage with me there was no reason why I couldn't carry on talking to her.

'You see, I have just had an extraordinary week and I realised that going up and down to London on the train to do a worthless and stupid job is a waste of my life and it doesn't make me happy. Can there be any point in living if the purpose is just to be *alive*? We all deserve more than that. Have you heard of Roger McGough?'

That at least garnered a sort of response. A shake of the head, still buried deeper in the magazine.

'He's a poet. He was part of the Liverpool Scene from the sixties onwards. He has a wonderful satirical view of the world. He wrote a poem that starts: *Let me die a youngman's death, not a clean and inbetween-the-sheets holywater death, not a famous-last-words peaceful out of breath death...* You see? He got it long before I did. Life is about living and letting that child within us all live and have fun. That's the purpose of living.'

This was going nowhere. How could they understand properly? After all, they hadn't had their eyes opened in the ways I had. I stopped the conversation, or more accurately my monologue, and sat back and smiled. Various stations whizzed by while I sat with a Cheshire Cat grin on my face, all the way back to Faversham. The carriage thinned out and somewhere around Rochester a man – a middle-aged man (whatever that meant) – stood up to exit the train. He looked at me as he headed for the door.

'I don't know what you're taking, but I could do with some. I know exactly what you mean. Have a good weekend.'

'You too,' I answered as he stepped out and headed towards the platform exit.

It had taken him forty-seven minutes to pluck up enough courage to speak to me, and I found that very depressing. My mood was dented further at Faversham. I knew my car was in the car-park but I had forgotten I needed to pay for parking. The windscreen was covered in tickets threatening more and more drastic action if it wasn't moved. I looked at them, and my dirty car. Standing in the open air, a car gets dirty so quickly. I collected up all the tickets and threw them in the back. They could be dealt with later. I had plans to make now, and a lot to do over the weekend. As I drove home, I thought of Jenny. In the past, she would have said something along the lines of "Oh, you're home at last. I'll put the kettle on," and she would turn away and walk towards the kitchen. I thought of the nodding dog she had become, but quickly put all my negative thoughts aside. I concentrated instead on my happiness and the plan that was forming quite quickly. Two realistic and deliverable plans within a week! I couldn't understand the change in me.

At the New Year we all make resolutions; like losing weight or going to the gym. I did those nearly every year. Not to be distracted by the road, I tried to remember those days. I'd arrive at the gym on a Saturday morning, immediately intimidated by my lack of appropriate clothing.

I was always in an old rugby shirt and off-white, far-too-tight tennis shorts showing clearly the extra pounds added since last worn. I would be confronted by a row of running machines and it was always the same: the only free machine plonked me between an ultra-thin woman wearing skin hugging Lycra running at a pace that defied belief, and a man, always older than me, impeccably dressed, loping along with an unhurried stride.

Before setting the machine into action I would stretch as if I had been doing this for months – if not years – before putting my glasses on to read and understand the instructions. Once set, I would start off at a rate that embraced far more optimism than capability. Within a minute I would be sweating profusely, a minute later panting like a puppy locked in a car; soon after I'd have to slow down, and in less than five minutes I was done and stepping off and away from my resolutions, leaving lycra woman and lolloping man to their exertions.

Today everything was different. There was change in the air and I knew it was not a passing phase and all thoughts of what I would ever have to say to Jenny were long gone.

I seemed to spend the whole weekend in my study, writing out lists and doing calculations, with only the occasional respite of a walk, on my own, around the countryside. I didn't have one alcoholic drink, about which I was very proud. I thought of phoning Scunt, but I didn't know quite what to say so I resisted the temptation; not something I do easily.

Monday morning came and the alarm sounded at five thirty. For once, I was excited to be woken up so early. I had got everything I needed together the night before and after a hasty cup of coffee I set out in the car. This morning, though, instead of turning off towards the station, I carried on towards London, joining an ever-increasing flow of commuter cars. I had a route planned which I was sure would take forever at this time of day. I stopped at the Medway services to stock up for the journey. I still didn't have Scunt's carefree attitude to take-away food and dallied forever over the choices. Then I grabbed some fizzy drinks and a large coffee for the caffeine.

I looked at the car as I approached it. It was in a state, but I couldn't see a car wash anywhere. Then, suddenly, it no longer seemed to matter. I got back in the car and drove on into London through the ancient Blackwall tunnel and on to the A13, which was heaving with commuters. I went two hundred yards on the A11 before heading north on the Commercial Road. I was close to Stoke Newington. With this degree of proximity, my plan seemed less secure. What if Scunt had taken another lover and I was met by a lanky youth with only a towel around his midriff? Maybe he wouldn't even bother with that. Thoughts of the film *Notting Hill* and Rhys Ifans meeting Julia Roberts naked flashed into my brain. Wasn't he also called Spike? Now *he* looked much more like the Spike I had been expecting but it was too late to change my mind. I had come this close and I wasn't going to chicken out.

I parked close to where we had parked the VW thingy a few nights previously. Actually the VW thingy was still there. Trust Scunt; she'd forgotten to give it back. Walking the same route back to her flat I felt nostalgia – even though it had only been three days ago. Nostalgia isn't what it used to be, I mused. I climbed up the stairwell steps and rang the intercom. Would she answer? I waited. I rang again. I thought of turning back, because in the films the door is only answered as the hero leaves and starts to walk forlornly away. Then the heroine races out after him. But this wasn't a movie and there were no heroes and heroines. I looked at my watch. It wasn't too early. It was ten o'clock. Maybe Scunt and a Rhys Ifans type were having sex and wouldn't answer. Maybe they had been together all weekend and I had been discarded within a minute of leaving. I was angry. How dare she do that to me. I rang the bell a third time.

'Hello,' the voice sounded gruff, even deep and angry, but at least it was Scunt's.

I used my Sean Connery Scottish accent. 'Interflora. I have a delivery for you.' It sounded cute and clever when I had rehearsed it, but pathetic when executed. I didn't want her to know it was me until she saw me. No. That wasn't true. I wanted to see her reaction when she saw me. I wanted to see her shorn of time to adapt and mould the face. Now I had to continue.

'Can you open the door please? Is it Flat C?'

There was no answer but the door opened with a click. I knocked on the door of the flat.

'Hold on a minute,' came the voice. I knocked again. 'Can't you fucking well wait?'

This idea was getting worse by the minute. Scunt was not a happy bunny. I stood there shuffling while I heard her finally come to the door. Latches were unlatched and keys were turned and she opened the door. She was a real mess. Her hair was flattened and looked like it needed a wash. She was in the same tee-shirt she had been wearing when I left, but now it was stained with food. She had no makeup on and her eyes were puffed up and red.

'Tommy?' Her voice was strained and questioning.

'Yes, it's Tommy.' How pathetic could I be? I thought I

might soon find out. I'd expected to find the old Scunt, the Scunt I remembered, the positive and resourceful Scunt – not a washed-out, tired and deflated Scunt. I had to rethink my plan. I could go with the original and ignore what was in front of me, or I could start to show empathy and enquire after her well-being, and generally just be nice. I chose to stick to plan A. We were still standing in the doorway.

'When you said you loved me, was it real or just in the moment?' I asked, with little confidence in my voice.

'What sort of fucking question is that? Men are absolutely useless. Of course I friggin' well love you. Why do you think I've spent the whole weekend crying and waiting for at least a phone call? I thought you had gone! Tommy...' Her voice reached a crescendo and subsided. 'You really are so stupid, but so loveable. Come here,' and she pulled me inside and with her arms around me and I back-heeled the door shut. I wasn't able to ask another question as she gagged me with her lips in the longest kiss I had known. Finally I was released but Scunt had the first word.

'Why are you here, Tommy? Shouldn't you be in your office?'

'I needed to know how you really felt. I have the answer and, yes, I should be in my office. We need to talk. By the way you look a mess. Being unhappy doesn't suit you. Go and shower and get dressed and I'll make breakfast. We need to talk.'

I guessed she hadn't eaten for a while so I fried up a full English, with bacon, eggs, tomato and bread. I wished there had been black pudding and sausages – they make all the difference. I checked the cupboards. A good marmalade but no HP sauce. Things would have to change.

We sat quietly over breakfast. The way she devoured every mouthful, mopping up the egg yolk with the toast, I don't think she'd eaten much since I left. When she finished, I said: 'Scunt, we need to talk. There are things I need to know and you need to tell me. It's very important. Can we talk?' She looked perturbed as rightly she should; although it wasn't easy, I had tried to add an edge to my voice.

'Of course, Tommy. Let's go to the lounge.'

I deliberately sat on one of the chairs and not the sofa. I wanted to face her and I didn't want to be distracted by her leaning against me.

'What do you want to talk about?'

'Well, I sat at home over the weekend and had time, for the first time I might add, to take stock and look at the last week as a whole. In the middle of it, it was all a bit of a storm and you, of course, were very distracting. And Scunt, you know, the more I looked, there were all sorts of discrepancies.'

'I'm not sure I know what you mean. What *do* you mean, Tommy?'

'There were a few things. For instance, I never saw any heavies chasing us. I never saw this boss, but he undoubtedly exists because he sent us an email. Actually that's not true – *someone* sent you an email. I don't know if it was a Serbian bad man. I've checked the *Evening Standard* and there's nothing in there about it. A guy called Spike hacked into a website. It could have been all perfectly legitimate. The truth is, if I went to a court and was asked to prove any of this, I couldn't.'

I looked at Scunt and couldn't make out what she was thinking. Maybe a little anger? Or was it fear? She looked at me intently.

'You want a game of truth or dare, and the only option is the truth. Is it that important to you?' she said, recovering some of her defiance.

'Am I that important to you and your future happiness?' I answered.

'Yes, Tommy.'

'Then knowing the truth is that important to both of us.' I was not going to be distracted.

'So, Tommy, if I fill in the gaps of what you don't know, then you'll tell me the truth too?'

I looked at her fondly; the impudent, cheeky Scunt was back. Now I was heading again onto the back foot.

'Okay,' said Scunt. 'I agree to your request, Mr Tommy but there's one condition.'

'Which is?'

'I ask the first questions.'

Tactically I knew this was a very bad idea. I didn't know what she had planned, but knowing her, even after a week, I was now fully on the defensive. I might never get my answers, and I needed them. They were crucial to the next stage of my plan. We could argue over the point of who went first all morning. I knew in the end she would win. So I gave way quickly. I still had a lot to do this morning.

'Okay. You go first.'

She sat upright in her chair and composed herself. 'Let me find the right words. Okay, Tommy. When did Jenny leave you? Or is she dead?'

This was out of the blue. What did she know? But I had promised honesty, and honesty was what we would have.

'It was about five years ago. She walked out on me one weekend and she left me for a director in another bank who was going further and faster than me. What's worse, I knew him and I didn't see it coming. I doubt she ever sees him during the week – maybe even the weekends; he's known to be a workaholic, but she will see his money and she will spend it.' I closed my eyes. I really didn't want to be reminded of Jenny right now. 'How did you know? Have you had a private detective check me out, or was I a mark for you at the very beginning? Oh, please, Scunt, tell me you didn't.'

'Stay calm. It was none of that, Tommy. It was woman's intuition. We know a married man. We know when a man is cheating, and when a man is just lonely. You had no sense of guilt when we had sex. A woman knows when a man is cheating and, Tommy, you were one of the loneliest men I've ever met. You're so sweet, so vulnerable. I just couldn't let you go.'

'Why did you let me carry on with the pretence? I mean, you could have confronted me anytime and I would have told you.'

'No, you wouldn't, Tommy. Jenny was a good barrier for you. You could always fall back on the "wife" excuse if you got cold feet or scared. But you never did.'

'So was that just a good guess just now, or did you know for sure all the time?'

'Not all the time, but I was very sure after we left the hotel in Glasgow.'

'How?'

'You phoned Jenny from the hotel phone.'

'So?'

'There were no phone charges on the bill. I asked them to check and they confirmed you hadn't made a call. That was when I knew for sure. It was a one-sided conversation. There was nobody on the other end, was there Tommy?'

'No,' I must have looked as crest-fallen as I sounded. 'But it was only a lie by omission.'

'No, it wasn't, Tommy. It was a lie. You wanted me to believe you were married.'

I sat quietly. Plans fucked again. Well, no, maybe not yet. Maybe even enhanced. As I thought about it, I had to smile.

'Why are you smiling, Tommy? I thought this was a serious conversation.'

'It is a serious conversation… but I would bet I'm the first man who's ever tried to con you into thinking he's married when he isn't. I bet when most men chat up other women they do all they can to give the impression they're free and unattached. It just seems ironic. Now can I ask you my questions?'

'No, Tommy.'

'Oh, Scunt, you promised.'

'I'll tell you everything. It will be faster than if you ask questions, and then you can ask your questions at the end – to fill in the gaps. Is that okay?'

'It sounds a lot more civilised.'

Again Scunt took a moment. I guessed she was wondering where to start. 'You're right. It's not all a true story but I promise you, the core of it is. That Serbian bully did everything I said he did – and to a lot more women and girls than I probably know about and honestly the means did justify the end. Whatever you take away from this, you can be sure that you've done some real good in this world. He did real and heart-breaking damage to me and my family but I didn't shoot him.' For a moment she hesitated and looked around searching for the right words as if they were written on the ceiling or walls, 'and he never chased us.'

Scunt's head had dropped. Her chin was on her chest and her eyes closed in submission, and I hoped a big dollop of humility. If this was a film, the music would slow down now, as I took in her words and their impact. I had been misled and led on a wild-goose chase. What a stupid idiot I'd been. I wanted to be angry and shout, but I couldn't. I felt crest-fallen yet again, and sad. I started to interrupt and cleared my throat to speak, but Scunt stopped me.

"Let me tell my story first and then you can ask questions, or castigate me, or walk out.'

I nodded.

'I told you about Sharon, my sister?'

Again I nodded.

'Last week, when I met you in the pub, I had just come from a funeral. It was Sharon's. Both Mandy and Margie were there. Sharon worked as an escort – for London Elite. The story I told was Sharon's. It was Sharon who met Sarah and became a prostitute. We were always close and I knew what she did and I knew her friends. She wanted to stop and get out, but the boss sent his heavies in and they did a bit of "enforcing".'

Scunt reached for a tissue and dabbed at her tearful eyes and continued. 'Sharon became more and more desperate and she tried many more times to get out and give it all up, but each time she did, the enforcers came with bigger and worse threats, which finally included harming me. Sharon was going mad. She hardly ate anything. She drank, too, and finally, especially when she heard that I was at risk and in danger, she cracked, and after nearly nine months of all that crap she decided there was only one way out.'

There was a distressing silence. I didn't know what to say. Any thoughts I had of becoming angry wilted into the melancholy I saw in Scunt's eyes and at that moment all I could see was an image of Scunt, dressed in black, standing at a graveside. She had my total sympathy but then she grabbed my soul with total force.

'Just over two weeks ago she committed suicide. She took a whole load of tablets.'

I had to make her take a break there. The tears were starting. I reached out and held her hand. We sat in silence, next to each other, while my mind raced over all that had happened during the week, culminating in that moment when she faced the man who had driven her sister to the ultimate moment of surrender. At that moment I was so very proud of her. If it had been me, I thought ... but then that would never have happened. I would never have had the courage to go into his house, but had I been standing above him with all that power I would have done much more than cover his cock with penetrating heat cream. My anger would have grown so big I might have stuck a knife in his chest. But Scunt, my beautiful Scunt, had exerted more self-control than I could ever muster. My Scunt, my beautiful Scunt, my clever, resourceful Scunt. I pulled her closer and held her tighter.

'Oh, Tommy we were so close and I didn't know how bad things were,' she sobbed. 'She lay in her flat for nearly two days before anyone found her. Tommy, I had to do something. I couldn't just let her memory fade away.'

Both of us were crying now. 'I'm so sorry, Scunt. I didn't mean ... I mean I didn't know. Oh fuck, what have I started.'

'No Tommy. You're right. We need a clean slate.'

'Did you work for the Serbian as well? I mean, did he know you were sisters?'

'There's another story there I'm afraid. It was Sharon who had the hard times,' she stopped. 'Oh, that was one of your jokes, wasn't it?'

At least, even in the worst of times, humour has its place. I smiled. 'Actually that was better than most of mine.'

'I was never an escort or a model. Everything I told you about being an escort was Sharon's story. We were very close and I hated her doing the job, but she kept telling me it was safe. I feel so responsible for her death. I keep thinking I should have done more for her. But even now, I can't think what I could have done. I didn't have money to support her and she wouldn't take what little I had. You know, at first, she actually thought she had a glamorous job. Mandy was her friend first, and we all met when she came to London for a weekend break. I'm exactly as I said to Granny: I'm an interior designer and I'm getting reasonably good. Don't you agree?' she said, waving a hand around the room.

'Much better than reasonably good. But I did what you asked me not to – I interrupted you. Finish the story.'

'I had been to Sharon's funeral. There was me and some of her friends. Some I knew and some I didn't. Margie was one of those I knew, as well as Mandy, of course.'

'What about Q,' I asked. 'Was she there?'

'No, and I feel so guilty about that. I didn't have the courage to tell her when we visited. I can't tell her what happened. It will break her heart because I would have to tell her that she took her own life and then she would have to ask why. I didn't have the courage then and I still don't.'

'But don't you think that she would rather know than sending Christmas cards every year? You have to tell her,' I said. I thought that I was being heartless, but I knew this might be my only chance to make these points.

"You're right, as ever, Tommy.' Scunt was now having problem getting any words out. 'And Granny has guessed something's wrong. She asked me lots of questions while you were out. Mum was just too ill to be there. This has done her recovery no good. After the funeral, a few of us went for a drink but I couldn't stay with them. I went home and changed. I was going to drink, wander around a bit, and drink some more. I wanted to drink all the thoughts out of my system. I was distressed and I just stumbled into the pub where you were and I just sort of sat down in front of you. I didn't *choose* you, but then you started talking and you were so kind and nice, and I needed someone to hold me and take care of me, and you looked so lonely, as well. I thought you would hold me longer and more tightly than anyone else. Then you asked some questions and I just made it up as we went along – to be with you and then I started to think you were funny and you made me laugh and I wanted to be with you even more. And then …'

'And then?' I asked.

'And then I fell in love with you.'

'Scunt, you can't fall in love with someone in just a week.'

'If you have, then so can I.'

A hesitation. 'You think I've fallen in love with you?'

'I thought this chat was about honesty?'

'Okay, hold that thought for a moment. What about all the fuss in Glasgow and wanting to get out quickly? What was all that about?'

'I made it up. I'm sorry, but I wanted to keep it all exciting for you, so I could stay with you. It was a total coincidence when Granny said the same thing at her house. That really was just coincidence. You know sometimes some things just happen by chance. And then in Woodstock my funny Tommy became my brave Tommy and you had your plan. Everything from then on was just how we planned it.'

'When you went to his house that night I thought you were going as an experienced escort. That was the only reason I let you go. I thought you had experience and knew how to take care of yourself but it was your first time! You are brave, Scunt.'

'Don't worry, Tommy. I had Sharon on my mind.'

'That's a bit of an understatement,' I said. She was the *only* reason you were there. How you stopped at Deep Heat now amazes me. I am surprised you didn't do much worse damage.'

'She gave me strength and I did use an awful lot of that cream. I wanted him to feel excruciating pain. Anyway, his cock might have fallen off by now. Maybe it wasn't eye-for-an-eye revenge, but then there was you to consider too.'

'What do you mean there was me? What have I got to do with it?'

'Tommy, you really are dense. If there was no hope then I might have done more, but you gave me hope. I need to be here to look after you. I couldn't do more. You were the reason. I got the revenge I wanted.'

'I hope his cock has fallen off. I really hope so. So that's why you could be so sure he wouldn't recognise you. He never knew you at all. Now I understand, I think. Do I understand it all?'

'I think so. There will always be bits to fill in, but that's the main story. That's the gist of it all. So it's really with you now. Are you going to stay, or are you going to leave?'

'Scunt. I'm going to go. I'm going to leave you.' She looked horrified. 'But I'll be back at the latest by six tonight, by which time you'll have invited Margie, Spike and anyone else to free drinks and a party this evening. You choose where. I have to go into the city now but before I do, tell me one more time that you really love me.'

'If you tell me that you love me.'

'I love you, Scunt, with a passion that is so deep, a fire that is so strong, and a desire so unquenchable that my love will never be extinguished.'

'A simple "Yes" would have been enough. I love you, Tommy. Will you come and live here with me forever?'

'I might just do that but now I've got one more task to complete, and you have two more things to do. First, fix the party.'

'And the second?'

'Book me a cab!'

'Yes, sir.'

Scunt was back to being her vibrant self and again stood on the pavement to wave me goodbye. But this time there was a smile on her face. She knew I was coming back. What she didn't know was that I really might move in with her. The cab arrived. Did the company only have one driver?

'Good morning, Mr Tommy. Where to today?' said Turban man again.

'Gutter Lane, please.'

Maybe, I thought, we should invite him to the party as well; after all, he was almost one of the family now.

'Where is Gutter Lane? Is it around here?'

'No. Head for St Paul's and I'll show you.'

What a change. I was even being polite to cab drivers and not complaining about the music they played. The drive gave me a chance to rehearse the next part of this little plan. I had worked on two different speeches over the weekend. I still wasn't sure which I was going to give. After a few directions, we arrived in front of my office. I walked in and the receptionist and security guards nodded, expecting me to go to my office but I didn't. I went to the reception desk.

'Can you check with Lauren and see if the CEO is in now. I need to speak to Mark urgently.'

'Mark Erin?'

'Yes, Mark Erin. The CEO.'

I sat in reception and waited. I didn't want to go to my office until I had this sorted. The receptionist called over. 'Lauren says that Mr Erin can meet you in forty minutes. Is that okay?'

'Fine. Tell her yes,' and I checked my watch and stayed where I was.

Some colleagues walked by and said hello and I waved a sort of greeting at them. I relaxed and admired the opulence of the foyer. No wonder we had to charge so much. I watched as colleagues and customers came and went; an army of financial wizards, both good and bad. Was there a white wizard, a Harry Potter of the financial world, among any of them? Probably not. They were all Voldemorts, with different degrees of evil. I marvelled at how I had managed so quickly to dissociate myself from the crowd. Now I was on the outside and they were 'the mob'. That was why I was in my Scunt-purchased clothes, casual and smart, while they wore dark pin-striped suits. Forty minutes passed quickly and when the time came I had to get security to let me in. My pass was in my jacket in the company flat. It reminded me I still had to collect all my stuff.

I exited the lift on the top floor. The top floor of a merchant bank is always plush and this was no different. Mark's office was at one end, and at the other was the

Chairman's. Lauren's was between the two. There was more space here than in most large family houses. The carpet was more opulent and the collection of paintings was, to the initiated, as good as the Tate's.

'Lauren, hello. Is Mark ready?'

'Yes, but he only has fifteen minutes.'

'That's enough. Thanks for fitting me in,' and I headed down to Mark's office. Mark was in shirt sleeves behind his desk. Of course I had been there many times, and I felt very at ease as I settled into one of the deep armchairs.

'Hi, Tommy. What's so urgent? I hope this is important. You look very relaxed today.'

'Yes, Mark.' We briefly went through the normal pleasantries before I got to the point.

'Mark I had two versions of what I was going to say and I'm still not sure which to give, so the easiest way is to tell you both. You know I was away last week?'

Mark nodded. 'We thought you were ill.'

'Well I could have said that I was ill, and then told you that I'd had a sort of breakdown, and now, at the end of it – for medical reasons – I need to retire and find a more gentle job. I could have asked for a release on medical grounds.'

'But it wouldn't have been true. Is that what you're saying?' he said.

'I'm afraid it wouldn't have been true.'

'So now you're going to tell me that you've been speaking to some large American bank in New York who have offered you twice as much and you want to see if we can match their offer here?'

'No. That was last year's story, and I turned them down because the thought of living next to people who claimed they spoke English when they didn't was not worth any money they could offer.'

'I'm very pleased to hear that. So what are you saying?'

'I'm telling you the truth now. I have had a very eventful and life-changing week. I've been away from work without authority and I've toured the UK and met real people, the sort of which I haven't seen in the Bank in all the time I've been here. I no longer have the stomach for what I'm doing. I don't believe in the system or ethos any more, and I want to resign immediately.'

Mark looked at me carefully while randomly shuffling some papers on his desk. He fiddled with his pen. 'Tommy. Despite what you think, honesty is one of the virtues of the Bank and the City of London. It's the basis on which the Ridley family built this institution. Privately, maybe I share some – if not many – of your concerns. Since the recession, we've been viewed as outcasts across the world and that's for some very good reasons which I don't need to elaborate on. You're a good man, and you've been here for a long time. With all your experience I would much rather have you in the team. I can forgive last week. I would like you to withdraw your resignation.'

'I'm sorry, Mark. I can't.'

Mark sat back in his chair and looked both at me and around the room. 'No, listen to me. Withdraw it for three minutes and let me make my speech. Will you?' he said.

'Okay, consider it withdrawn. But just for three minutes.'

"Tommy, this is confidential. We've been running a project for the last six months reviewing and considering the structure of the Bank and we're going to make some organisational changes later in the summer. They are not finalised and not yet ready to be released in full, but I can tell you now that in six months' time, I'm sorry to say, we're probably going to have to make you redundant. We would of course like to be able to call on you for special projects where your knowledge and expertise would be invaluable. It may amount to about a couple of days a week on average over the year. We had thought a three-year contract as a retainer may be appropriate. If you agree with this we could make it take effect immediately. There would of course be a good redundancy package reflecting your length of service. How does that sound?'

I didn't have to think at all. 'I accept your terms with great pleasure. Thank you.'

'Very good,' and he picked up the phone. 'Lauren, get Simmons from HR up here right now.'

'Are you going to tell me about this week? It sounds special. Is it a course we can send others on?'

'I don't think it's very appropriate and maybe I can tell you over lunch sometime. It will take some time, though, and even then you won't believe a half of it.'

'I admire what you've done. I look at my job sometimes and wonder why we all do it. It surprises me every day that we have such loyal staff. I often wonder why they all stay so faithful. We have to build on that loyalty and return it with real and meaningful job satisfaction but if you tell anyone I said that, I'll deny it immediately.'

Simmons arrived. I liked him from all our previous meetings. Vertical pin-stripes elongated his already tall and thin body. He had a mass of hair totally out of place in an office where short or slicked-back was the norm. Subconsciously I ran my hand through my own newly styled hair.

'Bill. Thanks for coming so quickly. Tommy and I have

just had a long meeting and I've agreed with him that we will initiate his redundancy with immediate effect. The terms are as we discussed with the consulting retainer. I know it will take time to get the papers all drawn up, but everything should be dated as from today. Now, we need to appoint a stand-in for his role. Any views, Tommy?'

'Yes. Rick Pangan is a good fellow with a fine brain.'

'You know him, Bill?'

Bill, who had not yet said a word, had the stage. 'Yes. A good man. I agree.'

Mark again picked up the phone. 'Lauren, ask Rick Pangan to come here immediately please.'

Now there were three of us waiting and none of us knew what to say. Mark broke the silence. 'What do you think you'll do, Tommy?'

'A bit of this and a bit of that. I have some personal things to sort out as well.'

The silence was broken when a very nervous Rick Pangan knocked on the door and walked in.

'You wanted to see me, sir?'

At times like this, you never know if it's good news or bad news. With his boss, his boss's boss and HR all sitting there, it could go either way.

'Mr Pangan,' Mark started. 'We've been talking to Tommy for some time about his role in the Bank.' It was clever of Mark to make it look as though this was all part of some great plan and not a knee-jerk reaction.

'We all agreed that Tommy will become a consultant to the Bank on an external contract which will give him the chance to do some of the things he wants to do while we continue to have access to his knowledge and deep understanding. In the meantime we would like you to take on his position – and I have to stress this – on a temporary basis, while we consider all the issues including the long-term management of the Strategy group. And before you ask me, there will not be a salary increase until we make final decisions. Is that alright with you?'

Pangan looked startled. For the first time in a long time he was almost at a loss for words. Almost. He stuttered: 'W-wh-when will this take effect?'

'In about an hour I should think. Tommy has a little business to undertake for me with Bill Simmons.'

'Thank you, sir. I would be delighted,' Pangan said. What else would an ambitious man say?

I looked at him and said: 'I'll be with you shortly. We'll tell everyone then.'

'Thank you, Pangan,' Mark said and dismissed him with a wave of his hand. When he had gone, Mark looked at me. 'This is not goodbye, Tommy. We'll be seeing quite a lot of you. I don't think a farewell party is necessary under the circumstances. Do you?'

I nodded my head in agreement. Such thoughts had never even crossed my mind.

'Off you two go then and sort it out. Thank you, Tommy,' and Mark returned to his papers. The fifteen minutes allocated had become thirty and Lauren now had other problems to solve. It was all in a day's work for a CEO and his PA. Sorting out the details with Simmons was easy. I hadn't expected or planned for anything from the Bank and the offer was extraordinarily generous. I would be getting almost two-thirds of my salary on a consulting contract. I headed back to my office, or I should say my ex-office, where Rick Pangan was sitting at his desk with a smile a mile wide. Jane said hello but was slightly frosty, no doubt thinking about all those unfunded coffees she had bought over the last week. She followed me into my office.

'Tommy! Where have you been? There's correspondence a mile high to sort out.'

'Later. Can you get the team in here now, please?'

'Now?'

'Yes, now.'

When they were all in the office I told them what was happening. I tried to judge whether they were pleased or sad about me leaving. I emphasised that I would be coming in once in a while to check up on them and make sure they were up to scratch. Jane was the first to ask question.

'What now then, Tommy?'

'I think you need to ask Rick. He'll be taking over. So I think Rick ought to answer that question. Rick – if you will take the team outside you can brief them while I clear all *my* things out of *your* office. Thank you all.'

As I looked around the office there was not too much I now wanted to keep or take with me. Any information I wanted was already in my head. There was no personal or confidential information. I didn't have any nick-nacks on my desk. The pictures on the wall belonged to the Bank. As I looked around, all I really wanted was my favourite pen. That would be easy to carry but I had a few important phone calls to make before I left, which I completed before I called Rick into the office.

'There's nothing I want to take Rick. It's all yours now. One piece of advice. Just call me whenever you want help. Don't wait until you *know* you need help – call me when you *think* you need help. I want you to be successful. I'm no threat. I have a much better life ahead of me now.'

And with that, I walked out. My life as merchant banker

was over. As I departed one life and moved into another I had no regrets at all. I was leaving a fantasy world to return to reality, taken there through Scunt's own fantasy. I had the taxi wait outside the company flat as I collected my things, then I stopped for some urgent shopping, before returning to Scunt. I was back well before the six o'clock deadline.

'I'm home,' I shouted, and for the first time in a long time I thought that might be true. 'Do we have a plan for this evening?'

Scunt came running to meet me, throwing herself into my arms. While in the embrace she told us where we were going.

'I was out this afternoon, Tommy. Have you seen the paper?'

'No. Which one?'

'The *Standard*,' and she raced off and returned with the paper and thrust the front page at me. I looked at the headline.

POLICE POUNCE ON LONDON PIMPS

'What?'

'Just read it, Tommy.'

Which is what I did.

The Metropolitan Police today confirmed that following information provided by the London Evening Standard they have arrested three Serbians on charges of living off immoral earnings. Further charges are expected.

Last week a number of websites owned by the arrested individuals were hacked into and prospective customers were presented with a message from a previously unknown organisation called OBOC, Our Bodies–Our Choice. This organisation also provided information to the Evening

Standard on the individuals behind these web sites.

A spokesman for the Police said: "These are violent people who are abusing women by forcing them into prostitution. We will be widening our investigation on the basis of the information received."

A spokesmen for a leading woman's group said: "We do not condone prostitution in any form, but recognise that there will always be men who will search out sexual services and women who will provide them. Until attitudes change, it is better that these are fully consensual. We thank the police for finally taking this matter seriously and we support the actions of OBOC."

The article continued on a later page, but finally I was like Scunt – exhilarated. I could read the rest later.

'Let's go and party!'

Scunt had chosen a trendy wine bar and by the time we arrived Margie and Spike were already there, together with a couple of her girls. I ordered two bottles of champagne while first Margie and then Spike read and reread the newspaper.

'How are you doing, Margie, getting your business going?' I asked.

'It's going good,' she said. 'When the London Elite site was done over by Spike I phoned the girls one by one and told them what had happened and asked if they wanted to re-join me in a new business to be run as a collective. We would all share in the business. Some said yes straight away and others were scared. But now there's this article and we know he's been arrested, I'm sure many more will come over. And we have a man in the collective.'

'Spike?'

'Yes. Spike has compiled our new website. We won't be hacked by OBOC,' she said laughing.

'If you don't mind me asking, Margie, how well did you know Sharon?'

'Not well at all. She was on my site and I knew her just as well as any of the girls. Of course we met at the beginning, but thereafter it was just on the telephone. I wish I'd known her better. I might have been able to save her. That's why we're having a collective. We'll look after each other and never let it happen again.'

'You may be made a saint one day,' I proffered.

'I think for what you've done you might get there first! I don't think you realise quite what you have done yet. It will change very many lives. Is there anything I can do for you?'

I looked askance at Margie. 'If you're offering a free lady for an evening I think I already have one,' and I looked across at Scunt and raised my glass. She smiled back and returned the greeting with her glass.

'Have you and Scunt decided what you're going to do? Are you together or apart?'

'Together tonight, but then we'll have to talk it through.' I was thinking about Margie's offer of help. 'There's one thing you can do for me, actually. It will be very enjoyable and not at all onerous.' We had a quiet conversation away from Scunt's prying ears as I explained my request.

Back at Scunt's flat, I told Scunt that tomorrow we were going on another drive.

'But aren't you supposed to be at work back in the office?'

'I've arranged for us to be together this week. You might call it compassionate leave.'

'Where are we going?'

'Now who's being impatient? You'll find out tomorrow.

Now we need some sleep.'

The day was sunny when we woke.

'Come on, Scunt, hurry up and pack. We need to leave soon.'

We drove out of London, retracing our route back towards Oxford. 'We're going back to Oxford? Woodstock?' Scunt asked.

'Nope. Past both of them. We're going to see Q again and we're going to tell her the truth about Sharon. She needs to know. As each day passes it will become more difficult. We need to do this so we can be free.'

This jolt into reality upset Scunt and she sat quietly as we drove north. We were about an hour out from Leek when Scunt asked me to stop the car. I looked for a layby and we pulled over.

'Why are we stopping?'

'Because, Tommy, I want to kiss you and tell you I love you. You're right – we have to tell Granny but please don't say what Sharon did and why she killed herself. We don't need to break her heart too much. Please let me do that. We can take honesty too far.'

'Of course. You do that.'

As we drove to the outskirts of Leek and towards Q, the bungalow already had that familiar feeling of comfort and Q already felt part of my family. We drove up to the house and decided it was better if she was alone with Q while I went and bought the food.

'There are some things that really are only for family. Scunt, you'll find the words. I know you will. I'll be an hour or so.'

'No, Tommy. I need you there as well. Please come

with me.'

'Really, Scunt. You need to do this by yourself. I'm sorry.'

I watched as she walked up to the front door and saw first the surprise and then the happiness on Q's face. She waved at me and I guessed she was telling her I was about to get some food. I drove away. The shopping didn't take an hour but I found ways to waste the time. Scunt needed that time. I knew how bad it must be, but I was going to be there to see them through the evening. I knocked on the door and it was answered by a tearful Scunt.

'How's Q?'

'She's had better days.'

I went into the kitchen and found her making some tea. She looked composed. Was it denial or the stoicism of the old who have seen it all before?

'Hello Q. I'm really, really sorry. This time we will stay until you feel better. We're here to help you through the news.'

It was a sad evening. We ate and we talked about Sharon. Q retrieved the family photograph album from the sideboard and we looked at pictures of both the sisters, mostly as children. They were playing in the sand on a holiday, or sitting in the garden, or holding hands on their way to school. The memories were happy, and the wounds were being treated. When we went to bed, Scunt cuddled up close to me and cried onto my chest.

The following morning, breakfast was subdued, but at least the initial shock had worn off.

'I've got a nice treat for you both today,' I said. 'We're going into town and I'm going to buy some beautiful dresses for you both. It will cheer you up.'

'Thank you, Tommy. But you don't have to do that.'

'Yes I do, and we are going to do it. Where should we go Q? Leek or Stoke?'

Q looked just as apprehensive as Scunt.

'Come on ladies. Two new outfits? You can't say no to that. I'll buy shoes as well!'

'But, Tommy, I'm too old. When will I ever wear a new outfit?'

'Well, we promised you a wedding this year. You could wear it then. Come on Scunt, you convince her.'

For whatever reason, Scunt saw some benefit in getting out of the house so off we went. Q nominated Stoke. With me driving, the mood lifted. We stopped talking about Sharon and Scunt was telling funny stories about some of the rooms she'd designed. I knew shopping with one woman was bad enough, but shopping with two I couldn't take. I gave Scunt my credit card and the pin number. What was I thinking?

'Don't break the bank, please.'

'What do you want me to buy? Sexy and silky?'

'No. Maybe something more sophisticated. Tell you what we can do. When you've chosen one or two outfits give me a call and I'll come and look for you and help you decide. Would you like that?'

'I would. Thanks.' And I went off again to find a Starbucks. I bought and drank two coffees while waiting and I read every newspaper they provided. I'd even begun reading the classified adverts when the call from Scunt came, with directions to their chosen shop. Scunt had exceeded my expectations. She had chosen a beautiful dress and jacket. It was both sophisticated and sexy. In truth, she had learnt how to exceed my expectations in every way. Q had bought an outfit, too, and we persuaded her to slip in to the changing rooms again and model her purchases for us. Both my women were beautiful, but better still they were smiling again. Maybe shopping really is a therapy.

'You two need another early night,' I said, 'especially because there's another surprise and treat coming for you both tomorrow. I'm going to keep you busy.'

'Oh, come on, Tommy, tell us. You can't keep us in suspense. Tell him, Granny – we want to know!'

Q shrugged. 'At my age, every treat is a reward. I'm not going to tell him anything of the sort.'

'You're a big tease, Tommy. You know I'll make you tell me before you go to sleep.'

But in that she failed. I was resolute despite her wiles. I'd set the alarm for eight o'clock and it took an age longer for Scunt to wake up.

'Wake up. Wake up,' I persisted. 'You have a special treat today. I need you at your best.'

I jumped out of bed and went into the kitchen. Q was already there and she made me a mug of tea as Scunt wandered in wearing an old dressing gown Q had lent her. It wasn't pretty and it wasn't sexy but it was warm.

'Right ladies. I need your attention, please,' I said when we were all seated round the table. 'I need you to make yourselves beautiful in your new clothes because we're going to have visitors at lunchtime and then we're going for a special lunch. I've organised a party. Can you do that?'

Scunt and Q exchanged glances. 'You are devious, Tommy. Will we like it – the party?' Scunt asked.

I wasn't totally sure, but showing no concern I said, 'You'll love it, Now *chop chop*,' and I tried to usher them out to get ready. Nothing happened. 'You only have until midday…'

'Okay. We'll be ready, won't we Granny?'

'I'm quite excited about it all,' Q said. 'I haven't been to a party in a long time. You have to admit that Tommy makes life quite thrilling, doesn't he?'

Scunt lent towards me and placed her hand on top of mine. 'Yes. Life with Tommy is always exciting. But … you're not going to tell us anything, so we'll just go and get ready.'

While Scunt dried from her shower and started to put on some makeup, I told her what had happened at the Bank and the outcome.

'Are you are still in love with me?' I asked. 'I mean, you fell in love with someone who had a job and some money. Now I have less money and only a part-time job.'

'Tommy, when I fell in love with you, I didn't know what job you had or even if you had a real job. It makes no difference. Where are you going to live?'

'With you, of course. Wherever you want. We'll have to work that out. We're a two-house couple now.'

'Who's coming to lunch and where are we going?' she ventured again.

'Wait. You'll find out.'

I started to get changed into the only suit I'd brought with me. With my new-found confidence, I left my shirt collar open without a tie. Scunt dressed and stood beautiful in front of me, straightened the lapel on my jacket, and combed my hair with her hand.

'My handsome man. I love you.' I had not felt this wanted for a very long time. If ever.

Eleven thirty and we were all in our finery, sitting round the kitchen table once more. Q was relaxed with the waiting and was reading a magazine. The old do a lot of waiting. Scunt, in contrast, sat down and stood up and sat down again; she made some tea which she didn't drink, and she sat down again. She was not very good at waiting. At last the doorbell rang. We looked at each other. Who was going to answer it?

'It's Q's house. Maybe she should go and see who it is?'

'Quite right, young man,' she said, and went to open the door. The scream was not expected. It was not a scream of pain but of happiness and joy. Scunt jumped up and ran to the door and then in seeing the guest she also screamed.

'Mummy! Mandy! How? What?! … Tommy?'

The words were coming out randomly and she didn't know who to hug and kiss. Mandy had done as I asked and dressed rather more demurely than when I'd seen her before. Scunt's mum was elegant, but you could see the fragility of her illness. I finally corralled everyone out of the hall and into the lounge, only just, and each of us had somewhere to sit. I talked to Mandy while the three generations of family chatted and cried and laughed in cycles. There was no way Mandy or I were going to break into that group for some time. I asked Mandy about the journey.

'It wasn't too bad at all. I guess the total driving time was about three hours. I had to wait a bit for Tracy's Mum and she kept asking me questions about where we were going. It can't just be for lunch, she said. And I said that Tracy was with her Gran and she wanted you all to be together and that I was a friend who was going to drive her there. She was over the moon with that. By the way. Tommy, I think it's amazing how you've brought the family together at this time. It makes up for all the dreadful stuff with the funeral. I hope it's the start of a bright new future for everyone.'

I appreciated her words enormously. 'It's all for the overall good. What a shame Sharon's fate had to be the thing that led to all of this but you know what, Mandy – what I've learnt about myself has been so important. Yet another reason for this party, eh!'

Then the doorbell rang again.

'Scu—' I stopped myself. 'I mean… 'I had to get this sorted. 'Look, everybody,' I looked around the room, 'everyone knows she comes from Scunthorpe, so can't I just carry on calling her what I always have?'

There was a group murmuring of agreement. I smiled.

'So – Scunt! Maybe you should get the door for Q or else we'll tire her out completely.'

'Yes, master,' she said, putting on a fawning bow. I heard the door open and another shriek. Scunt brought our new guests in.

'Mummy, Granny, Mandy – I want you to meet two of my friends from London. Margie and Spike.'

I wasn't surprised by Margie. She had dressed just right for the occasion. Spike had again managed to amaze me; he'd found a suit and a clean shirt with long sleeves. The floral tie was a little over the top, but at least he looked like a signed-up member of the human race. He even managed a little small-talk with the ladies.

Introductions over, Scunt turned to me. 'Are we expecting any one else, or is this the end of the surprises?'

'Well, as far as I know this is everyone – unless Q has invited anyone I don't know about. Have you Q? Have you been up to your own mischief?'

Q giggled and shook her head.

'But as to the end of the surprises – I don't know. By definition, a surprise isn't something we don't know about.'

'Oh, Tommy, please no more of your riddles or games. Come on tell me. Is there anything else? I'm so excited.'

They were all watching our conversation and waiting expectantly for my answer.

'Well, the first reason I've gathered you all together is so that you all have a chance to be together and remember Sharon.'

There was a general nodding of heads and a poignant silence.

'Then,' I continued, 'we've also had a good week and achieved a lot, and how better to celebrate our successes with our closest family and friends.'

More nods from everyone. Q and Mum had their own interpretations of our successful week.

'So I've booked a table in a big hotel for us all to have a sumptuous meal. That's more good news.'

Everyone agreed enthusiastically. Then Scunt asked: 'There's something else as well. I know you Tommy. I bet there was an ulterior motive. What's the other-reason?' She looked at Q. 'He can be quite devious when he tries,' she said. 'I know there's something else.'

I looked at her. 'Scunt, my darling, that really depends on you. I've made one other reservation.'

There were a number of ways to do what I had planned and I had considered them all. I walked towards Scunt and took her hands in mine. 'If you say "Yes" we can also turn it into an engagement party. Scunt, my darling, will you marry me? Because – in front of all of these people, your family and best friends – I want everyone to know that I love you. I want them to know you've liberated me. You're my muse and my heartbeat. I love you and I want to be with you for ever and ever and ever.'

My heart was thumping, beating faster than I had ever known. I could feel every beat in my neck. I waited for what seemed like forever. Scunt looked around at her friends. Mandy was nodding, Spike shrugged his shoulders. Q was wide-eyed with excitement. Scunt composed herself.

'Tommy. I can think of nothing that would make me happier. Yes. Yes. Yes!' and she hugged me and kissed me and everyone shouted out their congratulations. Everyone in the room was in tears. There followed a few minutes of hugging and kissing.

When things settled down a little, I turned to Mandy. 'Mandy? Did you manage to do what I asked?'

'You bet, Tommy! But I didn't know this was the reason. Give me a minute.' And she raced out of the room.

'Q, have you got any glasses? I do believe we may have some champagne very soon.'

Scunt was talking excitedly to her Mum and Q was almost skipping, as much as she could, to the kitchen. I went to help her.

'I promised you a wedding, Q.'

'You cheeky young man. Even I didn't expect that and I have a nose for these things.'

We heard a cork pop as we hurried through with the glasses. Spike had taken on the job of barman and was explaining to Mandy how to open the champagne without it exploding. With glasses full and raised, Margie gave the toast.

'To Scunt and Tommy, and all those gathered here, and all those who should be here.'

Scunt turned towards me and we kissed again. 'Tommy

– Mummy wants to know when and where we're going to get married? What do you think? And where should we go for our honeymoon?'

'Well, Scunt, again that depends on you. We have so much to discuss. By the way, I've booked cars to take us to the restaurant so we can all have a drink and no one needs to drive.' Then I took her aside and whispered: 'I've been very busy behind the scenes and there's yet another reason why we're all here – the cars could take us somewhere else first.'

'What do you mean take us somewhere else first?'

'So many questions…' I replied vaguely, and from my jacket I pulled out two small boxes. I opened the first, took out a white gold and sapphire ring and placed it gently onto Scunt's third finger. 'I think I was supposed to do that five minutes ago. Sorry.'

'It's beautiful, Tommy, and it fits – you're so clever. What's in the other box?'

'Ah, the other box. In there, Scunt, is a gold band. If we're quick, you could be wearing it later this afternoon. I rather assumed you would say yes to me – we have a reservation at the registry office in ninety minutes.'

'Tommy, no we can't. Surely you will allow a girl to be engaged for more than an hour before she gets married?'

'Darling, the choice is yours. You can say no and we can just go and eat.'

'What do you want to do, Tommy?'

'I want to get married and eat. I always want the best of everything,' I answered.

Scunt looked very serious for what seemed an eternity, but it was probably only seconds. Then she turned to the cacophony in the room and shouted: 'Anyone want to come to a wedding and a reception? Now?!'

There was mayhem! There was looking at rings, more pops of champagne corks, talking and shouting, back-slapping and as much happiness as I had been part of in a long, long time.

'Scunt!' I had to shout to make myself heard. 'Do I take it that you think you will marry me this afternoon?'

She was still surrounded by everyone looking closely at her ring.

'Yes, yes, yes!' she shouted back.

'And what about the honeymoon? If you'd like to, Mrs Blackaby has reserved the cottage for us. Now, come on everyone! The cars will be here in fifteen minutes. Drink up! Go to the loo, or whatever you need to do. We have a wedding to attend.'

Chapter XX

Scunt and I were married that day and we made our vows with family and friends about us, and in front of our nearest and dearest we made a promise that not only would we be faithful to each other but we would be forever *truthful* to each other. That's the more formidable challenge, and in the long run it's the one that will keep us together.

On the practical side, we sold both my house and Scunt's flat and we live now in Woodstock, where Scunt is establishing her new interior design business. Mandy still works in Leeds in her collective. Margie is back in business and flourishing. Spike creates websites and has set up a photographic studio for models in the collective, happily combining his hobby and his work.

The *truth* is so important. After all that happened to me, I still can't decide where I stand between Kant and the other philosophers on the moral imperative about lying. As I said, Kant could never justify a lie. He said it removes our moral integrity. When I said to Scunt 'I love you and I want to be with you for ever and ever and ever' it was unconditional. It wasn't 'I will love you while you stay pretty' or 'while you still love me'. It was a promise from deep in my heart. Yet once before I had said similar words to Jenny. In breaking my word to her, can I simply claim that time has moved on? Or that we both changed? There again, does it really matter? Kant was right: telling a lie – or breaking a promise – does remove our moral integrity.

Scunt told me a thousand small and large lies. None were malicious, yet in total they had taken me on what could have been a disastrous journey. If things hadn't gone as well as they did, would the end still have justified the means? At work every day, at the Bank, I used to tell 'white' lies – either to amuse myself or for personal aggrandisement. Occasionally I lied to improve the profits of the Bank. It was fair play because, after all, we all did it every day, and no one saw any moral issues. I guess some of us might have had private concerns or questioned the morality of our actions and those of others, but we easily slipped back into familiar patterns.

The truth is, if Scunt *hadn't* lied to me, if she had told me the truth from the very beginning, then we may not have achieved the same outcome, nor had our adventure on the way. She was right when she said I wouldn't have become interested, and I wouldn't have become involved, and certainly we wouldn't have got married. So, because of our little adventure, based as it was on omissions and lies, reluctantly and uneasily I now go along with the Utilitarian view which accepts lying as a means to balance the overall benefit or minimise harm to society. Yet this ease with which we can justify a lie has led to problems in western society today, because we tend to disbelieve everything we hear. We are cynical observers of information. Our first assumption is always that we're being lied to, and we're less and less concerned, therefore, about anyone who gets trampled in an avalanche of modern world greed. And we have a word for people who try to trust – naive. But maybe it has been like this forever. The avarice required even to survive – let alone succeed – becomes greater and greater as the number of people we can't trust increases. It's a truly vicious circle of the worst kind.

So here I am. Always hard at work and consulting for the Bank, but now I also teach at Jesus College in Oxford and when someone asks me 'How are you?' I always answer: 'I'm very much in love. I couldn't be happier.'

Chapter XXI

The train slows and gently shudders to a halt and my fellow passengers are already standing, chasing luggage off the racks and queuing by the doors. *Whoosh!* The doors slide open and the race begins, no doubt with Jonathan leading the charge.

Me? I wait for the carriage to nearly empty before finally standing and taking my first steps on to the platform.

I walk strong and tall – a hero facing another day on the battlefield

ABOUT THE AUTHOR

Gerry Cryer is a full-time writer who now lives in Surrey in England. He is also an actor, business mentor, innovator, coach - and one-time guitarist in the rock-covers band *Mid-Life Crisis*. After a university career contemporary with a British Home Secretary and the Editor of a daily national newspaper (neither of whom he knew because they didn't play rugby), he embarked on a long and successful series of jobs in business management and consultancy, which others have kindly called a career. Gerry has the useful knack of staying relaxed and calm especially in a crisis, not least because of his motto: 'Expect the unexpected'. This has proved particularly useful as his natural inquisitiveness and sense of adventure have caused him to be at the centre of many a situation.

Gerry is a tenacious observer of the human condition and the complexities of modern society, and his story-telling draws on his experiences of many cultures, having lived or worked in over twenty-five countries across Europe, the United States and Middle East.

Blah Blah is his second (genre-breaking) novel. His first is a more serious tome, entitled *The Masterful Manipulation of George Cove,* which reached the top 300 books in the Amazon Breakthrough Novel of 2014. His third book is due for publication early in 2015.

The Masterful Manipulation of George Cove

The book is about Ukrainian nationalism during the 1970s, and culminates with the Chernobyl disaster. It was written long before the current troubles but it offers a fascinating insight into the people of the Ukraine and their political and social struggles.

"Much enjoyed Mr Cryer's first novel. Very well crafted and good characterisation. Look forward to the next! John le Carre should look out – he has a rival now!"

"Highly recommended! The shocking climax dominates the story, but along the way there are important issues about destiny and complicity, personal identity and responsibility, all seen through the eyes of one lucky (or poor) individual."

"The whole of your life has been manipulated in ways you cannot imagine. Since you were young, everything you've achieved was scripted in advance - even what happened at Chernobyl. And you need to know that I was part of the team that managed the process."

These were Aleksandra's words to George as they talked for the first time in over twenty years. In one go, George found out he had played a pivotal role in one of the greatest human tragedies of the twentieth century, and that everything that had mattered in his life—his education, his job, where he lived, how he lived, who he loved and who he lost—had been orchestrated by an unseen hand. George had no idea that he and Anna, a fellow student at Oxford University, were "destined" to become each other's' first loves; and neither knew they had been singled out for a future of international espionage. They seemed to live charmed lives, unaware of the doors being opened for them as they were snow-balled towards events that would haunt George for ever.

. If you want to buy or read more reviews of **The Masterful Manipulation of George Cove** , they are available at Amazon.com (Kindle and Paperback) and Lulu.com (for iPod).